Tree
of
Dreams

Tree of Dreams

LAURA RESAU

Scholastic Press · New York

All rights reserved. Published by Scholastic Press, an imprint of Scholastic Inc., *Publishers since 1920.* SCHOLASTIC, SCHOLASTIC PRESS, and associated logos are trademarks and/or registered trademarks of Scholastic Inc.

The publisher does not have any control over and does not assume any responsibility for author or third-party websites or their content.

Library of Congress Cataloging-in-Publication Data available

ISBN 978-0-545-80088-4

10 9 8 7 6 5 4 3 2 1   19 20 21 22 23

Printed in the U.S.A.   23

First edition, April 2019

Book design by Carol Ly

To the trees

"My heart lives here in the jungle."

BAI NENQUIWI, HUAORANI MAN

El Corazón

I pluck a chocolate heart from the counter and drop it into my mouth, just as I've done a zillion times before. Letting it melt a bit, I slide it around on my tongue, then nibble off the stubs of veins and arteries. I push it toward one cheek, then another, maximizing taste bud contact. By now the aorta has dissolved, leaving only the ventricles and atria. I maneuver the now vessel-less heart directly onto the center of my tongue and nestle it beneath the roof of my mouth. Then, with my crooked front teeth, I bite the heart in half.

This heart comes from the rare Nacional cultivar of cacao, straight from the deepest depths of the Amazon jungle. And that's precisely how it tastes. Notes of earth, wood, flower, nut— maybe almond? There's a hint of amber honey . . . and some kind of fruit I can't put my finger on.

I close my eyes, swallowing the last bits. The flavors linger on my tongue . . . subtle, mysterious, enduring. Nearly perfect. For the next batch I'll tell Mom to roast the beans at 320° instead of 310° to heighten the smokiness.

In elegant script, I pen my description on a creamy card and stick it behind the display glass. Then, with plastic-gloved hands, I grab the chocolates one by one from the tray and arrange them on the counter, this time in a spiraling pattern, starting from the outside and working my way in. These hearts are my latest chocolate concoction, the beans sourced from a little co-op Mom's been working with in Peru.

The word *weird* might come to some people's minds when encountering a thirteen-year-old girl who cares so much about chocolate. I prefer the term *rare*. If I were writing a description of myself on a creamy card, it would be something like this:

Of the Rocky Mountain cultivar, Coco Hidden possesses a solid maple complexion with tender layers of petals beneath. A bright touch of acidity at the edges. Subterranean hints of sorrow and fear. Undercurrents of longing, sweet notes of caramel with a burning touch of bitterness. A rare mix of steadfast and passionate.

Once the heart spiral is finished, I step back and survey my work, making a few tiny adjustments. All our chocolates are heart-shaped—that is, molded from a small but anatomically correct model of the human heart. This was Mom's ironic take on the whole chocolate-sweetheart-romance thing. El Corazón—*The Heart* in Spanish—is the name of our chocolate shop and factory in one. The sign features the bloodred human heart of the famous Mexican *lotería* card, complete with veins, arteries, and aorta.

Since there's not another soul in the shop, and I don't feel like delving into algebra homework yet, I stare out the window at snow-tipped peaks, imagining the best sipping chocolate recipe for this particular bean. Even though it's nearly spring in some places, here in the mountains of Colorado, late February still means snowy ski season. Ideal hot chocolate weather.

I breathe in the scent of the hearts. Maybe I'll add a touch of vanilla? And almond? And maybe cinnamon? Petals of some sort, too, I'm thinking, to bring out the floral backdrop.

My gaze flickers over our shop—high ceilings, exposed brick, wavy glass skylights, old-fashioned arches, swirly antique molding. Four framed black-and-white photos of a jungle hang from the walls—a bug-eyed frog, a tropical flower, a palm hut, and giant aboveground tree roots—all as familiar as my hand-writing. For all practical purposes, this has been my home for thirteen years, since before my birth. From the time I was the size of a cacao bean, the aromas and tastes of chocolate have been seeping into my blood. And in all those thirteen years, I don't remember El Corazón ever feeling quite so empty as it does now.

My own heart has a unique place for four things—well, technically three people and one thing. The one thing is our chocolate shop, located in my left atrium.

I pop another heart into my mouth, appreciating the endorphins and serotonin zipping around my brain cells. A hint of happiness ripples through me. And the theobromine adds to my freshly relaxed-yet-alert state. The perfect combination. As I always say, chocolate makes everything better.

At the edge of my vision, I notice movement outside the window facing Main Street. Customers? My pulse races, and not just because of the cacao's phenylethylamine speeding it up. *Please be customers! Please be a whole big rich extended family of skiers in fancy down jackets craving loads of chocolate after a long day on the slopes.*

But then I see who it is and my heart screeches to a stop.

He's practically hidden inside a cluster of kids from school, the royalty of seventh grade, the faces that everyone knows, even the eighth graders. Which actually isn't saying much because the middle school's small, just fifty kids per grade. Although it *feels* bigger. Leo and I did kindergarten through sixth at a bilingual elementary school with a grand total of fifteen kids in our grade. Anyway, there he is, smack in the center of the little throng.

Leo de la Cueva. De la Cueva is his last name. *Of the Cave*— it makes you wonder what exactly his ancestors did to earn such a mysterious title.

Leo has always occupied the right atrium of my heart, which, incidentally, has started beating again, disturbingly fast. He was my best friend for twelve years—that is, if babies can have best friends. All our lives, his mom has worked in the small law office upstairs. Nieves and my mom used to share the cost of babysitters to watch Leo and me in the chocolate shop. When we were old enough, the babysitters stopped coming, but Leo and I kept hanging out together, making chocolate and experimenting with recipes, playing by the stream and climbing the cottonwood in the back courtyard.

Now he glances into the shopwindow, and for a terrifying second I think he's caught me staring. But no, it's so bright outside with the snow and sunshine, he's probably just looking at his reflection. Lately, he's actually started caring what he looks like. Dark floppy hair half covering his eyes, cold-rosy cheeks, a creamy wool sweater, worn jeans. I want to look away, but I keep staring. It's weird watching him, knowing he can't see me, like a one-way mirror. And that's how it's felt all year.

Leo turns away to follow the others, who are staring at their phones while cutting across the street toward Donut Delite.

Donut Delite, the reason why El Corazón has been near empty for a year. Donut Delite moved in once the art gallery closed after a year of fires and floods and a terrible downswing in tourism. Donut Delite, with its enormous, fluorescent yellow banner advertising ninety-nine-cent donuts and hot chocolate. Never mind that their so-called fresh-baked donuts come in shipments of frozen dough, chock-full of preservatives and bursting with artificial flavor and color, assembled at some factory in China.

And their "hot chocolate"? Makes my soul shudder, and Mom's, too. Watery brown stuff too sweet with corn syrup and fattened with partially hydrogenated oils and whey products. Worst of all, they vent their ovens straight to Main Street. You can't walk within a block of the place without getting bombed by chemicals specially designed to make your mouth water. Atrocious.

There's a line in Donut Delite stretching out the door and down the icy sidewalk. Leo and his friends are shivering and stamping their feet but apparently they think it's worth the wait. Every once in a while Leo glances over at El Corazón. Does he feel guilty for betraying us?

I turn away, start wiping the counter, even though it's sparkling clean.

The bells on our door jingle, and I glance hopefully at the entrance. But it's just Mom, carrying grocery sacks of toilet paper and cleaners. She sets the bags behind the counter, unwraps her alpaca scarf, and sweeps her gaze around the shop. Takes in the emptiness.

It's nothing new. Business has been sluggish for so long that we don't talk about it anymore. We've cut way back on how much chocolate we produce; still, most of our truffles have ended up going to the homeless shelter the day before they expire.

"Hey, Coco," she says, nervously tightening her ponytail. Her hair is red and wavy and long, bordering on frizzy. She used to do elaborate inside-out French braids with little fringy curlicues, and weave in blooms from the flower shop next door. Now she's using a grubby terry cloth scrunchy.

"Hey, Mom." I feel my own hands mirroring her nervous hair-fiddling. My own hair is long and wavy, too, but it's caramel brown, the exact color of the unusually large freckles on my nose. I wear my hair swept partly back in a simple braid, and always have. Once I've found something that works, why change? I'm practical that way. Loyal. A creature of habit, Mom says. A hobbit, Leo used to say.

"How's it going, Coco bean?" There's something way too cheerful about her voice.

"*Más o menos,*" I say, twisting my braid, feeling guarded. I speak Spanish fluently because of the bilingual elementary I went to, but Mom just knows a few basic phrases.

"Listen, sweet bean, I've been wanting to talk to you about something."

My insides freeze. No good can come of a conversation that begins with false cheer. "About what?" I ask warily.

She pauses, tugs off her fleece jacket, sucks in a long breath. "About El Corazón, honey." And from her voice, I can guess what she's about to say. The top left quadrant of my heart suddenly aches, as if a window has opened, letting an icy wind shoot inside.

Quickly, I mumble, "I can't talk now," and rush to the back office and lock the door. But no, I can't stay here; any minute now, she'll knock and I'll have to answer. I shuffle through the dresser beside the pullout couch and grab my red swimsuit. I tear off my clothes, drop them in a heap on the floor, and put on my swimsuit. I can't find my robe or flip-flops, so I just fling open the office door, and before she can say anything else, I rush down the hall and out the back door.

Barefoot, I step into the snow.

A shock of cold on my toes. It zips straight to the hole in my chest. Holes, really. It's not just the left atrium that's abandoned. It's Leo's spot, too, in the right atrium. He's barely spoken a word to me all year, ever since seventh grade started.

And while I'm spilling my guts, I'll admit that the right ventricle—my mother's spot—is pretty drafty, too. For the past year, she's been like a robot, running the chocolate shop with pretend joy, but her batteries have been draining, and any day now, she might just stop.

Goose bumps pop up over my bare skin. I hug my arms tightly, cradling my bony elbows in my palms. I'm proof that chocolate doesn't make you fat; at least high-quality chocolate like ours doesn't. I ingest about a pound a day, and still, my body is all sharp, awkward angles. My legs and arms are basically twigs. When girls moan *OMG-I-wish-I-was-naturally-skinny*, trust me, this isn't what they have in mind.

With the red swimsuit as my only insulation, I head deeper into the snow to try to warm my flesh and bones and heart. My heart that feels like our nearly deserted truffle freezer.

The Underground Heart

Our town is called Heartbeat Springs because of the hot rivers that thrum beneath the earth, like pulsing veins of blood. They make a deep, rhythmic bubbling, a *thump thump thump*. And the heartbeat is strongest in our courtyard, right here in the nook in the stream where I've settled under the giant cottonwood tree. In this spot, hot water gurgles up from the earth and mixes with cold mountain snow runoff to create the perfect temperature. Upstream and downstream, the river is mostly iced over, except for a smattering of other cozy nooks like ours.

Beneath me, underwater stones are arranged just perfectly to sit on, a mostly submerged throne. The foaming surface of the creek skims my collarbones like the lacy neckline of a magical gown. Every couple of minutes, when my head feels chilled, I dunk it to warm it up.

Around me, the courtyard is a nest-like space, tucked in on all four sides. To the east and west rise tall fences, where trumpet vines and honeysuckle climb in the summer. On the north side stretches a row of three-story-high, century-old buildings, one of which—the Roost—houses our chocolate shop and its porch where we arrange tables in warm weather. About fifty paces away, on the south side, towers a craggy gray wall of mountain—a Rocky mountain, to be exact. Leaning against the stone, and scattered around the courtyard, are dozens of rusted metal robots, sculpted creatures right at home in this strange habitat.

In the middle of it all, the cottonwood tree's four limbs rise from its base, close enough to the ground to form a perfect sitting spot inside. It's almost like four separate trunks that have joined into one to form a royal throne or pirate ship or hobbit nook, depending on how you look at it.

Not that I can see much of that now. The rising steam shrouds me in a mysterious cloud, and I let myself float off, somewhere far away, somewhere like a sultry jungle. My eyes drift closed, and tendrils of steam move through my pores, and the tree roots reach deep into my vessels, sending a silent song through my blood, planting the seed of a dream . . .

Clang! Clang! Clang! My eyelids shoot open. I sit upright, jarred out of my dozing. Blinking, I situate myself back in the hot springs in this snowy courtyard. Footsteps are clanking on the metal staircase, slow and careful. Gali must be coming down from his upstairs apartment. I can't see him through the steam, but I call out, "Hey, Gali!"

Galileo Gallo occupies my left ventricle. Gali is any kid's dream grandfather, even though he's more of an adoptive one for me. He owns the Roost (his last name means *rooster* in Spanish), and rents us space for El Corazón for an unusually small fee. In the thirteen years we've been here, he hasn't raised the rent once.

He's a creator, too—he doesn't use the word *artist*—he just makes stuff, specifically robots of all sizes made from old parts of cars and tractors and machines and tins and cans. Some of the robots are twice my size and some are as big as my pinkie. Each of his robots has a tiny treasure hidden inside, like a smooth pebble or snail shell or glass bead.

"Hello, Coco!" he says, and I can tell by his voice that he's truly happy to encounter me. He's from Spain and speaks English with a slight accent, each syllable precise and thoughtful. His footsteps come closer, and once he's a couple of paces away, I can see him, all wavy and ghostlike through the steam.

"How's your heart, my dear?" That's his standard greeting, his equivalent to "How's it goin'?"

"My heart," I reply, "could be fuller."

"How so?"

I can't see his eyes well, but if I could, they'd be concerned and kind, I'm sure of it. I can make out the cloud of white hair around his face, just grazing his shoulders. He's wearing his favorite tattered, stained mechanic's jacket that must be even older than Mom. His version of an art smock.

I'm not usually a complainer, and I pride myself on that fact, but there's no other way to say it. My voice is grave. "El Corazón might be . . ." I search for the word that captures the tragedy of it all. ". . . dying," I finish.

Through the mist, he shakes his head sadly. "Oh, Coco, my dear, remember the secret to happiness."

He knows ten thousand secrets to happiness, and tosses them around like confetti. Which one is he thinking of now?

"Chocolate makes everything better?" I venture. "I tried that. But lately, it's not working so great."

"I'm thinking of a different one, my dear."

The thing about feeling hopeless is that it's hard to recall secrets to happiness, even if you've had hundreds of them memorized for years like multiplication facts. I twist my fingers around my crystal necklace—the comforting one I've worn my whole life—shuffling through the few secrets I can remember. *Smelling flowers, walking in nature, breathing deep.* None seem promising at the moment. "Which one, Gali?"

"Every day, even just for a minute, think about whom and what you love."

"I've tried that one, too," I admit. And I let the truth pour out, because if anyone can handle it, it's Gali. "Everything— everyone—I care about—" I begin, searching for words. "The more tightly I hold, the more they all slip away."

"Then you'll have to find some other way, my dear."

I take this in, shifting my feet to rest on an underwater footstool-rock, letting my bony kneecaps poke up through the surface like steaming volcanic islands. "Like what?"

He tilts his head, pondering.

"For starters, have you considered smiling?" There isn't a trace of sarcasm in his voice, only genuine curiosity.

And he has good reason to ask. I was once kind of famous in Heartbeat Springs for my smile. Not that it's anything special—in fact, my upper left front tooth overlaps my right pretty significantly. It's just that my smile showed up a lot on my face, without any effort. Probably a side effect of chronic, long-term chocolate exposure.

As a little kid, when I brought customers their steaming cups of sipping chocolate, the smell of it made me want to smile, and so I did, and I noticed that my smile made the customers smile. Or maybe, now that I think about it, they were smiling at the chocolate headed straight for them. Either way, it was like my smile had a life of its own and wanted to be onstage on my face, in the limelight. And I let it shine.

Even with our occasional grumpy customers, I would assure them, "Chocolate makes everything better," and toss in a free heart. They'd always smile back at that, and listen attentively when I listed the delightful neurotransmitters released by chocolate.

But lately, even with truffle-induced endorphins and serotonin and dopamine, my smile has been hiding in the shadows, paralyzed by stage fright or something. I tell it to come into the light, but it just lurks around offstage. Like if it shows itself, there might be no one out there watching or caring.

"Okay, Gali," I say finally. "I'll consider smiling." I pause, the tiniest hint of a grin tugging at the corner of my mouth. "And I'll keep my eyes open for . . . *some other way.*"

He bends down in a strained, creaky motion, and places a wee robot on the wet stone in front of me. "For you, my dear Coco."

Ever so slowly, he turns and shuffles down the path, then clanks up the stairs. Even in the snow-muffle, I can hear him wheezing, pausing every few seconds to catch his breath.

Gali's always been as reliable as a big, old-fashioned ticking clock, but he's changed this past year, cutting our conversations short, leaving when the party's just getting started. He used to give off a long, steady heat, like a cozy fireplace that made you feel loved and unique in the universe. And that's been flickering low lately, as if his flames need more oxygen.

With stream-slippery fingers I open the miniature hinged door of the robot's chest. Inside is another door, even tinier than the first. Inside that, the heart, a bright red seed.

And, accidentally, I smile.

I'm just getting water-wrinkled and light-headed when Mom comes outside. I'm glad for the mist, because who knows what my face will do once I hear what she has to say. Luckily, it's already wet, which might disguise any tears that sneak out.

"Hey, Coco." She dusts snow off the little bench on the bank and sits down, adjusting her jacket and scarf. "Sweetie," she begins. "Listen."

Thump thump thump go the springs and my chest, pounding louder by the second.

"I know you've been avoiding this conversation, Coco bean."

I want to run, far, far away, but I'm dizzy and in my swimsuit and surrounded by snow.

In a rush, she says, "We have to close El Corazón."

"No!" It spews out of my mouth like bubbles from a shaken-up seltzer can.

"Coco, I don't want to shut down either. El Corazón—it's been my entire life with you. It's everything."

I'm glad I can't see her face well through the mist, because the way her voice is quivering, I imagine her chin is doing the same. "We're losing money, going into debt, Coco. And we need to think about our future. Braces. College. Retirement. A decent house. Ours is beyond repair."

I clutch Gali's robot with its hidden treasure. I think of his words. "We have to find a way, Mom. Let's see if things turn around this summer with the art festival crowd. Maybe it'll be too hot for donuts. This spring I'll invent some new recipes, some really delicious, irresistible chocolate shakes. Please, stay open through summer."

Mom buries her face in her hands. "I don't know . . . I don't know if we can even last another month, sweet bean."

I'm about to faint, which could be problematic in a partially iced-over creek. I stand up slowly, and Mom reaches out to steady me, then offers me my thick robe and flip-flops. Bundled up, I sit beside her on the bench, letting the cold air clear my head. I look at Mom in her box store sweats and bare earlobes. Most of my life, she's worn funky dresses and bangles and dangly rhinestone earrings from Viv's Vintage down the street. An eccentric complement to her fancy updos. But lately her wavy red hair's just been pulled back in that boring ponytail, and it's probably a matter of time before she cuts it in a short, no-nonsense mom style.

I suck in a breath, roll the tiny seed in my palm. "I don't care about the braces. Please, promise you'll give El Corazón more time."

She sighs, stays silent for a long time, maybe doing math in her head.

"Okay," she says finally. "Six more months. Till August. But if business hasn't drastically improved by then, we close. And you'll have to promise to accept it and move on."

"Move on?" I echo. Something in her voice scares me, something she's not saying. "As in . . . move away from Heartbeat Springs?" I can barely believe the words are even coming out of my mouth.

She nods, squinching her eyes to hold back tears. "Honey, real estate is ridiculous here. It's a resort town. We can barely afford the mortgage on a beat-up trailer on the outskirts. And there aren't jobs here beyond the service industry, you know that." She rubs her face. "I'm too old to bus tables."

As we walk inside, I let her put her arm around my shoulders and pull me close. Then it hits me: If El Corazón closes, everything I care about will vanish—the shop, Leo, Gali . . . and in some ways, even Mom. Who would she be without the cloud of cacao around her? Without roasting the beans and running the melanger machines and doing all the things she's done my entire life, all the things that make up who she is?

Mom's my only family by blood, and even though she's been weird lately, she's *buena gente.* A good person. I know that most thirteen-year-old girls wouldn't willingly admit this about their moms. And it's true, there's plenty about her that drives me crazy. But here's the thing: How many mothers celebrate their pregnancy by using their inheritance to open a chocolate shop to welcome their kid into the world . . . and then making it successful for a decade, even though the father has hightailed it out of there?

Mom, Gali, Leo, and El Corazón. The pieces of my world.

Which is currently whacked out of orbit and hurtling through empty, cold outer space, about to be gulped by a black hole. Unless I can find a way to save it.

Later that afternoon, as Mom breaks up a chocolate bar to melt into French *chocolat chaud*, I perch on a café table and soak in every tiny detail of the shop, trying to memorize it all, even the chips and cracks in the brick . . . until my gaze lands on the old-fashioned photo of giant tree roots. Now that I look more closely, I notice a blurry, khaki-clad figure leaning against a mountainous root taller than him, nearly hidden in its shadow.

Funny, I've never even wondered who took these pictures, or where, or when. They're like the features of a friend's face . . . you know them so well you don't think about them. At least, not until they're on the verge of vanishing.

Mom sets down two mugs of steaming, cinnamon-dusted chocolate and sinks into a chair.

"Thanks." I wrap my palms around the warm clay cup. "Hey, where'd these pictures come from anyway?"

"Oh, they were here when we started renting the place." She takes a sip, licks the foam from her lips. "I guess they're Gali's. I just kept them there. Thought the rain forest theme fit the shop. You know, since most of our cacao comes from the jungle. Shade grown, no clear-cutting involved."

She moves her face close to the bug-eyed frog picture till her nose is practically touching the glass and she looks a little cross-eyed. "That's one reason I got into the bean-to-bar chocolate business. Did you know that?"

I shook my head. It's weird how you think you know everything about someone . . . and then you discover a whole new room in the house of the person they are. "I thought it was just 'cause chocolate's the most mind-blowing food in the history of the universe."

"Well, that, too. But something like a hundred acres of rain forest are razed every minute, Coco. Can you imagine?"

We're quiet for a whole sixty seconds. And then I think of how a piece of jungle the size of Heartbeat Springs was just destroyed. It adds a whole new layer to my sadness about El Corazón, like melancholy frosting on a fresh-baked cake of sorrow.

Mom takes a sip of chocolate. "And these past thirteen years, we've done our teeny-tiny part to prevent more destruction. That's why we only use cacao sustainably grown in the rain forest."

Eyes misty, she breathes in the sweet chocolate steam, squinting at the pictures, as if she's saying good-bye to all these things already . . . the distant jungle, the cacao, the teeny-tiny bit of goodness we do. "That's a tree frog," she says, pressing her fingertip to the glass, not worried about leaving a smudge. "And that flower's a bromeliad. In full color, it would be orange or red or pink."

"And what's this?" I stand up and trace the enormous roots.

She speaks softly, as if reaching the end of a story. Or maybe, the beginning. "A ceiba tree."

The Ceiba Tree

AMAZON RAIN FOREST

Let me tell you about my world.

　　The world of a wizened old tree.

　　Listen carefully. Listen with your heart. It's a different kind of listening, you see. A kind of dream-listening.

　　You know, of course, that I have no mouth for talking. I have no legs for walking. Yet in silence, I speak. I travel without moving. My roots soar and dive and speak with trees of all kinds.

　　For most of my three hundred years, our talk has been peaceful, a gentle hum moving beneath the forest floor.

　　Yet lately, the soft murmur has risen to a shrill cry. So many loved ones butchered, more than ever before. This is a time when legs might be helpful. Or a voice. A loud one.

In three centuries of my branches towering and my roots delving deep, I have learned to whisper, to teach young trees to speak. I've even known some animals who have learned our tongue. Humans included.

Ours is a quiet language, and you must listen very closely, and you must want to hear it very badly. It often rises through the earth as you dream, when your mind is drifting and open. We speak in these heart words, this invisible movement, this secret song. In the darkness within my roots, I pass along dream whispers, dream rain, dream flowers, dream pain . . .

Here is what I must tell you: At this very moment, I feel the rumble of the trucks coming closer, the whir of the deadly blades, the screams of loved ones.

I hope other trees pass along my plea. I hope that someone, somewhere, hears. Someone near or far. Someone with legs and a mouth. Someone who cares. Someone who will act.

Someone who will help me save my world. Someone like you.

And why would you care? Oh, there are more reasons than stars in the sky. So I will give you a simple, bright one: Within my roots, a treasure awaits.

The Dream Tree

Later that day, as dusk falls, a few loyal locals trickle in and buy a truffle or two each.

"Storm's a-comin'," warns little old Permelia as she blows into the shop on a wintry gust. She's our most faithful patron, the owner of Permelia's Flower Boutique next door. Every day, she pops in with her tiny dog, Gooey Marshmallow, tucked in a bag.

Today, because of the impending blizzard, she devours a chili-lime truffle at lightning speed—a change from the molasses-in-January way she usually nibbles at them. Afterward, she pushes open the door against bitter winds, tucking the bag containing Gooey Marshmallow against her chest. "Oof! You'd better stay here tonight, Mara," she calls over her shoulder to Mom.

Snow's already swirling hard outside the shop. I'm dreading going home. Our mobile home park is just outside town, down a winding, unlit road that's treacherous when unplowed. The roof of our trailer has been caving in more with each snowfall this winter, spreading the cracks and leaks. There's an obstacle course of buckets inside the house to catch drips from roof holes when the temperature rises above freezing. I turn hopefully to Mom. "Can we stay here tonight?"

She blows out a long breath, considering the pros and cons. The pro is that there's something magical about spending the night here, where chocolate melts into our dreams. The con is that we're technically not allowed to stay overnight since it violates some zoning code. Finally, she says with a smile, "Okay, sweet bean. Just for tonight."

"Yes!"

By candlelight, in the iridescent white-blue twilight, I finish my algebra homework, then skim the latest issues of *Discover* and *Bon Appétit* magazines while Mom starts roasting a new batch of beans in the chocolate factory. The blizzard is swirling, and no new customers come in, so I blow out the candles on each table, flip the front door sign to CLOSED, and lock up early. I climb the narrow staircase to the factory, which is nothing like Willy Wonka's place. Ours is a modest cluster of five small rooms—more like interconnected large closets—just across from Leo's mom's office.

Nieves de la Cueva, Attorney at Law. She doesn't do exciting cases like murder or sabotage—mostly stuff that makes you instantly yawn, like copyright infringement and real estate. I peer through the glass door in case Leo's in there helping her with files. Nope. Empty and dark. Just like my own empty, dark right atrium.

I walk inside our factory, blink under the bright lights that reach into every corner. It's all shiny, smooth, sterile surfaces, wiped and cleaned and mopped daily. I glimpse Mom in an adjoining room pouring some freshly roasted Venezuelan cacao into the winnower—basically an upcycled juicer rigged up to a high-tech vacuum cleaner. Like a friendly and competent pieced-together robot, it whirs and sucks the husks from the roasted beans.

Breathing in the smoky chocolate scent, I put on a hairnet and shoe coverings and go over my shirt with the lint roller. I try to savor all the details. This place might not be . . . *alive* anymore after summer's end.

Slowly, I shuffle past the roasting room, with our two special ovens still warm from the latest batch. I linger there for a moment, breathing in the rich, nutty, fruity roasted cacao scent that has seeped into the walls.

As I walk past Mom, I call out, "Hi!" over the machine rumble, just as I've done hundreds of times before. An arrow of nostalgia pierces the center of my chest. I imagine El Corazón already gone, just a sweet and painful memory.

"Hi, Coco bean!" She waves a plastic-gloved hand. Tendrils of red escape her hairnet.

I head past the grinder room, where the cacao—now cute little nibs—will go next. The machine looks like those peanut butter grinders at the health food store. When the cacao oozes out in the liquidy form of cacao liquor, it looks like deep brown peanut butter.

Finally, I enter my favorite area—the melanger room—where our four machines are smoothing and mellowing older batches of liquid chocolate. They're silver cylinders the size of mini-fridges, and since I was little, I've thought of them as patient and hardworking old friends who need no sleep. Day and night, their granite discs rub against each other, making hypnotic river-circles of sweet, flowing brown. *Mélanger.* French for *blend*, though we pronounce it with a glaring American accent.

Mesmerized by the white noise hum of the machines, I open the lid on the left, stick a spoon in, and taste, gauging how much longer this batch needs. It's already been in for seventy-five hours. It's mostly silky, but still a touch gritty. By tomorrow morning it should be ready.

It's a slow process, and you can't rush it. It can take nearly a hundred hours, depending on the bean, but you have to be patient and trust that little by little, something delicious and happiness-making is being created. It's an art and a science, a mix of control and luck. And oh, how I'll miss it . . .

I trudge past the shelves of still-untempered chocolate chunks. They look like rocks, with mottled white stripes and swirls of light cocoa butter. I pause in the tempering room, run my hand along the machines that heat the chocolate ever so slowly and carefully to the exact right temperature to make it velvety smooth in consistency and color. These guys are like finicky old perfectionists. All of these machines feel like childhood friends—childhood *robot* friends. What would we do with them? Sell them to some clueless amateur chocolate hobbyist? Spine-chilling.

I sink onto a plastic swivel chair in the final room, beside metal shelves full of cooling and hardening chocolate. I help myself to a few pieces of still-warmish café au lait chocolate hearts. Chocolate makes everything better, right?

In front of me hangs the poster Leo and I made for a school

project about bean-to-bar chocolate-making back in second grade, back when we used to be default partners. It's an illustrated flowchart from seed to mouth.

In the jungle, plant a seed, grow a tree, wait a while, let the pods ripen to pretty colors, split the pods open, remove the gooey cacao beans, let the cacao ferment (rot), dry the cacao. Ship the cacao beans to the factory, roast them, crack them, winnow them (separate the husks), grind the nibs, smooth them in the melanger, temper them with controlled heat, shape them in heart molds, EAT AND BE HAPPY!

This is the process at the hub of my life. The burning star my planets spin around.

I have to save El Corazón. *I have to save my world.*

I suck on the chocolate heart and swivel around on the chair, faster and faster, as if I'll figure something out if I go fast enough. Soon my head's dizzy and echoey and buzzing, like a thousand insects are trapped in there, flailing around for a solution.

My head's still buzzing a few hours later, on a pillow on the pullout bed next to my sleeping mom in the back office of El Corazón. The wind has calmed, the blizzard ended, leaving snow frosting the world outside. With my eyes closed, I can feel a *thump thump thump*—maybe the underground springs, maybe the melanger machine upstairs spinning and grinding.

Then there's the rush and trickle and ripple of the warm stream outside, flowing through the frozen world. The drip of steam-melted snow from the cottonwood branches just outside the window. It's a strange music, a jumbled collection of rhythms.

The insects are buzzing, along with birds calling and frogs chirping—thousands of them, all at once. And the dripping isn't melted snow, but rainwater falling from giant palms. The rain is just letting up, but the air stays heavy, almost vibrating with a zillion droplets, and it's so hot and damp, I'm gushing sweat. The ground beneath my feet is soft mud, and above me stretch layers of leaves, all shades of green, with sunshine filtering through. This is how it would feel to be inside an emerald, bathed in green light.

And I hear a faint voice, a distant song.

I follow it down the muddy path a short way, through a tunnel of green, as the voice grows louder, stronger. I can almost make out the words now.

At a small clearing, I slow to a stop.

First I see the woody roots, like little mountains, as tall as me. And then I lean my head back and move my eyes up, up, up the impossibly thick trunk to an enormous umbrella of branches, a perfect half circle towering above all the other trees.

My eyes slide back down, down, down to the roots, like giant ribbons pooling out and forming nooks, almost rooms—places where magic might live.

And here, now, the words ring clear and light as raindrops. Singsong words so clear it's as if I feel them in my blood more than my ears. "Within my roots a treasure awaits."

The words float on the currents of my circulatory system,

out to the tiniest capillaries of my fingertips and toes, filling me. They are somehow light and deep at once, in the voice of an old grandmother. "Thank you," I say, flooded with gratitude. But it occurs to me I have no idea where in the world this place is. "Where am I?"

My voice breaks the spell, tugs me back to the waking world. I try to stay in that jungle, but it's fading and now there's only the *drop drop drop* of the thawing snow, and the *boom boom boom* of my chest, and the *thump thump thump* of the underground spring, and the *thrum thrum thrum* of the melanger machines, and the *zzz zzz zzz* of Mom lightly snoring beside me.

The hot, humid air dissipates and now I feel only the soft cotton of worn sheets and the fuzz of my spare pj's . . . and I *try, try, try* to go back down that path, into the emerald dazzle. I strain to listen for the tree's answer.

There's only the echo of the singsong voice in my blood.

Within my roots a treasure awaits.

Reluctantly, my eyes drift open. The room is dark except for the white-blue snow glowing through the window over the desk, silhouetted by the cottonwood's limbs. A treasure awaits? El Corazón flashes in my mind. The pulsing heart of chocolate, on the verge of vanishing.

A treasure would save El Corazón. Gold coins, rare jewels, ancient artifacts . . . who knows, but if it's really something of value, we could sell it and use the money to pay off our debts, and maybe even invest in an upgrade to the shop. And this supposed treasure is just waiting for me out there in the jungle. A smile sprouts on my face . . . until I realize there's no jungle anywhere near Heartbeat Springs, Colorado. Nothing close—not even a temperate rain forest.

I sit up, prop my head against the pillow, careful not to wake Mom sleeping beside me. My dream mind fades away and the logical, sciencey, wide-awake part of my brain takes over. And here's what it says: Not only are we thousands of miles from a jungle, but this was a dream. A weird dream, a strangely real dream, a dream like no other I've had . . . but still a dream.

Right?

I rub my eyes, stare out the window at the glittering snow. On the other hand . . . *what if* . . . just what if a miracle has been offered to me? What if there's a treasure waiting out there? And what if somehow, I discovered where it was and how to get there?

It's a dream, Coco. A dream.

I lie flat again, force my eyes closed.

Just a dream tree.

But as I drift off again, this dream tree nestles in my left atrium, just beside the chocolate shop.

When I wake up the next morning, my heart feels a little fuller. I fix myself a cup of hot sipping chocolate, made of heavy cream frothed and blended with a melted bar from Ghanaian cacao. I put on my coat and boots and hat, shove my phone in my pocket, and head outside into the courtyard, my insides still thrumming with the rhythms of the dream jungle.

I shuffle through sunlit snowdrifts toward the white-laced cottonwood. The air is mostly still, just a soft westerly wind blowing the rooster weather vane on the storage shed's roof. I hold my steaming mug with fingerless gloves, and without spilling a drop, manage to climb into the nook in the giant boughs, my favorite place to think. The snow is light and powdery and easy to brush clear from my sitting spot. The scents of almond and vanilla swirl upward, with a touch of lavender from the dried blossoms I sprinkled overtop.

As always, my elbows and legs are arranged just so, as if the tree has tailored custom spots for them. My mug balances on the top of one pointy knee, my phone on the other, and my hands hold them steady. Despite the snow, I'm not too cold, thanks to the hot spring steam and roasting cacao scents and happy neurotransmitters released by the chocolate.

I begin my online search with *Ceiba Tree*. Because yes, now that I'm awake, I'm sure of it. The tree in my dream was the same kind as the one in the picture in the chocolate shop. I sip and tap and swipe and scan, pausing here and there to read a description, unsure what exactly I'm looking for. And the whole time, I remind myself I don't actually *believe* I'm on a dream-inspired treasure hunt . . . I'm just expanding my arboreal horizons. (*Arboreal*, I've just now learned, means *of or relating to trees*.)

I have the urge to show these arboreal pictures to Leo. Only, he's not here beside me. It still feels strange to hang out in the tree without him. This used to be our place. Every once in a while, I'll see him out here by himself, waiting for his mom to finish her work upstairs. I'm always careful to avoid going into the courtyard at those times, and am extra careful not to let him see me watching him through the office window.

Ceiba. The common name in English is kapok, but ceiba sounds smoother. Out of habit, I imagine telling Leo all about these trees. My whole life, whenever I come across something cool, he's the first person I want to share it with. Ceibas, I would tell him, are sacred trees for many indigenous people, including his ancestors, the Maya. Ceibas are deciduous, losing their leaves during the dry season, unlike many other tropical trees. And they have fluffy seedpods that people use in blowguns and fire starters. Their flowers give nectar to bees and bats and birds.

And their roots! Their roots alone can reach fifty feet high— taller than the Roost or any other building in all of Heartbeat Springs. They're buttress style, like the stone supports for ancient, magical castles . . . and yes, they look like something straight out of Middle Earth. Even though the curmudgeonly-old-lady part of my brain is insisting *it was just a dream*, endorphins are dancing inside me. I drain the last drops of chocolate from my mug, licking bits of foam from the rim.

But as I read further, my hope sinks. Ceibas are found in Mexico, Central America, South America, West Africa, Southeast Asia . . . on more than half the continents on this planet. I can't just wander around every jungle on earth searching for my tree. Especially being thirteen years old and completely broke.

A *clank clank clank* breaks through my disappointment. Footsteps on the wrought iron stairs. It's Gali, heading ever so slowly down into the courtyard.

"Hey, Gali!" I call. "Up here!"

He squints through the branches and greets me as if he

hasn't just seen me yesterday, as if it's been decades and we're old friends. "My dear Coco!" he declares like a song. And then, predictably, "How's your heart?"

After a beat, I say, "Searching, actually."

He waddles closer down the path, cautious with his footing on the icy stones. "For . . . ?"

Another beat. If anyone would understand magical dream instructions, it would be Gali, but it would sound too crazy to say out loud. Not to mention, I don't really believe it myself. All I say is: "A treasure. A treasure that probably doesn't even exist . . . but, if it does, I've narrowed its location to four continents on earth."

He nods appreciatively. "Marvelous. Now just narrow it down a smidge further."

"How?"

"Have you tried asking the cosmos for a sign?"

"A sign?"

He nods. "Keep your eyes open, dear. Magic is around us all the time, but if we're not looking, we miss it."

My dream, even the memory of it, is practically oozing magic. But my real life feels painfully empty of it, crowded instead with distinctly unmagical problems. Donut Delite is the opposite of magic. As is a leaky house. As are the piles of bills on Mom's desk.

"But, Gali, what if you're looking for magic, but you still can't find any?"

"Why, then, you make your own magic, Coco."

The Ceiba Tree

AMAZON RAIN FOREST

My roots are screaming messages today.
    Cries of pain.
    Warnings.
    The saws, the blades, they're growing closer.
They have slain another mother tree. She saw
them coming. She tried to pass her knowledge,
her nourishment, on to the others, the younger
ones, but this cannot protect them from the
whirring steel.
    We mother trees oversee our own pieces of
jungle. We are ancient, and enormous, and we
each host our beloved creatures, from ants to
humans to monkeys to jaguars. And we
welcome other plants—like waxy, bright bro-
meliads that collect pools of water where still
more creatures live, tiny frogs and lizards. We

are little worlds unto ourselves, worlds within worlds.

In the past, humans living in our forest have spared us mothers. They know if they cut one of us down, that children trees of all kinds will suffer. And the thousands of creatures and plants who live on our bark, our branches, our roots, our leaves . . . they will be homeless.

But lately, different humans have come in, humans from faraway places, humans with machines, chopping down any tree in their straight path, sparing none in their way, no matter how big or old or wise.

I am not so much sad that I will die, you see.

What makes my heart ache is that my wisdom will die with me. Three hundred years of it, passed along from so many trees, our web of life, broken.

These humans with their killing machines do not understand the silent things we mothers do in the dark shadows of soil, deep beneath their feet, their wheels.

But maybe there is a human somewhere out there who understands, who hears my calls.

Are you listening?
Do you feel our roots touching?
Can you imagine our strength together?
Will you join forces to help?

Magic

Every night, for a whole week, I dream of the ceiba. If it were once, or twice even, maybe I could ignore it. But her call is growing insistent, desperate. She needs me, and I need her treasure. Not that I *believe* the dream, exactly . . . it's just that the tree's voice has become part of me, like a song I can't get out of my mind.

Then, one early March afternoon, on my wintry walk home from school, something catches my eye.

It's a poster taped to the lamppost outside the chocolate shop. And on the poster is a tree, the roots forming elegant arches, like an elfin condo complex. Above, a perfect half circle of branches stretches into the sky. A ceiba. A glorious ceiba.

My dream tree. I freeze, my backpack dropping off my shoulder to the icy pavement. Inside, my chest is quivering from some strange, invisible instrument. The flyer must have just been hung; I run my finger over the edges, so crisp and white, unlike the worn, yellowed fraying of the surrounding signs. Along the bottom, a shadowy green river at the base of the tree serves as a banner for some kind of announcement.

Through my breath-cloud, I squint at the wavy words on the river-banner, the oddest words, in a font that's so swirly and old-fashioned it's nearly impossible to read. It's as if the task of deciphering the script is supposed to weed out anyone who isn't passionate, or at least, desperate.

HOME SWEET HOME

A Dessert Creation Contest

Heartbeat Springs City Park ~ March 15, 11:00 a.m.

Open to concoctors of all ages.

Complementary trip for winner and a guest to the Amazon Jungle.

A sign. My sign. The roots of the dream tree are reaching into my veins and arteries. And the murky-rich river is tugging at me and the cosmos are breathing *yes, yes, yes, we will help you.* The valves in my heart open and shut, doors swinging back and forth, sweeping the blood through with new gusto.

My entire body thrums with hope. It's as if this contest has been created just for me.

And yes, this is beyond strange—I mean, wouldn't you think the owner of the town's chocolate shop would already know about a dessert contest?—but I try not to question it. It's like when you're flying in a dream and you suspect you're dreaming, but you don't want to think about it too much because you'll wake up.

Just to be sure, I pinch myself on my forearm. Ouch. My fingernails leave two indentations. This is no dream. So I tamp down any further thoughts that I'm asleep or crazy, and focus on winning the contest. I spread my twig-skinny arms wide open to the magic.

March 15, two weeks from today. Soon. It'll give me enough time to save El Corazón.

I kind of sway in this dreamy stardust mode until voices ring out across the street, moving closer. I glance up.

A fist clenches my chest. It's the seventh-grade royalty, recognizable as a flock of noisy parrots. Apparently, the fake donut smells are luring them into Donut Delite. Soon the fluorescent-lit chain store swallows them up.

All except for Leo. He's wearing a dark green sweater today, and he's paused in front of the lamppost opposite mine, just beside the enormous 99 CENT DONUTS sign.

From across the street, I notice the air around him moving differently as he studies what must be the same poster. Halo-waves of warmth. He tilts his head one way, then the other, moves it forward then backs it up. He must be trying to decipher the tangled-up lettering. A long ray of winter sunlight finds its way between mountain crags and illuminates his face. There's an intensity to his expression. The same intensity that must have been shooting out of my freckles as I read the words myself a couple minutes ago.

I'm smacked with a flashback to our decade of chocolate-making together—an era that ended last year. Our heads close, our noses sniffing the chocolate subtleties of our latest invention.

Back then, every day was possibility. Enchanting concoctions shone on our horizon like gold-lit, snow-topped peaks.

The feeling vanishes. If there's one person in Heartbeat Springs whose chocolatier skills rival mine, it's Leo. I taught him everything I know, and then he ran with it. And while my discerning taste buds might give me a slight advantage, he's surpassed me in carving skills. He's the Michelangelo of chocolate sculptors (thanks to the tools I gave him as a birthday present).

I have to stop him.

But I never approach him when he's with the royalty. Well, once I did, last year, and quickly decided, *never again.* There's an unspoken rule, it turns out. Inserting myself in their group is as preposterous as a scullery maid trying to hang with a prince. It's not like his entourage actually wields swords, but that's how it feels. As though, if I infiltrated their little procession again, one of them—possibly Leo himself—would say something to stab straight through the flimsy armor of my rib cage.

This time is different, though. For one thing, he's alone, sort of, only in eyesight of the royalty through the Donut Delite window. A few of them are waving their arms, trying to get his attention through the glass, motioning for him to come in. But he's absorbed in the poster. In his left hand, he's holding a big plastic bag full of something, which he lets drop to the ground without noticing.

On impulse, I race across the street—jaywalking, not typical for me, but luckily the cars are just chugging along and slow down even more when I zip in front of them.

I stop at Leo's side, breathing hard, diaphragm expanding, contracting. So much pounding inside me, I might burst. He looks up, surprised to find me within arm's reach of him. The closest we've been in a year. He pushes his floppy bangs from his face. Our eyes meet for one, two, three seconds.

I haven't seen his eyes in their full, close-up glory for ages, and I can't look away. His irises look exactly like thick liquid milk chocolate right after it's done in the melanger machine. After it's spent eighty hours being ground with sugar and cream powder between two granite discs. The particle size is down to an invisible twenty microns, the smoothest of the smooth, heaven on your tongue. The volatile compounds have been released, the acidity and sharpness gone, leaving only sweet mellow silk.

And yes, that's what I see now. Sweet mellow silk irises . . . with a large dose of something else. Confusion? Caution? Discomfort? If he were chocolate, I'd grind him another twenty hours to dissipate that extra gunk.

Self-consciously, he glances away, at his friends in the store, who are looking his way and raising their palms to the ceiling in puzzlement. He picks up the plastic bag of stuff he's dropped—a heap of library books, by the look of it—and starts turning to leave.

I need to find something to say, some string to reel out and snag him and keep him here, or else he'll go into the shop. I can already see his body shifting, and in a moment an excuse to leave will come out of his mouth.

So I speak. "How's your heart, Leo?"

Only it doesn't come out sounding kind, like Gali's question. It shoots out of me, accusing, a dagger dripping with something . . . blood, sarcasm, acid. And then it flings itself back at me, like a boomerang.

What was I thinking, asking him that? Sounding like a twisted thirteen-year-old mean-girl version of an eccentric old man. I want to dehydrate myself into powder and fly away on the wind.

Leo's face wrinkles up in bewilderment or self-defense or who knows what. He's always been the type to think about what he's about to say before he says it. I can practically see him trying out words on his tongue. But then he must decide I'm not worth it, because he shrugs a shoulder, just a few millimeters. He turns toward his friends.

My hand shoots out, grabs the soft wool on his arm. *I'm touching Leo.* My fingertips dig in. My insides are grating together like granite slabs. "Are you doing the contest?" I ask him. Or more like *demand* of him.

A little part of my mind is thinking maybe we could partner together, bring each other as the winner's guest. But my words smell rotten, like cacao beans fermented too long.

He shrugs again, glances at my hand on his arm, mumbles, "I think . . . I think I *have* to . . ." His voice trails off.

I snatch away my hand, tuck it under my other arm, holding myself in. I look at the poster, at my dream tree, my chance to save El Corazón. And I want to ask Leo *why* he has to enter the contest, and maybe scream or cry a little. Still, I keep my lips pressed together because who knows what new variety of over-fermented rot might find its way out of my mouth.

He follows my gaze to the poster. Visibly, he swallows. "Coco—"

But now Caitlyn Bland, who's as famous to any local middle schooler as say, the president of the United States, pokes her head out the door and locks her eyes onto Leo's without even skimming over mine. I am as invisible to her as her aorta.

"Dude, Leo, what're you doing out there? It's freezing." Caitlyn Bland shivers in her camisole. Like the rest of the princesses, she prefers spaghetti straps over sleeves, and sees no connection between her goose bumps and poor clothing choice.

Leo takes one last look at the poster, and then at me, and I vaguely wonder what he was about to tell me. But it doesn't matter, because within seconds, he's inside Donut Delite, firmly in the blue-manicured clutches of Caitlyn Bland, being led to a vinyl booth. He squeezes in beside the princes, who aren't stately, but slouchy and piggish and stuffing entire donuts in their mouths. From what I've gathered, they're into fly-fishing and Xbox and Frisbee golf and snowboarding and karate and ice hockey. Definitely not bean-to-bar chocolate.

I curse Caitlyn Bland and curse Leo and curse his new buddies. And then I curse myself because as much as I hate that place, its chemical smells are making my mouth water. Disgusting thoughts of cheap, hot donuts fill my head.

I cross back over to El Corazón and let my curses stay outside in the slushy snow and feel myself melt into the comfortable smells of the chocolate shop. I answer Mom's standard, distracted questions about school. (*How was your day, sweet bean? Fine. Anything interesting happen? No. How'd the science quiz go? Okay. Any homework? A little.*) Questions that have absolutely nothing to do with the heart of anything.

Soon she gets on the phone with one of our distributors, and I make myself a cup of hot chocolate and start experimenting. A whirlwind forms, of cacao dust and sugar, violets and lavender, cinnamon and vanilla. I enter the eye of the hurricane, the place where I create, my zone where time moves differently, where everything disappears except the taste of chocolate . . .

You know that expression "pouring your heart into something"? Well, that's what I do. Heart-stuff is my main ingredient and I dump a few gallons of it in there, because really, there's nowhere else for it to go.

It used to feel like a storm when Leo and I made chocolate together—a good, exciting storm, like wild lightning and rain and thunder crashing into a heavy, hot summer afternoon. But the very last time we made chocolate together, it was a bona fide hurricane that destroyed everything in its path.

The week before that final chocolate-concocting morning, these winds and electricity had been forming inside me. It was a half year ago, the first week of seventh grade. We'd always been inseparable: Leo-and-Coco, Coco-and-Leo. But most of the kids in our new school didn't know that. Not to mention, half our classes were different, and in the ones that were the same, even though I'd gotten there early to save him a seat, he chose to sit on the opposite side of the room. He paired up with other partners. He barely looked at me. I didn't say anything about it; I felt embarrassed, hot-faced, and shaky.

So that fateful Saturday morning, Leo and I were alone together. Mom was grocery shopping. The shop wasn't officially open yet for another two hours. Leo's mom was upstairs in her law office, catching up on some work. And Leo was hanging out with me in El Corazón. As usual, before the shop opened, we were in the kitchen experimenting with recipes.

I remember the precise moment when our chocolate storm became deadly. We were standing beside each other at the cacao-dusted counter. The windows were open, and late summer birdsongs drifted inside, and beyond that, the sounds of cars and voices faint outside. Leo was carving a chocolate ninja sword using the tools Mom and I had given him for his tenth birthday a couple years earlier. Every few seconds, he jutted his lower lip forward to blow his long bangs out of his eyes.

I inched closer to him by the counter, so that our elbows bumped. He was focused, bent closely over the half-sculpted chunk of chocolate. He moved his elbow, shifted his body away from me.

After a whole week of feeling ignored and rejected, I wanted his attention. Desperate, I held out a spoonful of my mixture of heavy cream and chocolate and almond extract and rose petals. "Taste it, Leo!"

"No thanks."

"Why not?"

He shrugged. "Just not crazy about flowers in food."

"What? Are you joking?"

He said nothing, just squinted at the hilt of his ninja sword.

"Come on, Leo, try it!"

He kept his head down, quiet.

I thought he was kidding—or at least I wanted to believe he was kidding—so I forced the spoon up to his mouth. He pursed his lips tightly like a baby refusing to be fed. Chocolate smeared all over his mouth and chin.

I laughed, because still, I told myself he was being funny. I told myself this was just the same horseplay we'd been doing since we were little. Then—and here's where I'm ashamed to admit what I did next . . . I tackled him to the floor. He's a reasonably strong guy, but I was strong, too, from dragging around giant burlap sacks of cacao all the time.

So I pinned him there and straddled him and sat on his chest and tried to jam the spoonful of chocolate into his mouth. Still, I was laughing, but now that I think about it, there was maybe a tiny bit of vengeance in my laughter. He strained against me, his jaw muscles clenched with effort.

Then, in a sudden wild movement, he threw me off. I thudded back against the counter and the chocolate on the spoon went flying.

He stood up, looked down at his shirt. It was white, and new, with buttons and a collar. And now brown goo was splattered all over it. "What the—?"

That's when I realized. He was mad. Raging mad. "You just ruined my shirt!"

I could only stare. Leo never got mad. He was always as calm as his chocolate lake eyes. Smooth, unrippled liquid. But now his face was red and veins were popping out. He wiped the chocolate from his face with his arm. "Coco, you're so . . ."

"So *what*?" I challenged.

"Weird." He shook his head and rubbed at spots of chocolate on his cheek. "You're all caught up in your own weird world. You don't even care about anything else."

"That's not true," I said, suddenly weak-kneed.

"And you're embarrassing. Everyone at school thinks so, too. Just—just stay away from me and my friends!"

He slammed the door behind him, leaving the brass bells frantically ringing. I stood up and watched the door, expecting him to come back any moment. Minutes passed. Finally, I half crumpled to the counter, a messy, chocolate-coated mix of humiliation and hurt.

For a week he avoided me. That next Saturday, I took the sharpest of Leo's tools and stabbed his half-finished chocolate ninja sword over and over, ferociously, until it was a pile of chocolate crumbs.

Over the next week, I felt bad about it, so I cleaned his carving tools and arranged them in the little leather case. Inside it, I tucked one of our creamy cards where we write chocolate descriptions.

I went through eleven cards before I got the wording and my handwriting near perfect.

Leo de la Cueva, of the Rocky Mountain cultivar: smooth, mellow, creamy. The brightness of sunshine sparkle on snow. Flavor as quenching as water bubbling from a cool spring. Layers of sweetness like summer-warmed peaches at the farmer's market. A rare mix of softness and toughness. A hint of hidden mystery and magic. Unforgettable honeyed notes of loyalty that linger forever.

In homeroom the next morning I set the leather case containing the tools and card on his desk. When he walked in the room, he quickly stuffed the case in his pocket without opening it, and without meeting my eyes. I waited to see what he would do after he read it, but by the end of the day, nothing had changed. By the end of the week, he was still ignoring me.

Just stay away from me and my friends.

The words etched themselves in my mind. Each one felt like the slice of a knife. If I was a chocolate sculpture, his words were carving me into something else, something like a monster. Was that really how he saw me?

Once upon a time, our friendship was a properly functioning heart, the two pairs of valves like doors swinging open, letting the blood move through, and closing again to keep it from backing up . . . open and close, open and close . . . a perfect rhythm like coordinated bird wings. But after that tragic Saturday, the blood started backing up, nowhere to go, the doors stuck, all those nutrients and oxygen trapped.

And instead, our friendship has become a foot fallen asleep, numb from lack of blood, devoid of energy and life. Supposedly when something's numb you can't feel it, but trust me, you can. It's all pins and needles stabbing at you, a kind of constant background pain that tells you, with every prick, *something's not right.*

And now, a half year later, Leo de la Cueva has officially become more than a dull ache. He's my competition, my opponent, my *enemy* in the Home Sweet Home contest. I'll have to use every trick in my chocolatier book to defeat him. He is the only thing standing in the way between me and my dream tree. My treasure.

The World Tree

Two days before the Home Sweet Home contest, right after school, I run straight through the back doorway of El Corazón. I skid into the office, shrug off my backpack, and tie my apron over my jeans and T-shirt. All day my concoction has been burbling and bubbling in my chest and now it's finally time to start on the real thing, using our exquisite new batch of Peruvian Nacional cacao.

From the desk drawer, I take out my pile of sketches and notes. Over the past two weeks, I've drawn up a detailed plan for my entry. I've done a trial run on a subpar batch of chocolate. Mom let me use our 3-D printer to create the model I'd designed on the computer. Then we dipped it in hot, liquid plastic to form a mold. Once it hardened, I poured in the melted chocolate, let it cool, removed the mold, and voilà, there it was . . . my dream realized.

I head into the kitchen, spread out my notes, and fling open cabinets and drawers, preparing my equipment and ingredients behind the counter. There's exactly one customer in here with me—faithful Permelia, sitting at her favorite spot by the window. She's crowned with frizzy purple hair with gray roots, adorned in wool socks and Birks, wrapped in mismatched flowy scarves and skirts.

The head of her little white dog, Gooey Marshmallow, is sticking out of her bag. The tips of his ears are deep brown, just like a perfectly singed campfire treat.

Over the counter, I call out, "Hey, Gooey! Hey, Permelia!"

Both lady and mini-mutt tilt their heads. "Coco, honey! You outdid yourself on these peanut butter truffles. I swear I've died and gone straight through the pearly gates. And Gooey adores the white jasmine truffles."

Gooey licks his chops, looking deeply satisfied and perhaps thankful the cocoa butter part of chocolate is safe for his species. I always make sure to have white chocolate on hand for him, since dark chocolate could poison this furry little truffle connoisseur.

A smile sneaks onto my face. Another secret to happiness: human and canine friends who appreciate your hard work.

Mom is leaning over a table near the back, doing yoga stretches with one arm and tapping something into her tablet with the other. "Hi, sweet bean," she says, glancing up for a second, then back at the screen.

Before she can ask her usual small-talk questions about school, I announce, "I'm starting my final concoction now."

"Cool. Good luck." She's already told me that she'd happily be my guest to the Amazon, that we could just close the shop during our trip. She can't resist adding, "I wouldn't be at all surprised if you win, honey, but remember, it's just for fun. If you don't win, don't be too disappointed, okay?"

This has been her refrain for two weeks. "You've made that abundantly clear, Mom." Secretly I think, *If I lose, my heart will be pulverized like ground spices.*

I've got my bowls and spoons and jars and petals ready on the counter, and now I'm scanning our climate-controlled storage cabinet for the chunk of Peruvian chocolate. But I can't find it. I run my fingers over the contents of the shelves, moving boxes and plastic containers around, searching. They're labeled Madagascar, Venezuela, Ghana, Nicaragua . . . But no Peru. The chocolate's vanished.

My insides tremble. Where could a chocolate chunk as big as a human head disappear to?

"Hey, Mom," I say shakily, fighting off a sense of doom. "Where's that Peruvian chocolate?"

She looks up from her tablet. "What? Oh, right, sweetie. Sold it today."

Beneath my skin, tectonic plates are shifting, dragging, cracking me, sucking me downward. Somehow, my voice comes out low and quiet. "You sold all of it?"

"Yeah." Her face softens. "Oh, no, you weren't going to use that, were you? I thought you wanted the Nicaraguan criollo."

"I specifically said I was using the Peruvian Nacional, Mom. You were just staring at your tablet and not even paying attention!"

She moves close, tries to hug me. "Coco bean, I'm really sorry. But the Nicaraguan is delicious, too—"

I step away, cross my arms tightly, blinking fast and trying to control the tidal waves of my lower lip. "The Peruvian is earthy and subtle and MYSTERIOUS! The Nicaraguan tastes like freaking tobacco leaves!"

"Watch your tone with me, Coco," she warns. Then she sighs, glances over at Permelia, who is still nibbling her chocolate with eyes closed, lost in blissful oblivion. Gooey Marshmallow lets out a few whimpers, distressed at my raised voice.

I breathe, try to calm down for his sake.

"Well," Mom says finally, "there's nothing we can do about it now, honey. The competition's in two days. We have more Peruvian beans, but we couldn't roast them and put them through the melanger in time."

I'm quiet for a while, gathering myself. "Who'd you sell it to?"

She looks at her feet, lets out a breath. "Nieves."

"Leo's mom?" All at once, I'm burning hot, smoking with fury. "He's my main competition."

"Keep perspective, Coco honey. It's supposed to be a fun contest. If things don't work out, it's not the end of the world."

Maybe I should've told her about my dream tree. But lately, conversations with her have felt like talking on a bad video chat, with stops and starts and glitches that make me wonder if she's even hearing me at all. It's as if only some of my words get through, not enough for her to understand the meaning. So I've stopped trying.

She doesn't understand that if I lose, it will be the end of my world. *Our* world.

Two days later, it's the morning of the Home Sweet Home contest, and Heartbeat Springs is all thawing slush and mud, slick and springtime slippery. A few brave crocuses have peeked through here and there, and shops have dared to plant cold-hardy pansies and violets in pots.

Mom's at my side and we're walking the four blocks to City Park, my three-pound concoction balanced on a five-pound platter. She holds one side and I hold the other and we're trying to keep it level while trying not to slip on the ice, which isn't easy in my special-occasion cowgirl boots with two-inch heels. There's never enough parking downtown, so it would be pointless to drive there.

Mom says, "Coco, no matter what happens with the contest, you should feel proud of this. It's . . . it's truly out of this world, sweet bean."

I have to admit, I'm happy with how it turned out. The World Tree. It was inspired by the research I did on the ceiba, which I discovered was the World Tree of the Maya . . . and that got me interested in other cultures' World Trees. The Tree joins all three realms of existence—Underworld, Earth, and Heavens. Some say the World Tree even holds up the sky.

In the center of my platter is a foot-tall ceiba tree made of chocolate. The branches form a precise crown and its mountain range roots spread across a sphere that is Earth, rejoining on the other side. It took me three different molds till I found a design strong enough to keep all those branches from breaking. I've painted the continents with white chocolate—cocoa butter mixed with vanilla and sugar—that I naturally dyed blue and green. And then I hand-sculpted hundreds of tiny green-dyed white chocolate leaves that I hung from the branches. My knuckle joints still feel stiff from those leaves.

Making the sky was tricky, too. I briefly considered blue raspberry cotton candy, but Permelia convinced me to go the all-natural route and sprinkle white petals from her special greenhouse-grown heirloom variety roses overtop its crown. "The sky's not always blue," she pointed out.

Rose petals. I haven't used them in a recipe since that hurricane with Leo. These petals have an ancient, slightly spicy fragrance that add the mystery that was missing without the Peruvian cacao. And not only is the rose petal sky a perfect accompaniment, but it will be a jab at Leo, that flower-hating traitor.

A gust of wind rises and blows some petals from the branches to settle at the base like miniature flowers. I'm worried they'll blow away altogether, but as we pass the flower shop, Permelia runs outside with Gooey Marshmallow. "Let us be your wind block, Coco."

She positions herself in front of me like a petite, pastel-clad superhero, raising her lilac wool cape to the winds.

"Thanks, Permelia," I say.

"It's the least I can do!" She smiles fondly at me and Mom. "You and Mara and your truffles have made life much happier for me and Gooey all these years. We'll really miss you—"

"We're not closing El Corazón." My voice is sharp, notes of bright acidity bursting to the surface. "At least not if I win this contest."

Mom gives me a strange look. "Coco, I've told you—"

"I'm not giving up, Mom. And I'm going to win."

Baffled, Mom presses her lips together and looks down at

the slick sidewalk. She has no idea what winning the contest has to do with saving El Corazón.

"Oh, of course you'll win, sugarpie," Permelia says with a vigorous nod.

Gooey Marshmallow wiggles his ears, then spews out a sneeze like an exclamation point.

We arrive at City Park ten minutes before the contest begins, with nearly all of my rose petal sky intact. A shiny, colorful throng of down-jacketed people are gathered around the gazebo, beneath a banner reading HOME SWEET HOME.

Most events here happen during the summer, when soft grass covers the block-long park along the river, and patches of coneflower and yarrow and sage bloom in pinks and yellows and purples. Now the river is half-frozen and only the broken debris from last year's flowers litter the dirt-patch gardens. At least it's sunny, with morning light reflecting off the white cloths on tables set up beneath the gazebo. Little kids chase each other around picnic tables, and dogs tied up to separate trees strain to sniff each other. Scarf-clad people are sipping hot chocolate from biodegradable cups and refilling at the giant silver samovars provided by Mom yesterday.

I recognize a few chefs from the nicer restaurants, along with some of our regular customers. A bunch of other shop owners from the DBA—Downtown Business Association—are here. They toss fond smiles and waves my way. I've known most of them all my life, and they spoil me, like aunts and uncles and grandparents, offering me treats from their shops. In some ways, they've been my teachers, too—Mad Matt from Mad Scientist Toys on his unicycle demonstrating the wonders of physics, elegant Nadia from the Atlas Gallery showing me how to peer beneath layers in art, mystical Kali from Gemstone tracing fossils with her ring-bedecked fingers and stretching my understanding of geologic time.

Caitlyn Bland and her royal cronies aren't here; in fact, no one else my age is. They must all be sleeping in.

Through the crowd, I can make out Gali, in his ancient mechanic's jacket and a gray skullcap and scarf, talking with Zephyr, the long-haired, spandex-sporting president of the DBA. Gali catches my eye and grins, looking like he wants to come over. Unfortunately, Zephyr is one of those people who talks without pause; you wonder how he can even breathe. He's tall and lanky, owns the bike store, and is constantly moving, tapping a foot, jiggling a knee, twitching a brow. I make a wide arc around to the other side of the gazebo so I don't get stuck in a one-sided conversation about the wonders of clip-on bike shoes.

The tables, cloaked in white lace, hold all varieties of sweet creations—cakes, pies, pastries, brownies. I let out a sigh of relief. There's nothing too original-looking, just your standard fancy desserts. And as far as taste, I'm hopeful that even though I had to use Nicaraguan cacao instead of Peruvian, my heart-stuff and experience will make my chocolate's taste stand out. On the platter, I've scattered chocolate shavings that represent soil and decaying debris, for judges and attendees to sample so they won't immediately devour the tree. Already, a small crowd has gathered around my concoction, oohing and aahing.

But someone is still missing. With a nagging feeling I look around. It's Leo I'm searching for, I realize. I don't want him to be here . . . but at the same time, things feel off without him. No sign of him anywhere. Maybe he's changed his mind. Which, weirdly, makes me a little sad. What was it he'd said about doing the contest? *I think I have to . . .*

Mom gives my hand a little tug, and we walk around with Permelia and Gooey, examining the other desserts. Gooey and I sniff every concoction. Blackberry tarts, red velvet cupcakes, lavender crème brûlée, *arroz con leche*, honeyed baklava, cream cheese brownies. By olfaction alone, I recognize which participants have used our chocolate. A flourless cake covered in sugared violet petals features our Madagascar trinitario, which my card describes as "fascinating and sophisticated with layers of grapefruit and raspberry flavors." And the chocolate mousse uses our Nicaraguan cacao as a smoky base, with its hint of molasses and mint, flaunting an edgy, rich touch of bitterness.

Nervously, I glance at the clock on town hall. One minute till ten. I'm just thinking I've got this contest in the bag, when Leo comes racing across the muddy dead grass. He's the only person on earth who manages to look cool while speed-walking. He's carrying his own platter, covered with an enormous silver dome. Pure drama. But practical, too, with this wind.

As he draws closer, I note he's avoiding my eyes, apparently guilty, as he should be. The only empty space on the table is next to my entry. His gaze rests on it.

"Mayan World Tree?" he asks, breathing hard, winded from the exertion of cool speed-walking.

"Not necessarily Mayan," I reply curtly, remembering his heritage. "Just the World Tree." And I add, "The concept is found in plenty of other cultures, you know."

He nods. "Rose petals, huh?"

"Yes, actually," I say. "Heirloom roses." I hope they're making him nauseous.

Nieves jogs up behind him in her yoga weekend wear and puts a hand on his shoulder. She greets Mom and Permelia and me with kisses on the cheeks. She acts oblivious to the icicles hanging between me and her son. "Coco!" she says in her delicate Spanish accent. "What a marvelous tree!"

The clock has struck ten and people are gathered around the table now, oohing and aahing and drooling. *"Momentito,"* Nieves says, jogging over to the electrical outlets where the speakers are connected. She plugs in an extension cord that's emerging from beneath the silver dome.

Leo's entry requires *electricity*?

He crosses his arms, rubbing the sleeves of his wool jacket, nervously rocking back and forth, looking everywhere but at me. When did he get that new jacket? I used to know his whole wardrobe as well as my own. He's like a stranger now. Nieves comes over and nudges him, pushes the hair from his face, whispering something in Spanish, too softly for me to hear.

He shrugs and lets his hair flop back into his face and I hear her say, *"Bueno,* then I'll do it, *hijo."*

With graceful flair, she begins lifting the silver dome from the platter. All eyes are watching. I bet Leo did this on purpose, came just in the nick of time so the unveiling of his piece would be the center of attention.

When his concoction is revealed, gasps of wonder dance around the crowd. It's a jaguar, nearly as big as Gooey Marshmallow, and it's standing at the base of a chocolate waterfall, posed as if lapping up a drink.

Stars fill my vision. A black hole is swallowing my world. I grab onto the table, sure I'm about to collapse. *Breathe, Coco, breathe.* Finally, I realize I'm not going to actually faint, even though my knees are wobbly and my stomach contains a stormy ocean and my brain has turned into burning mush.

A little sign in front of it reads: INTO THE UNKNOWN. As people take turns walking by Leo's waterfall-jaguar extravaganza, I find myself funneled into line with them. When I'm in front of the gurgling chocolate fountain, my nose can't resist leaning in to inhale.

It's undeniably tantalizing. Dang those subtle, earthy, mysterious notes of Peruvian cacao! My skin prickles, like my whole body has turned into a funny bone, not in a good way.

He's added some kind of berry liqueur to the waterfall, and something like cardamom . . . an exquisite blend, I have to admit, perfect for this particular bean. Then I notice something strange: White petals are scattered all over the scene, floating in the chocolate pool. Rose petals? I sniff. Yes, rose petals. Also heirloom variety.

Is he trying to rub it in? Remind me of our fight? The whole thing reeks of betrayal. He's used my chocolate, the tools I've given him, and now, he's even using my rose petal idea. And supposedly he hates flowers in food.

But he has this look on his face, the kind he used to get when Nieves would force him to go shopping or to piano practice. He looks like he'd rather be anywhere than here. Why *is* he here? When I asked him weeks ago whether he was doing the contest, he said, *I think I have to.* What does that even mean?

Zephyr adjusts his bike shorts and rings a little bell. "Attention, dessert lovers of Heartbeat Springs! Welcome to Home Sweet Home! The time has come for the judges to evaluate each and every concoction, in terms of both taste and artistic presentation. We have a panel of five esteemed chefs from our beloved local restaurants."

He drones on for too long, fidgeting the whole time, as the chefs move from entry to entry, tasting a small piece, taking notes in their little notebooks, conferring in whispers. Between entries, they chew on plain crackers and sip water to cleanse their palates.

I try to read their lips, to no avail. I squint at the scrawl in their notebooks. I get nowhere with that, either, and start watching people in the crowd instead while I wait. Gali is sitting on the bench beneath the gazebo, clutching a cane with one hand. Since when does he use a cane? It's alarming. But he doesn't look injured or weak. He actually looks like a king sitting there on a throne with a staff, secretly presiding over his little kingdom.

The judges finish their tasting and scribbling and conferring, and gather behind the tables, smiling, satisfied, buzzing from so much sugar. One of them—an actual French chef named Jean-Luc from the rustic bistro down the street—announces in his throaty voice, "Ladies and gentlemen, boys and girls of ze beautiful Heartbeat Springs, we have made ze decision."

There are plates beneath the earth's surface that move at the same rate our fingernails grow, and other plates that move even faster, at the rate our hair grows. And that's how continents form and drift over hundreds of millennia. All of a sudden, I can practically feel this growing and shifting in myself, in the world.

Supposedly right here beneath my feet, the Rocky Mountains were under an ocean millions of years ago. I feel an echo of it now, the currents surging, ancient tides rising, change happening.

And the source of the change? Who knows for certain? Gravity, tides, the moon, the sun, the revolutions of Earth. In my world—whether I win or lose—the source is simple: the words on the verge of exiting Jean-Luc's mouth, pushing fate into motion.

The Ceiba Tree

AMAZON RAIN FOREST

My fate, I fear, depends on humans. I do not know much about the ways of humans, especially the new ones with their killing machines. They are a frightening mystery to me.

But the other humans, the ones who have protected us, lived among us, listened to us—I have come to understand them. I have heard the stories they tell about the first ceiba tree, the Great Mother who created the entire jungle and all the creatures in it. I have felt the respect in the way they gather my silky fibers, nap in my buttress roots, use my leaves for medicines.

I have heard the tales of what happens to their own loved ones when they die, how their spirits live on in the wild cats who live among us—pumas and ocelots and jaguars. These humans do not kill such magnificent creatures, just as they do not harm us ceibas. These humans share our heart.

You may wonder where this heart is. It is outside our bodies. It is made of the countless connections with other plants and creatures, large and small. It is in the flow of knowledge, of nourishment, of love. It is an ever-changing yet constant thing, something you cannot pin down, something that can grow and grow and grow, sparking link after link in our web.

And now we will see if this heart can travel the farthest, grow the biggest that it's ever tried, ever even imagined. And if this heart can expand so much, clear across the world, then maybe, just maybe, there's a human out there whose heart will do the same.

Into the Unknown

Deep in the earth beneath my impractical cowgirl boots, the plates are moving and the steam is pulsing—*thump thump thump*—I swear I can feel the vibrations.

Jean-Luc is waxing poetic about the stellar quality of the dessert entries and the soulful community of Heartbeat Springs and how quickly the DBA pulled this contest together to counter the late-winter gloom . . . and I want to shake him and yell, *Get to the point!*

"And ze winning entry is ze fantastical jaguar-waterfall scene, Into Ze Unknown, created by young chocolatier Leo de la Cueva."

Applause explodes. Blood thuds in my ears. Chaos explodes in the right atrium of my heart—Leo's chamber. Bombs are detonating—a mix of anger, jealousy, hurt . . . and shockingly, some rogue fireworks of pride and joy. After all, this is *Leo*.

I look at my enemy. He's not smiling; he looks solemn, almost embarrassed. Nieves, though, is jumping up and down and whooping and hollering enough for both of them.

Jean-Luc settles the audience down with his hand. "And now, for a surprise! We have another winner! Zis was a tie!"

A confused round of clapping. A tie?

Jean-Luc continues, excited. "We are grateful to ze anony-mous donor of ze prize, who assured us zat in ze event of a tie, he would be willing to sponsor two winners and ze guests of zeir choice.

"Ze ozer winner, equally as talented, and also surprisingly young for such an accomplished chocolatier—Coco Hidden for Ze World Tree!"

Now Mom is cheering along with Nieves, and Permelia is screaming and Gooey is yapping. I wait for a smile to sprout on my face but there's only this blood whooshing, and this quivery about-to-boil feeling inside me. And part of me is aware how I must look from the outside: a stiff, wide-open-eyed plastic doll.

"Winners, start preparing for ze trip of a lifetime!" Jean-Luc raises his arms triumphantly. "A week in ze Amazon rain forest!"

I know I should jump up and down or something, but I'm still as a tree. I feel my roots leading to the Amazon, intermin-gling with my dream tree's, and the realization slams into me: *I'm going there.* To a place far, far away.

Did I mention I've never been outside of Colorado?

Mom and Nieves are hugging each other and squealing. And I'm whacked with another doozie: The moms think they're going to the Amazon. With Leo and me. *Together.* In two weeks, I will be in the middle of the biggest, wildest, most remote jungle on earth with the very person who turned my world upside down.

What was I thinking?

From his throne, Gali is watching me and Leo with lively eyes.

I dare to look at Leo. He's daring to look at me.

He tucks his hair behind his ears. His liquid-chocolate eyes are wide and terrified now, too. He's right here at the edge of a cliff with me. A cliff that we're about to leap from, together, into the unknown.

Over the next couple weeks, Mom and I prepare for the journey. We've agreed to schedule it over Leo's and my ten-day spring break in April. That way, we won't have to close El Corazón during summer tourist season and we won't miss any school. And supposedly, spring is relatively dry in the Amazon, meaning it's not raining *all* the time. I figured that might make my treasure easier to find.

But here's the thing. It's one thing to *imagine* yourself on a treasure hunt in the jungle, but when you're in a cold, fluorescent-lit doctor's office wincing at vaccines for hepatitis and typhoid and yellow fever, it becomes painfully real.

We take trips to the used outdoor gear shop and pretreat our clothes with special bug spray and dig out some flashlights from the depths of the closet. After a long hunt, we find our passports—issued years ago but never used—in the back of the junk drawer. We gather instant cold packs and insulated bags and mini-coolers and plan how to keep the chocolate we'll bring from melting. (We can't go a single day without our chocolate.)

Every day, I pore over the only books I could find in our little Heartbeat Springs library. The books look more ancient than the century-old building—battered, musty, clothbound, yellow-paged tomes with grainy black-and-white photos. They're packed with quotes from old-time explorers that make the Amazon rain forest sound like a death trap, a dungeon of tortures. Mosquitos eating you alive, injecting diseases of all kinds into your bloodstream; horrifying parasites that find insidious ways to set up camp in your body; predators, large and small, with the sharpest teeth and strongest jaws; deadly venoms and stings that hurt as much as a bullet wound; ruthless anacondas, pit vipers, electrical eels, caimans, jaguars . . . not to mention fierce warriors toting deadly wooden spears and poison blowguns.

Someone else checked out every single modern book on the Amazon—in both the kids' and adults' sections. There wasn't time to special order a book from a bigger library. So I got stuck with these nightmare-inducing artifacts.

And scariest of all is the company I'll be keeping: the boy who is painful for me to even look at. Chaperoned by our *moms.* Thus the refrain going through my head hundreds of times during the day and night: *What have I gotten myself into?*

The one bright spot in all this is Gali. He's coming on the trip with us. Imagining him there instantly calms me down, makes me think that maybe, just maybe, I can see this through.

Apparently, the anonymous contest sponsor decided we need a guide, yet no DBA member except for Gali speaks Spanish. His dialect is from Spain, where he grew up, and although it's way different from Latin American Spanish, it's more or less understandable—just a bit lispy with a distinct rhythm and rise and fall.

And as it turns out, Gali did travel to South America a few decades ago. Maybe that's where he got those old jungle photos hanging in our shop. Judging by how slow and frail he's seemed lately, I don't know how great a guide he'll make, but I'm glad he'll be along for the ride.

One early April evening, three days before the journey, Gali invites me to sit at a candlelit café table in El Corazón, then spreads out a map of South America between us.

Over the speakers, Andean pan flutes softly play. Mom is clanking around behind the counter, cleaning up and listening to a learn-Spanish-fast program on her earbuds. In whispers, she repeats basic phrases in her terrible American accent.

Mom's been unabashedly excited about the trip. She and Nieves have been drooling over the itinerary, which includes a night in a fancy boutique hotel in Quito. And it turns out that the ecolodge we'll be staying at in the jungle is run by a cacao co-op. Mom couldn't stop squealing when she discovered this detail . . . which makes me feel even worse for secretly wanting to back out.

Gali sips his cinnamon-almond hot chocolate and moves a liver-spotted hand over the mass of green at the top of the continent. He points a finger to the capital of Ecuador, Quito, marked by a star. I have to squint in the faint yellow flame glow to read it.

"We'll land here, my dear. After a night resting in a lovely inn, we'll take a car to the town of Shell."

Strange name. It's far from any ocean. "As in, seashell?" I ask.

"As in Shell the oil company," he says with a sigh. He taps on a small dot at the jungle's edge. "So, we'll fly on a small plane into the Amazon. People from the cacao co-op will meet us there." He moves his finger in an arc all the way to the center of the green blob.

There is nothing but green with ribbons of blue. No town dots or roads or anything. A prickly fear moves over me.

"They'll take us by dugout canoe to the huts where we'll be staying." His fingertip traces a river labeled Shiripuno. "See? It's in the Yasuní National Park, in territory where the Huaorani people live." He pronounces it wow-RAH-nee. "Then we'll spend a little over a week touring their bit of jungle and cacao co-op. Cooperativa Felicidad."

Happiness Co-op. The name is promising, but I've looked for more details online, and there's practically nothing about the place—just a single, amateur-looking webpage with an email address, a map, a paragraph in Spanish about cacao, a paragraph about indigenous Huaorani culture, and a few blurred, low-resolution photos. Mom hasn't been worried about the lack of online info; she and Nieves keep going back to video tours of the fancy hotel.

Hands shaking, I take a sip of my cardamom-dusted hot chocolate, lick the whipped cream from my lip, and look up from the map, into Gali's old gray-blue eyes. "Gali, I'm . . . I'm . . . I'm . . . *terrified*."

"Oh, Coco, dear. Remember the secret to happiness."

I wish I could see into his heart, *feel* his heart—I bet it feels as big as the ocean, filled with ten thousand secrets to happiness, like giant, flashing schools of silver fish. "Which secret?"

He leans in. "Do what scares you."

I take another shaky sip. "That sounds . . . dangerous."

He looks out the window, through the reflected candlelight from the shop, into the snow-blanketed night. "Well, then, my dear, remember the other secret to happiness."

I sigh. "Which one?"

"Try something new."

I frown, watch the flame flicker, golden at the tip, blue at the base. "I'm a creature of habit, you know. A hobbit, some people have called me." Some people, meaning Leo.

Gali laughs, a low wheezy chuckle.

I tug at my crystal necklace. "Gali, I've even worn the same jewelry every day for years. If I love something, why change it?" I swallow hard, imagine the vast unknown of the Amazon. "Why risk it?"

He reaches into his shirt pocket, pulls out a folded piece of paper, opens it up. It's the Home Sweet Home poster, featuring the giant ceiba tree. It's an echo of the black-and-white photo of the ceiba on our wall. An echo of the tree in my dream. A zing of familiarity warms my chest. *Within my roots a treasure awaits.*

"Think of why you entered this contest to begin with. Coco dear, you said you were searching for something."

I nod, drain my last drop of chocolate.

"Here's another secret to happiness, my dear. What you need—it needs you, too. It's only waiting for you to ask, *to act.*" His eyes blaze in the candlelight. "Be brave, Coco."

Three days later, the first day of spring break, we're in a small plane rumbling from the teeny Heartbeat Springs airport across the Rockies to the big one in Denver. It's only April, so there's still plenty of snow in the mountains. Out the window, they look like a rippling sea of meringue, rich and white, with glitter-dusted peaks and shadowed valleys.

The plane is nearly empty, so we have our choice of window seats, and we can shout to each other over the vibrations without disturbing any strangers. In front of me is Mom, who has donned a flowered vintage frock from the back of her closet. Two small braids on either side of her face join in back to form a French braid, ending in a curlicue over her shoulder. Across from her is Nieves, in her black yoga pants and matching zippered-up hoodie, her dark hair in a long, smooth ponytail.

And across from me is Leo. He's wearing earbuds, with a Nintendo 3DS in hand, but he's forgotten about the little screen. He's staring through a part in his long bangs, his mouth dropped open a tad, gaping at the snow-frosted Rocky Mountains and clear blue sky and dazzling sunshine. His T-shirt is the same white as the snow. If I wore a white T-shirt in winter, I'd look like a snowman, a pasty, pale, skinny blob. But Leo's skin is the golden hue of *cajeta*, aka caramelized goat milk, so he can pull off any color of clothes, from bright white to neon yellow.

I fiddle with the hem of my shirt—my favorite shirt that I've had for three years, and even though it's a little small, there's some life in it yet. A soft, nubby brown long-sleeve shirt with wispy, creamy lace trim like foam on a mocha latte. Mom's tried donating it to the thrift store three times already, but I always manage to grab it from her clutches. It's got a few *unnoticeable* holes, and once I've got a good, comfortable look going, why mess with it?

Behind me is Gali in his "traveling clothes," which consist of an old-fashioned suit, suspenders, hat, and striped bow tie. I wonder what he's planning to wear once we enter the Amazon. And how his brass-tipped cane will fare in the mud.

The moms are whispering together, and every once in a while shooting a concerned look at Gali. They doubt he's up to the task of tour guide. When I asked Mom about it last night, she said, "He's an old man who gets winded walking up ten steps! How's he going to lead us through the jungle?"

But they both want to go so badly, they accept him as a necessary burden. Personally, I'm glad he's here. I don't mind carrying his bags for him and helping him up and down stairs. While the moms gab, he can diffuse some of the *AWK-ward* between me and Leo. And there's plenty of it. I decide it will be easiest to just ignore him for the rest of the ride, maybe even the rest of the whole Amazon trip.

Once again, Leo's buried in his Nintendo, though, unaware he's being ignored.

I turn to Gali. "How's your heart?"

He sits up straighter, adjusts his bow tie, raises an eyebrow. His eyebrows are like wild, white-haired caterpillars. "Oh, just pondering death."

"Death?"

I can see Leo perk up with interest, but his eyes stay glued to the screen.

Gali looks at me gently, with crinkly-eyed compassion. "That's an ancient secret to happiness, you know. Imagining yourself dead."

"Dead?" Now the conversation's getting somewhere. Out of

the corner of my eye, I see Leo pausing his game and turning down the volume.

"One day we'll die, and it could be tomorrow." Gali speaks matter-of-factly. "So live life deeply, without regrets. Forgive and seek forgiveness."

I imagine a boa strangling me to death. It doesn't exactly make me happy. Now maybe the thought of a boa strangling Leo, or better yet, a poison dart heading straight for his chest . . .

Somewhere along the way, my hurt has morphed into anger. And instead of wanting to make up, I want revenge.

As if he's read my vicious thoughts, Leo stands up and mutters something about the bathroom. I notice that Gali is watching me watch Leo.

Once Leo's down the aisle and out of earshot, Gali leans in and whispers to me, his voice barely audible over the rumble of plane engine. "Coco, dear. Bitterness is tricky. You want to hurt the one who's hurt you—"

"By shooting him straight in the heart," I interrupt.

"Straight in the heart," he echoes, nodding, taking a breath to continue.

"With a poison-tipped dart," I clarify.

"With a poison-tipped dart," he agrees. "But here's the thing, Coco dear: The poison-tipped dart is actually lodged in your own heart. The heart it's hurting is your own."

And this is when it hits me: Leo's chamber of my heart hasn't just been sitting there, empty and abandoned. Over the months, it's been filling with poison, poison that's starting to overflow and seep out.

"Is it fixable?" I ask gravely.

He nods. "Pull out the dart."

I frown and try to picture this. Nope, imagining death by anaconda is much easier.

How will my heart survive a week in the jungle with this boy? The question feels like a thirty-foot-long boa constrictor wrapping itself around my chest and squeezing out every last bit of air.

That's exactly how I felt six months ago, when I dared to infiltrate the seventh-grade royalty . . . when I accidentally lit the fuse that set off the friendship bomb at the chocolate shop a week later.

Leo and Caitlyn and her escorts were in Heartbeat Springs Park, holding court on the playground. It was the first week of school, when summer changes to fall, and the aspens were just starting to flame golden, and the whole place seemed as welcoming as a birthday cake, aglow with freshly lit candles. Maybe that's what made me feel so brazen and hopeful.

The elementary schools hadn't released yet, so the middle schoolers had taken over the swings and jungle gym territory. They acted aloof, like they were *ironically* swinging and doing the monkey bars, but once in a while a pure, little-kid grin broke through. Leo was on a swing beside Caitlyn's, and they were twisting the chains around slowly and drifting back and forth in spirals. As I approached, iron ground against iron like sounds from a medieval torture chamber.

I should've taken that as a sign to turn back.

Instead, *"¡Hola, amigos!"* I said cheerfully, flashing my then-fearless smile at them both.

"Hey," Leo said under his breath.

I turned to Caitlyn, who was pressing pink gooey gloss between her lips. It matched the sparkly pink on her eyelids and cheekbones. She looked like a glob of aspartame-sweetened, chewed-up bubble gum, glistening in the sunshine. Politely, I said, "We haven't officially met yet. I'm Coco."

She half nodded, looking over my head, as if she had no idea what to do with that bit of information. To rescue her from her bad manners, I said, "I know who you are already—Caitlyn Bland."

Into my head popped a full, polished description I'd write for her if she were chocolate:

Caitlyn Bland, of the Heartbeat Springs Oppressive Regime cultivar: Artificially enhanced white "chocolate," made of cocoa butter derived from common, lesser quality beans. Chemically deodorized to mask its fetid stench, resulting in a plastic Tupperware aroma. Generous heaps of preservatives, corn syrup, and milk solids. Rounded out with a fair dosing of hydrogenated oils, vanillin, and other artificial flavors. Perfect accompaniment to Donut Delite.

Smiling to myself, I glanced over at Leo. He'd stopped twisting his swing and sat hunched over on the flexible rubber seat. He was shrinking down, caving in on himself. Instead of meeting my gaze, he pulled his phone from his pocket and started randomly, almost desperately, scrolling.

Leo had always been quiet at first in social situations. He hardly ever approached new customers in El Corazón, while I could just stride right up and engage them in a half-hour chat about ethical chocolate industry practices.

Suddenly it seemed extremely important to remind him— and enlighten Caitlyn—about the fact that I knew Leo better than any human in the universe.

"Leo and I have been best friends for ages," I informed Caitlyn. "Practically since we were the size of cacao beans in our mothers'—" And here I paused. Leo was so self-conscious nowadays, he might not want me bringing up his mother's womb. I racked my brain for a synonym, rejected *uterus*, *internal organ*, and finally settled on *abdominal cavity*.

Caitlyn screwed up her face. Leo shrunk farther down into the swing, staring at his phone screen like he wished it were a portal to another dimension.

My pulse was racing at warp speed. I had to change the subject, fast. I looked around and my gaze landed on the playground sand at my feet. When things aren't going well, I've found it useful to put the problem into perspective. Inspired, I picked up a handful of sand. Props are good when you're explaining something new, like the process of chocolate-making or astronomically big numbers.

In my most intriguing voice, I mused, "Did you guys know that there are more stars in the observable universe than grains of sand on earth?"

Caitlyn blinked, as if she simply couldn't process a number so large.

"I know, right?" I said, encouraged. "The latest estimate is seven hundred sextillion stars!"

"*Sex*-tillion?" she echoed with a sneer.

Leo's face was turning red now. He'd let his hair fall all the way over his eyes.

There was a long silence, which I felt the strong need to fill. "Now, of course, if we're just talking about our own galaxy, the Milky Way, the low-end estimate is a hundred billion stars . . . which isn't too far off from eighty-six billion—the number of neurons in a human brain!"

Another silence. By this time, the other members of the royalty had finished their ironic antics on the monkey bars and were standing nearby, checking their phones to see what updates they'd missed during their two upside-down minutes. In their peripheral vision, they watched me and Leo and Caitlyn.

I opened my mouth to tell them about how the growth of the universe parallels the growth of a brain, when Caitlyn said in a dragged-out voice, "TMI."

My first reaction: flabbergastedness. Too much information? Seriously? Nearly a hundred billion neurons in her brain, and they couldn't handle a few simple, interesting factoids?

Then, suddenly, my own face grew hot. The sand slid through my fingers. I wanted to convince her how enchanting the universe was, make her admit in front of everyone that I was a fountain of fascinating knowledge. But Leo looked like he was *this close* to actually digging a hole and burying himself in the sand.

Quietly, I mumbled, "Well, I should go. Gotta get a new batch of chocolate in the melanger machine. It needs a few days of mixing to get the particle size down—"

I stopped, reminding myself that Caitlyn Bland's eighty-six billion neurons could not handle any more information, especially that of a microscopic nature.

From my pocket, I pulled out a truffle. Chocolate makes everything better. "Truffle?" I offered her.

"What kind?"

"Madagascar trinitario with *cajeta*."

"What the ?"

"It's chocolate rolled with caramelized, locally produced goat's milk."

Her face scrunched up. "Goat's milk? Seriously?"

I wanted to point out that if she thought goat's milk was gross, she should take a good long look at the ingredient list in those donuts she devoured. But I bit my tongue and raised a limp hand. "Bye."

No one returned my "bye" except for Leo, and his voice sounded small, as small as a voice in a movie about some kid who's shrunk down so far no one can see him, but only hear his little insect-sized voice.

As I left, the autumn wind carried a round of laughter, including Leo's, which I could've easily picked out of a lineup, blindfolded, because for the past thirteen years it had been an essential part of my life . . . if not *the* essence, like chocolate. Not only delicious, but necessary.

Now there was a sharp edge to his laughter.

I set the whole truffle on my tongue and urged it to work its magic. But chocolate couldn't make this better. It couldn't even muster up a smile in me.

And a week later, chocolate would end Leo's and my friendship. That's when he would say the words that cut like blades: *Just stay away from me and my friends.*

When Leo comes back down the airplane aisle, he sits down and works his jaw back and forth, as if deciding something. Then, in a lightning-quick movement, he grabs something from the air. A red silk scarf, which has suddenly appeared out of nowhere. He waves it around for a moment, then tucks it into his fist, taps it with the other hand, then opens his fist. The scarf is gone.

Against my will, wonder ripples through me. Where did the scarf go? And where did Leo go? This is not the same Leo I've known for thirteen years.

Gali claps and chuckles, delighted. "Ah, the unexpected! Another secret to happiness, my friends."

"Where'd you learn that trick?" I ask Leo suspiciously.

Nieves tunes in and says, "Online magic tutorials!"

I scrunch my eyes at Leo. He's mastered a new skill without me, without me even *knowing* about it. I wonder if Caitlyn Bland and the royalty know about it, if he does tricks for them.

"Isn't he fantastic?" Nieves says proudly.

Leo shrugs a shoulder. "I figured magic would be a good way to break the ice with the locals, you know?"

Gali nods, adjusting his bow tie. "Ingenious idea, son."

Magic. So Leo's been finding magic, too. On his own.

The Ceiba Tree

AMAZON RAIN FOREST

I have witnessed many painful things. I have witnessed anacondas as thick as my limbs squeezing the life out of sloths. I have witnessed jaguars crush deer skulls in one bite, then drag their carcasses into neighboring branches to save for later. I have witnessed humans shooting darts at monkeys in my arms and then, once the animals fall, spearing them to death.

But that is all in the natural order, the eternal story of predators and prey, life and death.

Perhaps the most painful thing I've witnessed: a man shot dead for defending our forest. A brave man, a loving father, felled to make way for more destruction.

I wished more than anything that my arms could have scooped him up before the bullet hit. I would have kept him safe in my canopy.

For a long time afterward, the whole jungle mourned him. We still mourn him. Perhaps it is so painful because if humans themselves, the most powerful predators of all, cannot protect our home, then what hope is there?

I should warn you this might be dangerous. Please do not let this scare you away. Be brave.

Poison-Tipped Dart

From above, the Denver airport looks like an enormous circus tent with multiple peaks. Once we get off the plane and go inside, it's crowded and chaotic all right, but it's no carnival. We have to rush like crazy to get to our next plane's gate on time since it's in a different terminal altogether.

Nieves is used to airports—she takes Leo to Mexico to visit relatives every year—so her eyes just glide over the giant screens and she instantly knows where to go. She tries to hustle us along, clapping and kind of jogging in place in her yoga pants and sneakers like she's leading an exercise class. "Let's go, *chicos!* *¡Ya, vámonos!*"

Mom and Leo and I can keep up, but Gali straggles along as if he's in a slow-mo video. His brass-tipped cane *tap-tap-taps* the marble floors, slipping and sliding, doing more harm than good. On the rollicking underground train, Gali catches his breath and says, "A secret to happiness is slowing down, you know. Slowing down and noticing the world."

Nieves makes a face. "True, *mi amor*, unless we slow down so much we miss the plane."

Except for a few slips from Nieves, the moms mostly hide their exasperation from Gali. We take turns carrying his bag and backpack up and down the escalators, on and off the train. He seems lost in the giant airport, his bow tie crooked, his eyes befuddled, like a time-traveler embarking from long ago. "Oh, my," he mumbles at every blunder. "The old airport was so much simpler."

We barely make it to the gate before they close it, and by that time Leo's pulling Gali along by one elbow, and I'm pulling him by the other, and Gali's huffing and puffing so much he can't protest.

Getting through the airport is such a frantic whirlwind that I don't notice Leo hasn't said a word to me until we get settled on the plane for Miami, our layover. I thought I was ignoring him, but maybe this whole time he thinks he's been ignoring me.

It stings, this dart spewing toxins into Leo's space in my right atrium. And to be clear, I can't just pull it out. It's like a barbed fishing hook. If I did try to tug on it, the whole organ would just get shredded to bloody bits.

On the plane, Leo keeps his eyes glued to a screen—rotating among TV or video game or phone or tablet—and his mouth glued shut. He has a window seat, but instead of taking advantage of the view, he's shut the plastic shade, blocked out the view for the rest of us. I sit in the aisle, with Gali in the middle, buffering me and Leo.

Across the aisle, the moms are blabbing and sharing a little bottle of white wine. I thought I'd have Mom mostly to myself on this trip, free of distractions. But it's like she and Nieves are besties who haven't seen each other for years.

Mom nods sympathetically as Nieves says how burnt out she is on real estate law. "I mean, really, Mara, the whole reason I got into law was for social justice. Human rights. Environmental protection. And look at me now!" Usually Nieves is calm and professional, in and out of her office—as smooth as her glossy hair, as subdued as her neutral clothes. It's weird to see her so heated up about something.

"I know," Mom says, clicking her plastic cup against Nieves's in a toast. "I used to be all about saving the world with shade-grown cacao." She sips and sighs. "And now all I think about is paying bills."

I turn my attention to Gali, hoping he'll talk with me. But he's limp as a wrung-out dishrag. He's sleeping with his mouth open and his head tilted to the side, snoring lightly. I sigh and open a book.

At one point, while I'm reading, I hear Gali's name as the moms talk across the aisle. Their conversation has shifted course and they're on their second mini-bottle of wine. Nieves sips from her plastic cup and flails her manicured hand around and says in a very loud whisper, "He can barely make it through an airport, Mara!"

"It doesn't make sense," Mom says, shaking her head. "Why on earth did the DBA assign him as our guide? It's like we've got an extra kid to take care of."

My insides buck, not just at the idea that Leo and I are kids to be taken care of, but because Gali is my old-man superhero. Not only does he break up some of the *AWK-ward* between me and Leo, but he's nice to have around. It's like he's toting an invisible sack of butterflies with a hole in it, trailing behind secrets to happiness . . . even if the recent ones involve death and darts.

"Bottom line," Nieves says, slipping into lawyer mode, "I don't feel comfortable doing adventure travel with an unhealthy, elderly, incompetent man."

Ouch. Poor Gali. This is sounding dangerous, like they might kick Gali off our trip altogether. I feel my dream tree reaching deep into my brain, zapping a bunch of neurons into action. *Within my roots a treasure awaits.*

I can't give up. We haven't even left the United States yet. I lean across the aisle and say firmly, in my own lawyer voice, "I claim full responsibility for Gali."

Mom looks at me, startled. "What, sweet bean?"

I glance back at Gali beside me, still snoring, oblivious to how close he is to getting booted, ignorant of the mutiny being plotted against him. I feel strong, bigger than myself, with a solid trunk and giant roots. "I'll take care of him."

The moms exchange worried glances. "We're just not sure if he's up to this, sweetie," Mom says finally.

Then Leo, who's supposedly been listening to something on his earbuds, pipes up. "You can't dump Gali. Let him come."

And even though Leo's been ignoring me and hogging the window, I feel a swell of gratitude. He adores Gali as much as I do, maybe even more. Once he told me that with his dad mostly out of the picture, Gali was his best hope for a decent male role model in life.

I cross my arms. "Mom, if you make Gali stay behind, then I stay behind."

"Me too, Mamá," Leo says.

Together, at this moment, we are as solid as two trees. At this moment, Leo's six-month-old demand that I stay away seems more like a wispy cloud than a metal blade.

The moms confer in hushed voices. Finally, Nieves turns to us, says slowly, "Okay, we'll take Gali to Ecuador. But he might have to stay in our hotel in the city all week. We might not be able to bring him into the jungle."

"We can!" Leo and I say at exactly the same time.

In my head, I hear his voice, triumphant, calling, *Jinx! You owe me a truffle.* We used to say the same things at the same time all the time. We always owed each other lots of truffles, so many they'd evened out over the years. And I'm guessing he heard my voice in his head, too, because for the first time in hours, he looks at me. And for a split second I look back . . . without shooting daggers from my eyes.

Once when I was little, I got a splinter in my finger that Mom couldn't get out with a needle and tweezers. After a while, it stopped hurting, and after a while more I forgot about it, and after a while more, one day, it just popped right out of my skin, no pain at all, like an invisible force inside me had just poked it out.

I wonder if something like that's possible with poison darts.

I pull a *dulce de leche* truffle from my insulated chocolate bag and extend it to Leo. "I owe you a truffle."

Keeping his hands in his lap, he peers at me from under his long bangs, probably weighing the risk of me poisoning it.

We both know that chocolate's good at hiding the taste of poison. Back in colonial times in Mexico, there was a priest who told his congregation they could no longer drink hot chocolate in church. The ladies were all addicted to chocolate and it was the only way they could get through his boring service. So they added poison to his hot chocolate. He died and they got a new priest. One who supported their chocolate habit.

After a beat, Leo says, "No, thanks."

I smile mysteriously. "Thinking about that dead priest?"

"Yeah." A nervous snort of laughter.

"Thinking about death's a secret to happiness," I tell him.

"So I hear."

"Listen, Leo, if you're gonna get murdered, death by chocolate's a good way to go. You get a natural painkiller plus delicious endorphin release while you're kissing the world good-bye."

Meeting my eyes, Leo reaches out, takes the truffle, and as if on a silent dare, pops the entire thing in his mouth. As he chews, he mumbles, "Chocolate makes everything better, right?"

A few minutes later, he's looking out the window, a hint of a smile on his face. Maybe it's the endorphins. Maybe just relief he's not dead.

Sometimes I let myself remember the good things about Leo, the fun we had together, the way he would manage to humbly save the day. Back when things between us were easy—two years ago in fifth grade—we were partners for our social studies project on the Maya, who are technically his ancestors. We gave a short presentation, and then I served sacred ancient Mayan hot chocolate, complete with chili peppers so spicy they nearly burned off the taste buds of everyone in class. Our teacher narrowed her teared-up eyes at me between desperate gulps from her water bottle.

We were headed for a big, fat F until Leo rescued us with his small, carved milk chocolate replicas of Mayan creations—celestial temples, statues of ancient gods and monkeys and corn. When he announced the kids could eat them—and that the milk's casein would wash away the burning capsaicin of the chili—everyone melted into happy sighs. We'd used the criollo cultivar, true to its Mesoamerican roots—delicate, complex, floral, nutty, and rare. Since it's particularly disease-susceptible, the organic varieties are highly prized.

Let's just say that once everyone's taste buds recovered from the fire, they found themselves in paradise. And we ended up with an A-minus.

For the rest of the day, I try to remember these good things about Leo. And it's a long day. We debark our last plane, wait in a long line for customs, and finally, our strange little group steps out of the Quito airport into the sultry night. The air smells green and wet and feels thick on my skin. Taxi drivers swarm us, urging us to get in their taxis. Spanish words fly everywhere. Part of me wants to jump up and down and shout, "I'm in ECUADOR!" Another part wants to curl up and go to sleep.

As the rest of us look around in a drowsy daze, Nieves efficiently negotiates with a taxi driver to bring us to his brother's hotel. It turns out Gali never booked the rooms at that lovely historic inn on our itinerary—he was supposed to, but he hadn't realized reservations were necessary these days.

After a high-speed ride down a wide highway, the taxi drops us off at an unpainted gray cinder-block building on the edge of town that looks half-finished, then abandoned except for a slight fluorescent glow through a few windows. Because of some sporting event, it's completely full except for one room with two twin-sized beds. The moms let loose a flurry of exasperated sighs and exchange glances of impending disaster.

It's decided that Mom and I will sleep in one bed and Nieves and Leo in the other. In the *same room*. A room that smells like mold and mouse droppings. The single light bulb flickers blue, and the cement walls are speckled with large, mysterious, amoeba-shaped stains. The small window reveals a view of a tangle of electrical wires on the side of another concrete building, practically an arm's reach away. Even this late at night, traffic sounds and sirens and distant bass beats float into the room.

Gali insists he's fine sleeping on the sofa in the lobby. This gives the moms plenty of time to talk about him as they're doing bedbug checks.

"You know, Mara, we could just all go back home tomorrow," Nieves says, grimacing at a large brownish-red spot on the underbelly of the ancient flowered mattress.

Mom inspects the seams of a pillow. "Or Coco and I could take Gali back, and you and Leo could continue with the trip."

I'm about to protest, when Leo says, "No. We have to stay together."

Nieves studies her son for a moment, then says, "I think we should all just go back."

The ceiba roots move through me like waves, urging me toward the treasure. "No!" I hear myself shout, and then realize I'm yelling at someone else's mom.

Softly, I say, "Please. We can do this, all of us, *with* Gali. It's an adventure, right?" I resort to flattery. "I mean, come on, you're a brilliant lawyer, Nieves. And, Mom, you've run your own business for thirteen years. We can't let a couple little obstacles stop us."

Mom rubs her eyes, haggard. "Why don't we sleep on it?"

Looking skeptical, Nieves nods.

After we all take turns using the dinky, mildew-speckled bathroom, splashing cold water on our faces and brushing teeth, we hop in bed—Mom and I in ours, and Leo and Nieves in theirs. Leo says he'll sleep on the floor, but it's cold tile, and when a cockroach crawls over his foot, he quickly overcomes his embarrassment of sharing a bed with his mom and hops in beside her.

I giggle. I'm embarrassed by the whole situation, too. What on earth would Caitlyn Bland say about this? I'm still wearing my mocha latte shirt and soft, ripped-up jeans. No way do I want Leo to see me in my pj's. Which is kind of weird because up to about third grade, we used to have slumber parties together nearly every weekend.

And come to think of it, I have that slumber party feeling right now. A late-night snack is in order. I have to turn this trip around, make sure we continue on to the jungle. This is my one chance to find me dream tree. And despite a few glitches lately, chocolate does make everything better . . . about 99.9 percent of the time.

Even though I've already brushed my teeth, I take out some truffles from my stash in the insulated bag. Good. Not melted at all. Our instant cold pack system is working.

I hand a truffle to Mom. Briefly, I consider Gali's words: Forgive and let go. Then I toss a *dulce de leche* truffle to Nieves, and to Leo, I toss a jasmine truffle, chock-full of flower petals. I wait to see if he'll trade with his mom.

They each hesitate, Nieves probably thinking of her freshly brushed teeth and the late-night effects of caffeine; Leo probably wondering if maybe there's poison in *this* one. They throw caution to the wind and each take a bite of their own.

After the first round, I toss everyone another, and then another, and soon the theobromine is kicking in and showering us with happiness. Endorphins and serotonin and dopamine dart around like hummingbirds in our brains. Phenylethylamine sparks us wide-awake. Our mouths turn into a flashing, disco-ball-spinning night at Rollerland—hundreds of flavor compounds skating laps on our tongues. This entire batch was made from Madagascar trinitario, layer after layer of flavor, tart notes of grapefruit and raspberry. It makes our words suddenly bright and crisp and colorful, all joy and jokes.

The moms keep bursting into giggle fits. All the mishaps, combined with the chocolate, have pushed them over the edge into a land of snorting, helpless guffaws. It's like they've turned into kids. Nieves manages to look goofy despite her matching set of long black satin pajama pants and top. Mom's sleep clothes serve to make her look even goofier: sweat shorts and a polka-dotted tank covered by her red vintage Chinese robe embroidered with a dragon on back. I haven't seen that for ages.

They volley stories back and forth, mostly of me and Leo when we were little, and I can't help cracking a smile here and there, and piping in, *No, no, that's not what he said; it was like this* . . . And then Leo's cracking smiles and piping in, *No, no, no, it went like this!*

On impulse, I throw a pillow at his head. Probably a little too hard.

He throws it back more gently.

And even though the room is musty and bare, and the fluorescent light is buzzing and flickering, and the fan is rattling, and a few cockroaches are skittering here and there, and we aren't exactly sure where we're heading tomorrow or how to get there and I'm not sure if I'll still trust Leo after my neurotransmitters settle back down . . . it's a good night.

Once we finally turn off the lights, late, late at night, I'm smiling to myself. Lamplight filters through the gauzy curtains. I look over and see Leo sitting up in bed, tossing a red spark from one hand to another.

He sees me watching him. The red spark flies away toward the ceiling, and he reaches his hand way up to catch it, just in time. And who knows how he's doing this trick, but it's magical all right. The moms are so quiet they must be drifting off to sleep, so it's only him and me, watching these red sparks flying around. *Who is this boy?*

While I'm at it, who are any of these people who occupy chambers in my heart? This silly, giddy side of Mom is something new. This death-talking side of Gali is new, too. And then there's Leo with his strange new confidence, his red-sparking magic, the contents of his mind unknown.

And swirling in the center of the questions is my dream tree, beckoning to me.

Behind the Curtain

I don't play lots of video games, but Leo's into them, and there's this game we used to play—*The Legend of Zelda*—where you start off with three hearts at the top corner of the screen, and when your guy gets hurt, you lose hearts. But you can replenish hearts by sleeping, or eating, or finding little spirit orbs.

When I wake up to the sun shining through violet curtains, I've been replenished with more hearts in the corner of my screen. And looking around at the moms and Leo, it seems like they have, too. Must be the lingering effects of late-night laughter and chocolate.

Even Gali looks revived. In the light of day, he seems back to his old self. He's chipper in an old-time explorer's outfit, khaki pants with lots of pockets and a khaki shirt with even more. His white ponytail is poking out from under a wide-brimmed army surplus hat, the string tightened beneath his chin.

"A good night's sleep," he proclaims when we meet him in the lobby. "Another secret to happiness."

In the hotel café, over scrambled eggs and beans and rice and toast and melon juice, the moms plot and plan and Nieves makes a few strategic calls on her cell phone. Turns out Gali hasn't made any arrangements for transportation. Things must've changed plenty since he was here decades ago in a pre-reservation world.

Triumphantly, she announces, "I found a driver to take us to Shell—that's the little town on the edge of the rain forest. And I confirmed our flight from there to the airstrip on the Shiripuno River. We'll be in the jungle this afternoon!" She turns to Gali. "Now I couldn't find a contact phone number for the chocolate co-op. Please tell me you've been in touch with someone there."

"Oh, yes. I've corresponded by email."

Mom sighs. "Gali, it's one thing to arrive in a big city like Quito with no driver or hotel . . . but it's another thing altogether to get abandoned in the middle of the Amazon." She knits her brow. "You sure you got that part covered?"

"Of course, dear," he says, scooching his eggs and beans around on his plate. He's hardly touched his food. Sure, it's pretty average food, but who won't eat scrambled eggs and toast when you skipped dinner the night before? Is it because he's lying? Not feeling well?

Either way, he has to keep his energy up. His spot in my left ventricle has always been the safe, happy, cozy one. Free of drafts and problems. The pillow-filled, firelit chamber of my heart. I need to keep it that way.

I slip him a cinnamon truffle. "Eat and be happy, Gali."

Soon we're out of the city, our shiny SUV swerving around deep green mountains. Llamas and sheep dot the hills, and it's all so much warmer and lusher than my wintry Rocky mountains. Even in the early summer, with snow runoff, our Colorado mountains never look so Technicolor green. We pass small houses and shops made of painted cement with red-tiled roofs, and fringed with bursts of red and pink and orange flowers.

After a few hours, our driver, Jorge, stops in a town called Baños, which translates as *Baths*, as in hot spring baths, not so different from Heartbeat Springs. We don't have time to find the springs, but we make a stop for lunch at the edge of the town square, surrounded by green walls of jungled hills. We stretch our legs and arms, and outside the climate-controlled SUV, I'm suddenly swamped by the air—hot and heavy and sweet and tinged with car exhaust.

Instantly, I'm sweating and my T-shirt is sticking to my torso. It's the shirt I got from fourth-grade soccer, back when I used to play, and it's such a perfectly comfortable blend of cotton and polyester, it's still my favorite. And the color is a soothing robin's eggshell, which is proven to make people feel peaceful. Despite the tranquil blue, I have this fluttery feeling in my stomach, like it's been plopped in a winnowing machine and little husks are flying around inside me.

We're actually doing this! We're going to the jungle! We're heading to my dream tree!

Jorge leads us into a little restaurant, formally holding open the door in his sweat-stained button-down shirt. The walls are painted bright orange, with folk art hanging everywhere— woven llama tapestries, alpaca fur murals, pan flutes, painted clay sculptures, fiber and seed bags. We scarf down roasted chicken and salty potatoes and tart *agua de limón* while the moms chitchat. Jorge mops his head with a handkerchief and leans in to me and Leo. "Enjoy! You might be eating only monkey and caiman for the next week."

"Caiman?" I ask.

"Like crocodile," Leo says. "In the alligator family."

Jorge smiles and nods.

I take a swig of *agua de limón*. Who knows if he's joking, but just in case, I make a point to savor this last meal. Leo cleans his plate, too.

Afterward, Jorge offers to walk to the local grocery store with the moms so they can stock up on provisions for the jungle.

"Why don't you kids stay with Gali?" Nieves instructs, eyeing him with concern.

He still looks a little woozy from the steamy two-minute walk from the SUV to the restaurant. He has a far-off look on his face, staring out the window at the tip-tops of hills the color of lime snow cones.

Once the moms and Jorge leave, the bell on the door jangling behind them, Leo looks up from his Nintendo, straight at Gali. "How's your heart, Gali?"

"Ah, my heart," Gali says. "For decades, something sharp has been lodged in my heart."

"Wait, what?" I say, doing a double take. "You're, like, master of happiness."

He offers me a smile—a heavy, sad smile. "I thought I could live happily despite it. But as I inch closer to the end . . . well, I see that I can't bear it after all."

"What exactly is the sharp thing?" Leo asks, puzzled.

"A poisoned dart?" I venture.

"You could say that," Gali says after a pause. "But the poison in my case isn't anger."

"Then what?" I push.

"Shame. Stinging, burning, relentless shame."

Leo's brows furrow. We're both used to Gali speaking in riddles, but they're usually happiness-related riddles. What's this about *shame*?

A befuddled Leo stares at the llama fur mural for a few moments, then asks, "How'd the dart get there?"

Gali pats his chest. Something's inside his left chest pocket, something wrapped in a clear sandwich bag, something brown and leathery and mysterious. A small book? A journal? "Oh, Leo, son, that's a long story."

"Gali," I whisper, leaning in close, "what did you do?"

He loosens the string beneath his chin and tightens it again. "I can't bring it into the light. Not yet, Coco. Maybe, just maybe, on this trip, if I find a way to make up for what I did . . ."

He sips his *agua de limón*, dabs at his mouth with a neatly folded paper napkin. "Sometimes we think our little world is all there is. But it's a tiny piece in something much bigger. And all the pieces are connected, part of the whole. When we move outside our little world, we're startled. We see that what we've been doing has been hurting someone in their world."

"Wait a minute." Leo stares at Gali, hard. "So you have your own reason for coming here?"

"Indeed. For me, dear ones, this trip is a matter of life or death."

"Life or death?" I sputter.

"If I go back to Heartbeat Springs without finishing my business in the jungle, well, I'll die. And die a not-good death."

I'm rarely speechless. I usually have a thousand fascinating facts and flavors inside me just elbowing each other to get out first. But now all I can do is stare. Death? Dying? Shame? What happened to the ten thousand secrets of happiness? And what's this so-called business in the jungle? And was it all a coincidence that the anonymous benefactor of the contest chose him to be our guide? Like an elaborate root system, that question leads me to others, and others.

I tilt my head. "Was it you all along? The anonymous person behind the Home Sweet Home contest?"

He sighs, nods.

I exchange bug-eyed looks with Leo. Realization dawns. The shock of betrayal.

Slowly, Leo says, "You planned the whole thing, Gali. You came up with the prize. You knew me and Coco would win."

"Well, I *hoped* you would. I thought I'd toss the possibility out to the cosmos. I thought I'd give our destiny a little nudge. Sometimes you can't just wait around and hope . . . you have to take action. Make your own magic."

The pieces are coming together. I study the web of wrinkles on his face. "You needed our help but you knew our moms wouldn't let you pay for us all to take a trip to the Amazon."

He nods. "The doctor says I'm too frail to travel by myself. I wouldn't have been able to carry my bags. And in case something happens . . . well, I need travel companions."

Leo squints at Gali, as if he's peering through fog. "What if two random strangers had won? Or what if our moms hadn't let us come?"

"Well, then, I suppose I'd be making friends with two strangers now. Or staring out my window back home." He smiles at us. "I'm grateful that fate chose my favorite four people on earth."

The ground seems to shift beneath me. I struggle to stay steady. Should I feel thankful, too? Or angry? Now looking at Gali is like looking at one of those pictures of a vase that's also a picture of two faces in profile, nearly touching noses. For a second, I see him as a sneaky liar, and the next second as a kind grandfather. Can I really know anyone?

Leo's expression looks as muddled as I feel. "So really, this is all about you, Gali? You manipulated this whole thing?"

Gali lets out a long breath. "I'm an old man. I've learned to trust my gut over the years. And I had a feeling that you two and your mothers all needed something, too, something you might find on this trip. I had a feeling that our trip was written in the stars. Of course, that's a little too *out there* to explain to a lawyer and a businesswoman. But you understand, don't you?"

Leo and I look at each other again. It's strange that suddenly we're on the same side, in the same place. He looks comforted to have me near him, rather than wishing I'd stay away.

We glance back at Gali, both bewildered. You think you know someone, and then, like the Wizard of Oz, the curtain falls, and you see who he really is. You see how raw and aching he's been all this time. And then, when you look around, you see that everyone around you has their own tender ache from one thing or another. Maybe it's a matter of looking. Of asking.

Finally, I say, "Whatever horrible thing you did, Gali, I'll help you fix it."

Leo blinks, takes a long breath. "Me too."

"More secrets to happiness." Gali's eyes gleam, wet and shiny. "Sharing your truth with ones who care."

In the black SUV, we snake along a narrow road, with a deep canyon slicing through the jungle to our right, and walls of green rising so high I can't even see the sky from my window. Here and there, someone zip-lines across the valley, looking tiny as an ant in a towering jade palace. Out the other window looms a hydroelectric dam. Mist hangs low and turns into actual drizzle in some spots, then back to mist. Huge leaves abound—enormous versions of Mom's potted houseplants.

By midafternoon, we're in a clearing of grasses and concrete at the rain forest's edge—the town of Shell. Jorge motions to a strip of low buildings that look like storage warehouses. "The airports."

The moms look at each other.

He pulls into the dirt parking lot, points to a door. "Here's yours."

If the enormous circus tent airport in Denver had an opposite, this would be it. I've seen tool sheds bigger than this airport.

Within five minutes, we've paid Jorge, and after helping unload our bags, he gives us a doubtful look. *Buena suerte.*

Yes, we'll need good luck.

The airport is two adjoining yellow-painted rooms, about

the size of our mobile home, and only slightly more solid-looking. There's a garage-style door open to the street, and inside, a dozen hard orange chairs and an ancient computer on a small counter. Instead of a digital screen with departures on the wall, there's a dry-erase board with a sloppy orange chart, half filled out. But there's Nieves's name scrawled on it for the three o'clock departure.

A teenage guy behind the counter points to a scale in the middle of the room and mumbles, "Weigh yourselves and your bags, please." Apparently our plane is so tiny that every pound makes a difference. Disconcerting.

He leads us outside on the other side of the building, where we toss our bags on a cart, empty except for a woven green plastic sack with a chicken's head sticking out. It's alive and peering around with bewildered, beady eyes. And just beyond the luggage cart is a plane, which is smaller than the SUV we just came here in.

The guy—who's just a few years older than me—tells us the plane's delayed for mechanical reasons, and we'll have to wait. My adrenal gland has plenty of time to spew out cortisol, which, in turn, makes my mouth dry, my belly fluttery-sick, my palms sweat, and my brain scream, *WHAT WERE YOU THINKING?*

"You okay, sweet bean?" Mom asks.

I wonder what my face looks like to make her ask me that so gently.

"Fine," I creak, popping a passion flower truffle in my mouth to calm down.

I try to conjure the tree's singsong voice, the splendor of her roots, the promise of treasure. But all I can think is that I'll be trapped in that tiny plane just like that chicken trapped in the plastic bag.

Mom keeps patting my shoulder, giving me sideways hugs, probably more to comfort herself than me. Her shirt is ruffled, flowered Indian cotton, and smells like home, by which I mean El Corazón, roasting cacao and vanilla and old cedar and stone.

Nieves is making a halfhearted effort to get Gali to stay in this little town of Shell instead of venturing into the jungle with us. Gali listens politely and says, "Nieves, dear, if I die in the jungle, that's fine with me. Truly. Don't worry about me for a second. If you must leave me behind somewhere, then please do leave me in the jungle."

Lightly, Leo pats the place where Gali's shoulder blades touch like folded wings beneath his khaki shirt. "We got your back."

Nieves frowns.

Keeping her hand on my shoulder, Mom turns to Gali. "Listen, how will the people at the co-op know our plane's delayed? What time are they meeting us anyway?"

"Oh, I didn't mention an exact time in my email. But they'll see the plane coming."

His usually wide-open eyes are hiding something. Something he's not telling us.

Nieves senses it, too. "Did they email you back a confirmation of the date at least?"

"Well, no, but—"

The teenage guy comes out from behind the counter and calls out, "Nieves! Your group is up!"

The moms look at each other with a wave of panic.

Wiping her name off the board, the teen tells Nieves, "The mechanic finished up with your plane and the pilot's taken it for a test spin around the tarmac."

Which means there's no time to hear the end of Gali's sentence because, suddenly, things are moving fast. The airport guys are rushing us and tucking our bags in the back of the plane.

Nieves just blinks for a few seconds, but she's caught in the flurry of movement, too. It's as though a dam has been lifted and we're just carried along in the current, and next thing I know, my shaking chicken legs are walking outside and climbing into the plane.

Mom and Nieves sit in the third of three rows, and me and Leo in the second. The pilot is right in front of me, so close I could touch his curly black hair. Gali has trouble getting into the plane, but the pilot helps heave him up and buckle him in, right beside his own seat. The moms exchange looks.

"I'm cool with it," I hear Mom murmur to Nieves. Her eyes are hidden behind giant, sunset-colored 1960s sunglasses from Viv's Vintage. In a weird way, they make her look like an old-time hippie rock star. Her voice sounds as mellow as a rock star's, too. "It's crazy. But maybe crazy is what I need in my life."

I'd never thought about Mom needing *crazy* in her life—I thought she needed precisely the opposite—stability for El Corazón. A continuation of the steady, grounded, predictable, safe world that she'd created for us.

"Pura locura," Nieves says, shaking her head and smiling.

Pure craziness. She tosses up her manicured hands to the heavens, as if to say, *What happens, happens.*

They both let out low laugh-sighs, echoes of last night's slumber party.

The pilot adjusts the controls and the plane rattles and clanks along the runway like an old car and a hush falls over us and we hold our breaths—and then we're lifting up, up, up into the mists over the Amazon. And we breathe.

We breathe.

"The lungs of the Earth," Leo says, to no one in particular.

References to an internal organ and planet in one sentence. He's speaking my language. A peace offering?

And now my chest is soaring and my brain is gushing endorphins and serotonin, and sudden, strange, starry joy is swirling, galactic and euphoric, inside and out. It feels like I've devoured a thousand truffles.

Onward we fly, inside this capsule of rusted metal containing the beating of six hopeful hearts.

Seven if you count the chicken's.

Here I come, ceiba.

Inside the Broccoli Sea

From above, the Amazon rain forest looks like broccoli. An endless sea of broccoli. Ten minutes into the flight, in all directions are mounds of green florets, each one a treetop. That's the only way I can wrap my head around how gigantic this place is—comparing it to a side dish on a dinner plate.

Rivers snake through, ribbons of gold lacing through all that green. Here and there is a straight brown line, a road, and brown square clearings and rectangles of gray buildings. *"Petroleros,"* the pilot shouts over his shoulder, pointing with his chin. Oil drillers. Other than the *petroleros*, there's just this broccoli sea beneath us. And the farther in we fly, these naked patches are fewer and farther between.

The pilot is burly and muscled, his chest nearly bursting through his buttoned shirt. Sweat stains the fabric under his arms but he smells only like cologne. In a loud, rough voice, he explains that first the logging companies come and chop down strips of trees to form muddy dirt roads. They make way for the *petroleros* to set up oil wells and drilling operations. He shakes his head, taps his large fingers on the steering device. "Ten years ago, this was solid jungle, *amigos.*"

I can't see his eyes behind the mirrored lenses, but there's something sad in his voice, in the shrug of his shoulder.

We fly for another half hour over mounds of thick, rich green. I could never get tired of so much green. I'm gulping it down like a cool glass of water on a hot day. It's as if my soul sighs between swigs.

The first few minutes of the flight felt like a roller coaster, from the stomach-flipping takeoff to the upward swoop to the leveling off in the clouds. But now I'm used to the vibration and engine rumble and the way the wind tugs us here and there. It feels like cruising in a cozy, old car through the sky, comfortable enough that I can focus on the mind-boggling view out the windows.

Meanwhile, Leo doesn't even touch his Nintendo. And I wonder if he's feeling like me: 90 percent mesmerized and 10 percent terrified. Because if this jungle has a heart, that's where we're headed, deep into the secret, pulsing core.

"Any Internet or phone service out here?" Mom shouts over the engine roar. There's a waver in her voice, a shrill edge. I know that voice. It's when she's trying to sound casual but is actually on the brink of panic. The hippie sunglasses can only do so much.

He shakes his head slowly. *"Nada."*

Nada. Nothing. Which means that if something goes wrong, we're on our own. Absolutely, completely, and in all ways on our own, adrift inside this broccoli sea. All of a sudden

the balance flips to 90 percent terrified and 10 percent mesmerized.

Hands shaky, I unwrap a chamomile-honey truffle and nibble
nervously.

"Almost there, *amigos*," says the pilot. "Just another few
bends up the Shiripuno River."

Soon the plane slows and swoops and circles, and there,
ahead, stretches a strip of grass, a long rectangle of shallow
green cutting through denser green. Now the plane is lowering,
centering, dropping. My stomach drops along with it, as if
I'm whooshing down an elevator. I make sure my seat belt is
fastened tight and clutch my hands together in my lap.

There is no airport, no building, not even one made of
bamboo and dried leaves. Not a single road in sight, not even
gravel or dirt.

Nada.

We lower, lower, lower, and the pilot flips switches and the
engine sounds shift, and then we make a few gentle bounces on
the grass strip like a rubber ball slowing to a roll. The brakes
engage and we skid to a stop.

I peer through the window. Now that we're on the ground,
the forest no longer looks like broccoli. On all four sides of the
airstrip the jungle begins, thickly and greenly. These are no
dinky stalks of veggies, but enormous leaves and trees, fit for a
land of giants.

The pilot gets out, stretches, then opens the passenger doors
for us. Stiffly, I climb out.

And I'm in another world. The air is a blanket of a zillion
water droplets, sizzling, steaming, and wrapping around my

body. In seconds, I'm sweating, salty rivers gushing down slick skin. Blinking, I grab my hat from my pack. The light is misty but blinding. Sunbeams are zapping around in so many tiny mirror drops.

Leo and the moms are squinting and fumbling for hats, too.

Insects are swarming, but I don't know where the bug spray is, so I just swat them away. Now that I can see better, I look around from beneath the brim of my hat, turning in a full circle, scanning the jungle for signs of life. And there are plenty—all manner of birds screeching a riot of squawks and caws and chirps and peeps. Bright feathers darting here and there through the green.

But no sign of humans.

My insides are on the wildest amusement park ride ever. One second, my insides are laughing and screaming: *I'm in the Amazon! I'm near my treasure!* And the next, my gut is falling down a dark pit, crying: *We're all alone! We can't survive!* And the next, I'm reaching for another truffle. *Need some endorphins! Now!*

In the insulated bag, the chocolate is softening, so I break open another instant cold pack, mashing it with my fingers, then zipper the bag quickly to trap the cool air. With shaky hands, I bite into a nearly melting peanut butter truffle.

The pilot stretches, takes a long sip from his water bottle, then starts climbing back into the cockpit. "Have fun, *amigos!*"

"Wait!" shrieks Nieves.

He adjusts his large body on the seat, buckles himself in. "Yes, *señora?*"

"You can't just leave us here!"

He sighs, offers a sympathetic smile. "Sorry I can't wait till your hosts meet you, *amigos*, but I'm behind schedule already. I have a group of *petroleros* to take to another site before night falls."

I chew my truffle ferociously.

Nieves widens her eyes, looks at Mom, who is frozen silent. Slowly, Nieves says, "But. We're. In. The middle. Of nowhere."

"Just head downriver." The pilot wipes sweat from his neck with a hankie, points toward the jungle at the edge of the airstrip. "There's the village, just a few kilometers away."

"Village?" Nieves asks. "I didn't see any village from the plane."

"Well, it's more like some tiny houses, a few families. They're expecting you, right?"

Nieves looks at Gali, who's gazing around as if he's in a snow globe with freshly shaken snowflakes of wonder floating around him. Hot green jungle snowflakes. He's in his own world.

Rubbing her temple, Nieves translates for Mom. Now they're frantically talking in hushed voices. "We have to turn back," Mom says.

Nieves squints at the misty-bright sky. "Of course we do. We don't even have a radio or any camping gear." She shoots Gali an icy glare. "What were we thinking, Mara?"

I wipe chocolate from the corners of my mouth. I have no idea what to do. I glance over at Leo.

There's something protective about the way he's holding on to Gali's elbow, steadying him. Gali doesn't look like a wise old king at the moment, just soggy and woozy. Leo is staring into the jungle. His expression is determined, his jaw fixed in that stubborn way, the way it does when he's stuck on a hard part in a video game or carving a fragile piece of chocolate.

"Let's get back in the plane, kids," Nieves says.

No. No. No. We can't leave. I can't go home without my treasure. If I do, soon there will be no home for me at all anymore. And if Gali goes home without fixing things, he'll die . . . *a not-good death*, whatever that means.

I stare into the jungle, too, as if the answer lies there. And I see something that makes me catch my breath: a flash of red, yellow, and blue feathers—a parrot flying up from the rounded tip of a tree in the distance, a tree towering above the others, a tree that I know from my dream, from my research, a tree I'd recognize anywhere, even with just the tippety-top of it showing. The leaves and flowers have fallen off as they do every dry season, leaving a perfect crown of bare branches.

A ceiba, I'm sure of it. Could this be my dream tree?

"Hold on!" I yell over my shoulder, already running toward the tree. It has to be less than a mile away, and maybe if I just go in a straight line . . .

"Coco!" Mom screams.

I don't look back, but I'm guessing she's on my tail.

I try to pick up my pace, but I'm inside the jungle now, and plants are everywhere . . . growing up and down and sideways, sprouting from trunks, dangling from branches. I swipe aside the massive leaves, aiming for a straight line. Which is impossible in this tangle of green.

Here in the shadows, it's cooler, and the insect sounds are louder now, surrounding me on all sides. Mud squishes beneath my shoes, gives the air a rich, earthy smell. I scan the forest for some kind of path through the ocean of leaves and branches and logs and ferns and vines. The crown of the ceiba is already out of sight, blocked by a layered canopy of other treetops.

I pause, wondering if I should blindly barrel myself in the direction of the ceiba, or give up and go all the way back to Heartbeat Springs and admit defeat.

"Coco!" Mom's voice comes from behind me.

And then I hear a rustling, see a movement: Someone is peering at me from between palm leaves. I step closer, focus on the human form through the foliage.

It's a girl, and she looks about my age. She's wearing a lilac T-shirt and blue shorts, and her hair is long and wavy and tumbling over her shoulders like a dark waterfall. A circular strip of fiber forms a crown around her head. Slung over her shoulder is a bag made of woven fibers. She's looking at me with curious cacao-brown eyes.

We're not alone! I want to run up to her and hug her and spin with her in circles. But I don't want to scare her, so I hold back and offer a smile. A little crooked. Just a hopeful upturn of the right corner.

She smiles back, full, with teeth, big and white and straight.

At that moment, Mom catches up with me, breathing hard, sunglasses pushed up on her head.

"Mom, look!" I point to the girl, who's looking behind her. That's when I see that three more kids have gathered. They're little kids, and they're watching us like we're the exciting part of a TV show.

By now, Leo and Nieves are beside us, panting, their eyes

trained on the kids, too. Two boys around age four or five, and a girl who looks about six.

Leo's the one who makes the first steps toward them. Which is weird because in El Corazón, I've always been the one to greet new customers while he lurks quietly by the counter. Now I'm the one who's tongue-tied and hanging back.

He waves his hands in greeting, as if to show they're empty, as if to assure them we're unarmed. And then he snatches something from the air, closes it in his fist, and with the other hand, pokes his fingers into the clenched fist and pulls out a piece of red silk attached to yellow silk attached to blue silk and swirls the whole thing around his head, like a flying parrot, like a flag of peace.

The kids burst out laughing. Sparks of joy have leapt from that rainbow silk, right into them. Even though Leo's tricks are just sleight of hand, they make an unexpected kind of magic . . . the kind that somehow changes the story. The kind of magic that turns fear and suspicion on its head and replaces it with— *ta-da!*—warm smiles.

The oldest girl walks forward, her eyes lit up and dancing. Her outfit is strange, something that Caitlyn Bland wouldn't even know where to begin critiquing. But I like it. A large animal tooth hangs from a red beaded necklace around her neck, right over a fading decal of Smurfette. Below, shiny cursive lettering reads *Sweet Dreams* in English. The *s*'s on either side are partly flaked off. The lilac fabric looks old and worn and cozy-soft.

"*Buenas tardes*," Leo says. The rest of us echo his greeting.

"Buenas tardes," the girl replies, softly, with an accent. Each syllable is choppy and tentative, the sounds not quite Spanish. And then, "What are you looking for?"

Again, I can't find words. They've always come so easily to me before, like turning on a faucet. What *am* I looking for? What would my truest answer be? The ceiba? My treasure? A way to save my world? A way to remove my poison dart?

I glance at Mom and Nieves. They're speechless as well. What are their true answers? Looking for craziness? Giggle fits?

There's a crunch of twigs behind us, and Gali appears, slogging through the mud, his nice shoes and the tip of his cane already coated.

A noise rumbles through the jungle—the plane engine revving up. My stomach leaps. In moments the little plane is over our heads—I catch a silver glimpse of it through the treetops—and moments later, the rumbling fades in the distance.

Mom gapes at Nieves. "The pilot . . . he just . . . *left*?"

Between gasps, Gali says, "I told him he could go. That everything was working out fine."

Nieves looks like if she had a weapon, she'd use it on Gali. Mom just looks plain scared.

Everyone seems to have forgotten the girl's question, hanging in our midst. *What are you looking for?*

What's Gali looking for, really? A way to make up for whatever horrible thing he did?

"Gali's right," Leo says to his mom, patting her arm to keep her from pummeling the old man. "Everything's fine. There are people here. They can help us."

There's something strange about his calm determination.

What's Leo looking for? Why is he really here? He must have his own reason, a big one. Why else would he overcome his shyness to march right up to these kids and do a magic trick? Why else would he voluntarily come on a trip with the so-called weirdo he told to stay away?

He turns to the girl. The younger kids are tugging on her hands, asking her questions in their language, Huaorani. Wow-RAH-nee, I pronounce in my head. One of the boys is wearing a too-big Spider-Man T-shirt hanging past his knees; the other boy, a too-small Dora the Explorer T-shirt with his stomach poking out from beneath the hem; and the little girl, a red fire truck shirt and cotton-candy-pink shorts.

The older girl hushes the kids and looks expectantly at Leo.

"I guess we're looking for the Cooperativa Felicidad?"

She tilts her head. "Are you the volunteers?"

The moms glance at each other, confused. "Um, sure," Nieves says.

Meanwhile, Leo and Gali and I are nodding eagerly, as if, *of course we are, who else would we be?* Working for free wasn't part of the Home Sweet Home prize description, but I'm so grateful not to be abandoned in the jungle that I'll do anything.

"What kind of volunteering?" Nieves asks.

"Harvesting cacao," the girl answers matter-of-factly.

Mom understands this much Spanish. The deep lines of worries around her eyes smooth. And with all that sweat coating her face, she's suddenly shining. "Cacao! *Perfecto.*"

After some whispered conversation, the moms head toward the airstrip to fetch our bags and the live chicken, instructing us to wait with Gali and the children. "Stay put and don't let them out of your sight!" Nieves calls to Leo in English over her shoulder, as if she's afraid these kids will disappear back into the jungle.

Gali's caught his breath and now he's fuddling around in his pocket. Finally he pulls out a little robot, no taller than his pointer finger, made of an ancient mint tin. Using his cane to maneuver through the underbrush, he offers it to the oldest girl.

She opens it up and discovers a perfectly round, mica-flecked pebble inside. Delighted, she passes the tiny treasure around to the others.

As the kids are examining it, the moms straggle through the trees with the luggage. Beneath her arm, Mom has tucked the chicken. Apparently it's a gift from the pilot to the locals to thank them for keeping the airstrip trimmed. Its face, sticking out of the plastic bag, looks innocently curious about what's to come.

"*Gracias,*" the girl says, tucking the little robot carefully in her fiber bag. And then, as if that was the key necessary to unlock some door, she says, "Follow me."

Piranhas

Are we headed toward or away from the ceiba? I keep my face uplifted, trying to glimpse its crown, without luck. It feels like we're walking through a maze inside a green glass marble. I have no idea what direction we're going. In Colorado the sky is huge and uncluttered and I recognize exactly which peaks are to the north, south, east, and west.

This jungle is mystifying, but at least I have a whole week to figure it out. So I soak in the light that falls between thousands of leaves, casting tiny beams and patches of gold. I listen to the forest music—a soundtrack with the volume turned up—insects and birds, each calling their own song. I breathe in the air, which smells magical, of earth and plants and tree bark and the sweet rot of fallen fruits I never knew existed.

Even though he's got his own pack slung on one shoulder, and Gali's over the other, Leo has managed to get toward the front, right beside the older girl and the gaggle of little kids, who are begging him to do his magic trick, over and over.

I've positioned myself right behind him so that I don't miss anything. The moms are bringing up the rear, supporting Gali in the middle. To feel useful, Gali is carrying the bag with the stunned chicken.

After making the scarf disappear for the third time, Leo says, "I'm Leo," and reaches his hand toward the oldest girl's.

"I'm Isa," she says, touching his lightly.

"I'm Coco," I pipe in, sticking out my own hand.

The younger kids are too shy to say their names, but Isa introduces them—Dany, Marcos, and Lily—and I gesture back to the moms and Gali and introduce them.

As we walk, Isa and the kids point out plants and frogs and lizards. Sometimes they mention signs of mammals I've never seen, like ocelots and peccaries, noticing their tracks and scat and movements in tree branches.

At one point, Isa drops to her knees, traces something in the mud.

A huge paw print. The pad looks like an upside-down heart, crowned by four thick toes.

"Jaguar?" Leo says, breathless.

How would he know that?

Isa nods, stands up, glances around, and squints up into the tree canopy. She follows the tracks a little ways off the trail, into the foliage. The moms look unsure whether to be excited or nervous.

"How fresh?" Leo asks.

"Pretty fresh," Isa says calmly. For the rest of the walk, her eyes flicker regularly up to the trees, and every so often, she turns around and scans the jungle behind us.

Soon we reach the Shiripuno River. It's as wide as Main Street in Heartbeat Springs, only curving and golden, with the late-afternoon sun shining through the opening in the trees, making it sparkle, from the mica bits at the bottom to the tiny ripples on top. It's slow-moving and disappears around a bend into the misty light of more jungle.

A dugout canoe awaits us on the shore with enough room for us to all pile in with our packs. It's a huge tree trunk, cut in half, with the insides scooped out and the bark stripped off. It looks at least fifteen feet long.

And now Leo is holding out his hand to help me in the boat . . . Really? A gesture of a gentleman or Boy Scout or something. *So not Leo.*

His hand is stretched out toward mine and I'm planning to ignore it, but just then my muddy foot slips on the edge of the canoe, and on instinct, our hands find each other. Our fingers and palms press together, gritty and sweaty. With my other hand, I clutch the edge of the canoe, and as soon as possible, snatch back my hand. Even his hands have changed—gotten muscled, bigger, calloused. Disturbing.

He does the same for the moms and Gali—everyone except for Isa, who's so agile she could've spent her life climbing in and out of canoes.

She stands at the front of the dugout with a long pole of bamboo, and talks to us over her shoulder as she pushes and steers us down the river.

"How'd you know to meet us?" Leo asks.

"We heard the plane." She pauses a beat. "We hoped you'd be coming sometime soon."

"So someone in your village got Gali's email?" I ask.

"Oh, we can only check email a few times a year, when

one of us leaves for a town. Last time someone went was months ago."

I wrinkle my brow. "Then how'd you know we were coming?"

"We've been waiting for years."

Years? I want to ask for details, but now Isa and Leo have moved on to basic conversational Huaorani. *Waponi* is the greeting in her language, she says. Spanish is her second language, as it is for me. Maybe that's why it's so easy to understand her. She speaks slowly, pronouncing each word clear as crystal. Thanks to my seven years in a bilingual elementary school, my Spanish is about the same level as hers.

She has a gentle, easy way of talking, of moving, of being. She's the opposite of clumsy. You know she's the kind of person who never accidentally drops stuff or runs into things or stubs her toe. And if you accidentally dropped something, she'd probably swoop in to gracefully catch it. And if you were being stalked by a feline predator, she'd know it and take appropriate precautions.

If she lived in Heartbeat Springs, I'd want to be her friend . . . but then again, probably Caitlyn and the royalty would decide her outfit was ironically cool, that *she* was actually cool. They'd get to her first and drag her into Donut Delite and make her one of their own. And I'd be instructed to stay away from them all.

We float downstream, practicing *waponi* and other words, and Isa says this is good timing because she has a break from school for *Semana Santa*, Easter week. As we talk, the little kids shyly ask Leo to do his magic trick again, giggling into their hands. Meanwhile, the moms and Gali are pointing out macaws and parrots and toucans.

And I'm scouring the forest on either side for that ceiba tree because how many times can a person watch the same magic trick? Anyway, I have a treasure to find.

We've been drifting downstream for about a half hour, trailing our fingertips over the river's surface, when Isa asks, "You like piranhas?"

"Piranhas?" Leo sputters, pulling his hand from the water and looking at me.

Snatching my own hand away from the river, I widen my eyes. I've never thought about whether I *like* the creatures. "Aren't they, like, mini-sharks?" I murmur to Leo.

He turns to Isa. "Um, we don't know if we like them."

"I think you will," she assures us.

Now Isa pulls the canoe over to a little natural pool, letting the boat rest against a fallen log to stay anchored. From her pocket, she pulls out a piece of fishing line and a hook wrapped in paper. She breaks off a branch from the fallen log, then ties the line to the end of the stick. One of the boys has leapt out, dug around in the mud, and unearthed a grubby, wormy creature, which she passes along to Isa.

"We'll fry the piranha for dinner," she explains, piercing the worm with the hook.

And within minutes, she's caught one. It's the size of her hand and has rows of sharp little teeth and it's flopping and flipping around in the air.

I wince as she lays it on a seat and raises her pole. I look away just as she bonks it. When I look back, it's stopped flopping.

"Can I try?" Leo asks, excited. Right, he got into fly-fishing with his new friends this year.

He holds the stick with both hands as the little kids search for more grubs.

I stare into the jungle. My eyes fall on the bare crown of a tree that towers above the rest, a tree with a perfect half-circle canopy. A ceiba! Is it the same one I saw earlier? How many are there around here anyway? My pulse quickens. I wonder if I can get to this one tonight.

And then I notice Leo, staring at exactly the same point. "You know that trees can communicate with each other?" he says in Spanish, to no one in particular.

Isa looks at him, like she's interested and wants to know more.

Holding the bamboo rod, he says, "There are these fungi that live in the soil and they have these threads called mycelia. And the mycelia pass chemical messages from the roots of one tree to another, even trees of different species. And if some little saplings are sick or struggling, then the older, stronger trees can pass them extra nutrients. Like carbon, nitrogen, phosphates. Pretty sweet, huh?"

"Interesting," Isa says.

This encourages him to go on. "It's just like how neurons and axons in the human brain form a network. So it's like there's this whole underground forest brain!"

He's talking faster and faster now. His dark hair is damp

from sweat and river water he poured on it to cool off. He pushes it out of his eyes. Now I have a clear view of his face. It looks different than it used to. It's more angled now, as though the cheek- and jawbones grew more solid.

"Oh!" he says, "And the hub of the whole network is the mother tree. She manages how the trees share their resources. When the mother tree is about to die, she sends her nutrients and knowledge to the younger trees."

Even his voice is different from when we used to be friends. Lower and more crackly. Like if I heard him on the phone, I might not even recognize him. Disorienting.

"A secret to happiness," Gali pipes in. I thought he was dozing. But he continues, his voice strong. "Being part of the flow of wisdom. And understanding that all things in nature have their own form of consciousness."

Isa is nodding, like this all makes sense to her. She points to a tree ahead, with branches like a candelabra and leaves like flower-shaped parasols. Something's moving in its spindly limbs, ever so slowly. I lean forward, glimpsing gray-brown fur with odd green highlights that blend into the leaves. Its long white claws clutch the bark as it hangs upside down, its little round face staring at us.

Leo's eyes widen. "A three-toed sloth!"

Isa nods. "A thousand beetles make their homes in its fur. Once a week, the sloth digs a hole at the foot of this tree and leaves its droppings there. The beetles leap off and lay eggs in the dung, then ride on their sloth back up the trunk. The tree gets nutrients from the droppings, and when the eggs hatch, the baby beetles find a new sloth to be their home."

Isa pauses, looking around at the jungle with pride. "The insects and animals and plants all do their part to keep the forest alive. You're right, Leo. With so many parts working together, it's like the forest has a mind of its own."

Leo takes that as his cue to pipe in with the factoid that blue-green algae also lives in sloths' fur and camouflages them. "It's all science," he says, "but there's something so . . . magical about it, isn't there?"

Suspicious. He's never mentioned sloths or algae or fungal threads to me before. I stare at him. In English, I demand, "How do you know this stuff?"

"Library."

"But there weren't any decent books at the library. About trees or jaguars or the Amazon. Definitely nothing with modern science." And as I say it I remember the plastic bag jam-packed with library books that Leo was carrying that day we saw the Home Sweet Home contest poster.

He gives a sheepish shrug and offers me the bamboo rod. "Here, you can have a try."

I grab the rod, pull it back and send the string flying over the water, watch it settle. "So you're the one who hogged all the books."

"I didn't know—"

"Wait a minute! You got all those books out before you even knew about the dessert contest. Before you even knew about the Amazon prize, right?"

Again, a shrug.

There's a tug on my fishing pole. I let out a little yelp and clutch the pole with both hands. Isa shows me how to gently pull it in, winding the string around her hand, slowly and skill-fully. The piranha pops out of the water, floundering about, splashing and raising a commotion and baring its tiny sharp teeth.

Deftly, Isa takes the pole from me and bops the fish. This time it happens so fast, I don't look away. "Nice job," she tells me.

"*Gracias*." My pulse is racing with the burst of adrenaline from the fish and the dawning realization that Leo's had his own reasons to research Amazon trees.

The moms, who've been snapping pics in the back of the canoe, make me pose with the piranha. For a while, Leo, Gali, and I take turns holding the makeshift rod, and end up catch-ing six more fish between us, letting two escape. But only half my mind is on the fish. I have to figure out what's going on with Leo. What he knows. Without giving away what I know.

"That's enough for dinner," Isa announces, and tucks the piranha in another fiber bag. Then she resumes her place stand-ing at the front of the canoe, steering us downstream with a bamboo pole.

Leo is sitting in front of me, staring into the jungle, at the ceiba. My ceiba.

I tap his shoulder.

He turns to face me.

"Leo de la Cueva, what made you check out all those books?"

A pause. "Just—I had this weird dream."

I pierce my eyes into his. "What, exactly, was your dream?"

I can't read his reaction—fear, embarrassment, shame? His eyes shift. "I don't even remember it anymore."

But he does, I can tell.

Maybe the tree dream is a thing with a life of its own, making its rounds all over Heartbeat Springs, dropping by here and there for visitations. Or maybe it's more like a radio channel and Leo and I both happened to be tuned in to it.

And like me, he's kept it a secret. He's looking for the treasure, too. What would he do with it? Use it to impress Caitlyn and the royalty? No way will I let that happen, not when the existence of El Corazón depends on it. I need to claim it first.

All the newfound warmth I'd been feeling toward Leo flees. The charm of his magic tricks and scientific factoids disappears. Any thoughts of forgiveness vanish. And in their place, distrust and anger flood back in. I can't let him find my treasure.

Suddenly, a fish leaps out of the water and lands on my thigh. A piranha the size of my spread-out hand. It thrashes around, its toothed jaws open. I jump up, nearly falling out of the canoe. I grab the fishing pole, and whack the creature.

It becomes still. This is the first animal I've killed bigger than a bug.

Pulse racing, I glance at Leo, whose eyes are wide and shocked.

Leo, who is now my enemy.

Leo, who has witnessed exactly how I handle surprise attacks.

I give him a meaningful stare, as if to say, *Watch yourself.*

The Ceiba Tree

AMAZON RAIN FOREST

The nearest mother tree, a ceiba older than I, was felled today. A fate worse than simple death. Her body is not resting gently in moss, cradled in vines, being tenderly eaten by insects. No, her body has been taken away, and she will no longer be part of our jungle, even in her death.

These killing machines have no mercy. They tear through the forest floor, ripping and shredding the smallest shrubs, the network of roots, the nests, the homes, the food. And all this, only to make way for the drillers who pierce the earth and release oil that belongs deep below. Oil that oozes together with poisons and kills what the machines missed.

The forest is mourning. I feel their tears in my roots.

I watch these humans from afar, how they

cut the trees without regard for which ones are sickly or healthy, old or young. I watch these humans and I think I understand the problem.

Each believes his heart is inside his body, a small, fist-sized organ made for him and him alone. Containing his little world, and that is all.

I would like to tell them their hearts are seeds to be planted. I would like to tell them how very far and wide and big my own heart has grown. I would like them to try this, too.

And you, you are trying, I know you are.

Cacao

I'm the first one in the canoe who spots it—a shiny, bright purple pod through the leaves up the embankment. I squint up the embankment, into the trees, and there's another, lemon yellow, then a maroon one . . .

Cacao pods. In the flesh. I've seen them in pictures and videos, but this is real life.

"Mom, look!" I point, eyes bugging out. "Cacao!"

When she sees, she lets out an *eep* of joy. "Cacao!" She jumps up for a better look, so excited she nearly overturns our canoe.

"Cacao!" Nieves shouts.

Even Gali gets sucked into the excitement. "Cacao!" he yells, laughing.

Soon we're all shading our eyes and gaping at the pods. Most are well hidden in the forest—which makes sense, since they need to be shaded and protected from winds and rains by bigger trees. But a few are poking out from the jungle's edge, just up the riverbank. They're strange. Imagine a smallish tree with a bunch of Nerf footballs hot-glued to the trunk and limbs.

It's just like I've seen in pictures—both recent photos and

copies of ancient Mayan codices. It gives me a shiver. Mom runs her fingertips over her arm. "Goose bumps, Coco!"

Isa looks amused at our reaction. "You *really* like cacao," she observes. "We'll drop off your bags, then take you straight there."

We drift down a few more bends and soon a thatched hut comes into view high on the riverbank. A smattering of adults and babies and toddlers are waiting at the top, watching us and waving. They all have the shiny dark hair of Isa and the same thrift-shop-chic look going—mismatched shirts and shorts, too big or too small, well worn and soft. A few wear the nut-and-tooth necklaces and fiber crown that Isa does.

There's excitement in the air, passing back and forth among us all. Excitement and curiosity and anticipation, as plentiful as the tiny water droplets. We wave back and Isa steers us to shore.

"You can hop off now," she says.

I step out before Leo can offer me a hand. Instantly, the mud suctions my feet, nearly swallows my sandals whole. I grab onto a tree branch and pull my feet out and find more solid ground.

A couple of men skid down the embankment to help drag the canoe ashore. Somehow they know where to step to not get sucked under by the mud.

They start gathering up our bags and backpacks. I'm just trying to remember the Huaorani word for "hi" when Leo reaches out his hand and says with a big smile, "*Waponi.*"

They take turns shaking his hand, matching his smile.

The rest of us shake hands, and climb up the slippery river-bank, and then there are more people, more hands to shake, old and young. I repeat *waponi* with each hand I shake—about twenty-five, including the littlest kids. By now I know the word well. *Waponi.*

Isa chats with them in Huaorani as they nod and pepper her with questions. They look pleased with the chicken the pilot has gifted them.

Meanwhile, I glance around. There are three more huts farther down a trail along the river. Each is nestled in the trees, on low stilts, made of wood and thatched palm-frond roofs and screened walls. And each has a small porch and a hammock strung between the posts.

Finally, the conversation switches to Spanish, and one of the women motions for us to follow her. She speaks Spanish quietly. "I'm Isa's mother. Alma. My daughter says you want to see the cacao right away."

Actually I wouldn't mind lounging in one of those hammocks right away—I'm suddenly exhausted . . .

"Cacao!" Mom says. "*¡Sí, perfecto!*"

Mom's so ecstatic about the cacao that I muster the energy to nod along with her. "*Waponi*," I add. This seems to be a one-size-fits-all word meaning *thank you*, *please*, and *hi*, all in one. I manage to sneak the word in before Leo this time. Now that I know about his dream—and his own secret mission—I have to make allies to help me find the treasure before he does. It's like I've ended a short truce and now all my rage from the past six months has come roaring back.

Isa motions for us to follow her. "First you can drop off your bags."

"*Waponi*," Leo says quickly, beating me to it.

They show us our cabins—the huts with the beckoning hammocks. "Special lodging for volunteers," Alma explains proudly, opening the door. She looks younger than Mom, her face still smooth, and she's a few inches shorter. She wears a simple ponytail and a red seed necklace and a yellow Baltimore 10K race T-shirt from 1989. "Our community built the huts ourselves with fallen trees. We rotate cleaning them, and this is my family's week. We live in our own homes nearby."

"*¡Perfecto!*" Mom declares.

We walk inside our cabin, while Nieves and Leo head to theirs, and Gali heads to his, stopping often to tug his cane from the mud. The little kids are kindly heaving his bags onto his porch and propping open the door for him.

Inside, I shrug off my bag, rub my shoulders. The beds are simple, with white sheets and orange blankets. There are a few pegs on the wall—for clothes, I guess—and some wood shelves.

I open a little door and find a regular bathroom with a toilet and sink. Sweet relief. I start peeing just as Isa calls through the door that she'll have to turn on a special solar-powered pump so that I can flush. She seems extremely proud of this pump.

When I come out, she says, "We've had all this ready for five years."

"Five *years*?"

"That's how long we were waiting for you."

I imagine this cabin sitting empty for five years, waiting for us to come along. It makes no sense. "Well, it's great. *Waponi*."

When I translate for Mom, who's perched on the edge of a bed, she wrinkles her forehead. "Huh." And then she turns to Isa and her mom. "Sit down, please. Tell us more."

They sit on the edge of the other bed. "The first group of volunteers came five years ago," Alma explains. Her Spanish is slightly better than Mom's, only with a Huaorani accent instead of English. "They gave us cacao saplings and showed us how to plant them. They said they'd be back to help us care for them and harvest them. So we built these huts. We made the beds with fresh new sheets. But years passed, and they never came."

Once I translate, Mom gives her a look of sympathy and reaches across to pat her hand.

Quickly, Alma adds, "Don't worry, we wash the sheets every week just in case that's the week the volunteers arrive." Then, with a smile, she says, "We thought the organization forgot about us. Or ran out of money. Or got scared off. But here you are."

"Oh, we're not part of that group," I say, vaguely wondering what she meant by *scared off*. When I see Isa's crestfallen expression, I tack on, "But we happen to know a lot about cacao and we're happy to help."

Mom nods eagerly. "Yes, we want to help!"

Alma gives a slightly confused smile.

Mom pulls out an El Corazón promotional flyer from the outside pocket of her bag and passes it to Alma. As she and Isa peer at the photos, I point and explain. "That's our chocolate shop and that's our little factory and that's the back courtyard."

Isa traces her fingertip over the limbs of the cottonwood in the midst of the café tables and wildflowers and hot springs steam. "Beautiful," she says. "You think one day our cacao beans will travel all the way up there?"

I try to keep hope in my voice. "Maybe." I don't have the heart to warn her that the chocolate shop might not even exist in six months. Anyway, there's still a chance I'll find the treasure and solve our financial woes.

Handing back the flyer, her mother says, "Come on, we'll show you the cacao." She motions for us to put on two pairs of black rubber boots sitting by the door.

"Thanks," I say. "But my sandals are already muddy."

Isa shakes her head. "It's for the snakes. The poisonous ones."

"Oh, right," I say, picking up the boots and taking off my sandals.

"Shake them out first," Isa says.

"Scorpions?" I guess.

She nods. "And other creatures."

Holding each boot at arm's length, I shake them upside down. No creatures emerge. Mom does the same. Then we slide our bare, mud-coated feet into the too-big boots that have been sitting there for five years, waiting.

Before we leave to see the cacao crop, I dash over to Gali's hut to make sure he's all settled.

At least, that's my excuse to the others, but over the past few hours, my brain's been churning about why exactly Gali is here. What if Gali had the same dream as me? What if he's looking for the treasure, too?

But he doesn't need money—he has enough to live comfortably. He owns the Roost and gets a regular monthly income of retail space rent. Still, who knows what surprises he might hold. Maybe it was no coincidence he put the ceiba on those Home Sweet Home contest posters.

"Why, hello, Coco dear," Gali says, hanging his hat on a hook.

"Just came to see if you're settled in."

"Oh, yes. I'm going to rest now, but you all go on and have fun."

He looks exhausted, leaning against the wall and still breathing hard.

From my day pack, I pull out a rose-lavender white chocolate, which won't interfere with him sleeping. "Truffle?"

He accepts with a smile, and nibbles at the truffle. "Superb!"

I take a step toward him and say softly, "I'll do everything I can to help you. But you have to promise me something."

"What's that, Coco dear?"

My voice comes out low and determined. "Whatever's in the roots of the ceiba is mine. Okay?"

He cocks his head, furrowing his caterpillar eyebrows in confusion. "Oh, Coco dear, I'm not here to *take* anything. I've done more than my share of that, and it ended terribly."

He takes another bite of truffle. "When you find what you're searching for, well, then you'll have to decide what feels right to do with it."

I give him one last look, then leave, letting the screen door thud behind me.

Next I stop by Leo and Nieves's hut with Mom, and together, we all follow Isa and her mom down a path past the huts, and a little ways into the foliage. I clomp clumsily through the forest, my feet sliding around inside the rubber, slick and sweaty.

There's a network of trails, and we pass areas of less-dense jungle where they've planted papaya and bananas and a starchy root called yuca in the dappled light.

Between the fruit and mushrooms and flowers and insects, there's so much to look at that I nearly run into a beautiful garnet-red cacao pod. I reach out and touch the thick, shiny leaves, the bumpy, ridged texture of the pod. It feels luxurious, like cool silk, like something so precious you'd expect to see it through protective glass at a museum. But it's here, beneath my hand, and I can practically feel the chocolate magic dancing inside, just waiting to come out and start the next stage of its journey.

"So this is where it all begins," Mom says in awe, stroking another pod.

Yes, this is what makes El Corazón run, at the core of it. Without the miracle of these pods, we'd have no chocolate shop. How strange to think that thousands of years ago, people in this very jungle stumbled across precursors to cacao as we know it, and over the years, across the continent, domesticated it. Thanks to them, we've created chocolate at El Corazón nearly every day of my life, using scientific principles along with centuries of traditional knowledge and hard work . . . all to make our own delicious kind of magic.

I feel like kissing these pods . . . but I don't because that would be nutso, even for me. I look up to see Leo's reaction—I can't help it—force of habit, I guess.

But his back is to me, and he's walking toward a bunch of cacao trees a short distance away. Who knows what he thinks about this. Or anything, really, for that matter. He's a mystery.

With her machete, Alma chops a deep purple pod from the tree and breaks it open with the blade. The insides are white goo, with the seeds—the beans.

She offers it to Mom, who scoops out some gooey seeds.

"Criollo cultivar?" I guess.

"Maybe . . . but look, Coco! See how some of the seeds are white instead of purplish? That's a sign these might be Nacional."

Our smiles stretch even bigger. In Spanish, I explain to the others that Nacional is one of the rarest and most prized varieties. It tastes silky and delicate, with touches of fruit and flower. The cultivar dates back over five thousand years, and originated here in the Amazon. For a century, it was nearly extinct from disease, but recently, healthy Nacional trees have been discovered.

"These trees," I conclude, "are a chocolate-maker's dream!"

As if it were the greatest delicacy on earth, Mom slides a seed into her mouth. "Suck the membrane off, Coco. Isn't it sweet?"

I pluck some from the pod, and yes, it has a light honeysuckle flavor. I spit the beans in my hand, still covered with white slime, and stare at them. It all begins here.

Isa's face radiates excitement. "How do we harvest them?" she asks, planting the tip of her machete in the soil and sampling a seed herself.

Mom's eyes widen in surprise. How odd that the co-op doesn't know the next step. "Well," she says, taking a wine-colored pod in her hands, "just scrape the skin with your fingernail like this, and if the mark's yellow, it's ripe." She shakes the pod. "And you can feel the insides moving around."

She moves on to some yellow-and-green pods, shakes them gently. "Now, these are probably still ripening. The trees take about five years to start producing after they're planted. So the timing's perfect! We can show you how to crack open the pods and ferment and dry the beans."

It's hard to keep up translating as fast as Mom's talking. I haven't seen her so energized in ages. This joy here, this is something unrestrained, a downpour, a flood, something spreading through the whole forest. Something contagious.

After I translate, Alma's face beams bright enough to match Mom's. Alma gushes out a river of Huaorani words, as if she's too happy to slow down and speak Spanish.

Isa translates for her. "Now we can sell the cacao and make money without hurting the forest. We hardly have any money in our village—we hunt and fish and gather fruit, but we need money for medicine and clothes. Things have been getting so bad, we talked about moving out of the forest. Our men were considering working for the logging companies. Or the *petroleros*."

Isa spreads her arms. "But now we have the cacao." She looks like a bird about to leap into flight. "The most important thing is protecting our forest. And now, with the cacao . . . maybe we can do it after all."

The moms go off to survey more pods, while Isa and I stay together. She brushes her fingertips over the pods with reverence, and I see we have this in common: Both of our livelihoods are at stake. We both depend on cacao. We both might be forced to leave the homes we love. We both might have to sacrifice in order to survive.

At least she doesn't have a Donut Delite cramping her style.

But I have to admit, Donut Delite sounds better than loggers and oil drillers.

And another thing we seem to have in common: a distinct lack of fathers in the picture. Well, that's something she has in common with Leo, too. His dad's a decent guy—he comes to town once in a while for a visit—but his gambling addiction makes him too unstable to be a dependable father. For Leo's dad, gambling gives him a dopamine rush—the kind of happy, warm feeling that chocolate gives me . . . only times a hundred. And since I can't imagine ever giving up chocolate, I do have sympathy for the guy. Unlike my own father, who had no excuse for fleeing under the sudden weight of responsibility.

"Where's your dad, Isa?" It slips out before I remember how much I hate when people ask me that question. (Gone. Never met him. Has zero real estate in my heart.) But I usually don't admit that. I usually shrug and change the subject.

My question deflates her, brings her back to earth with a thud. She twists the tooth necklace around her neck, back and forth and back and forth. "He died."

"Oh." I feel like kicking myself. Way to dampen the conversation. Still, I'm curious how he died . . . but Isa doesn't offer any explanation.

Instead, she sucks in a deep breath and changes the subject. "Tell me everything you know about cacao."

"That would take years, Isa." Okay, maybe not years, but at least a hundred hours.

"I have time."

I'm an expert at telling customers the history of chocolate, so I dive right in. Here and there I have to grapple for the word in Spanish, but she gets the gist. I tell her archaeologists have found the earliest evidence of wild cacao trees here in the Amazon, but the ancient Mayas in what's now Mexico and Central America are most famous for their chocolate drinks. I tell her cacao beans were used as money at markets by the ancient Aztecs. I tell her that when the Spanish conquistadors came five centuries ago, they were captivated by chocolate, and named the cacao bean Theobroma, food of the gods.

I'm just getting to the juicy part—how the Aztecs used to mix chocolate with blood as an offering to the gods—when I realize Leo isn't anywhere in sight.

"Wait, where's Leo?" I ask, suddenly anxious.

Isa glances around, mystified. "I haven't seen him for a while."

I meander through the cacao trees, peering through the leaves. Isa follows, scanning the ground for his footprints. At one point, she drops down to her knees and examines something in the mud.

"What is it?" I kneel beside her, follow her gaze to a large paw print. That big, upside-down heart with four toes. My insides tighten. "Jaguar?" I ask.

She nods, grabs her machete. "Come on."

Together we follow the tracks away from the moms, off the path, away from the swimming half-light and into the dense, shadowy jungle.

I have to step carefully—there are plants everywhere, and I'm clumsy in my rubber boots. I jump when I spot a movement in the brush. A rustling of giant leaves. The hair on the back of my neck stands up. The jaguar?

But no, there's a flash of orange. Leo's faded T-shirt.

"There he is." I breathe out in relief. No blood in sight.

Isa is still eyeing the trees, probably scanning for the jaguar. "Let's tell your mom where we are," she says. "So she doesn't worry."

But now Leo has disappeared again. "Can you tell her?" I ask over my shoulder, and without waiting for an answer, I start running in his general direction, hoping no large feline will drop from the trees and crush my neck with its jaws. I locate Leo again and stop just far enough away that he can't see me.

At a distance, I follow him, stalking him like a predator. He's emerging from the thick part of the forest, walking toward the river, where the sky is visible with a break in the tree canopy. At the shore, he pauses and turns around, looking back at the jungle, shielding his eyes from the setting sun.

I take a deep breath and walk toward him, trying to keep the suspicion from my voice. "Hey, Leo."

He startles, glances at me, then returns his gaze to the tree-tops, as if whatever he's looking at might fly away. "Oh, hey."

I stand near him, but at an arm's length. I heard a famous saying about love once, about how love isn't staring at each other, but standing beside each other and staring at something amazing together. Which is exactly what we're doing now, minus the love part.

What we're staring at is the ceiba. Its crown towers over the jungle. It could be the same one we saw from the canoe. It looks like if you just walked for a few minutes, you'd get to it. Of course, easier said than done, since the second you reentered the jungle, the other trees would block the ceiba canopy and you'd be wandering aimlessly. But now that I'm looking closely, there seems to be a rough trail leading in the direction of the ceiba. Maybe . . .

It's just starting to get capital-A awkward with our silence, so many things unsaid between us. This staring at the ceiba together is *so* the opposite of love, although maybe the symptoms are the same: sweat, pulse pounding, blood heating up. Not that I would know firsthand.

Isa appears through the trees and waves to us, breaking the tension. I wave back, then return my gaze to the ceiba.

My ceiba is calling to me. I can hear her echoes from my dream. *Within my roots a treasure awaits.* I need to find her. And I'm beginning to understand that she needs me to find her, too.

I can barely resist making a beeline to the tree, zipping through the jungle in a mad rush. But if Leo comes, he could claim the treasure. And Isa's mission is to protect her forest—which might mean guarding any treasure it holds.

I have to wait till the time is right, when I can go alone, unseen.

Preferably, without a jaguar prowling nearby.

Later, when evening has fallen in deep blues and greens, Mom and I return to our little volunteer hut to wash up for dinner. She's still radiating sunshine.

"This is just what I needed, Coco!" she says, splashing water on her face. "To get out of my own little world with my own little problems. To help someone else. To connect, you know?"

"*Mmhmm.*" I glance through the screen wall of our hut,

through the trees, to Gali's hut, lit by a bare bulb. I'm still not sure what to make of his trickery. But he's the invisible hand that brought us here, together. That brought me to my ceiba tree. Whatever his motives, the important thing is that I'm here thanks to him.

Inside his hut, Isa and her mom are helping him put his stuff away. I see him sink down on the bed in the faint yellow light. I wonder if he'll be strong enough to do what he needs to do here.

He seems reenergized when we meet for dinner in the screened-in, candlelit dining hut. While Isa and her mom were tending to us, some others in the community were preparing fried piranha and yuca. They explain that they built this dining hut just for the volunteers.

The chef is Isa's uncle, José, a gentle and enthusiastic man who lived in Quito for a couple of years, working as a cook at a big hotel until he missed the jungle and his family so much he came home. "We've been waiting a long time for you to come! I have many menu ideas for you. Food you will like!" He smiles knowingly, eyes bright beneath his straight-cut bangs. "You don't eat monkey meat where you're from, do you?"

Compared with monkey meat, the piranha doesn't seem too exotic. It's actually pretty good once you get past all the sharp teeth and tiny bones. The flesh is white and light and much better than canned tuna. And it turns out this subspecies of piranha isn't aggressive to people—kids even swim in the river with them. Grinning at Isa, I announce, "I *do* like piranhas."

Our side dish is yuca—basically a giant, sweet, starchy, greasy, salty stringy French fry. In other words, it's the bomb. To drink, there's *agua de papaya*—papaya blended with water and sugar, which Nieves is thrilled about since it reminds her of her childhood in Mexico. For dessert we have golden fried sweet plantains, essentially sweet 'n' sour bananas, only less mushy.

"*Waponi*," I say gratefully, licking my fingers.

At dinner, Leo's asking about the various dangerous and deadly Amazonian animals that he read about in the books he hogged from the library. This prompts José to show off old wounds and tell tales of local creatures. He shows us the accidental machete nicks on his hands and deliberate diagonal scars on his cheeks. He explains how they were done with coarse vines rubbed over his flesh as part of a young man's ritual. Those look like they were painful, but what makes me cringe is the gruesome fer-de-lance snakebite on his ankle, now a tangle of scarred flesh.

His worst injury of all is a deep, jagged scar running across his forehead. "Guess what this is from."

We toss out guesses.

"Caiman?"

"Piranha?"

"Giant anteater?"

"Jaguar?"

"Monkey?"

José laughs, shakes his head. "A car wreck in Quito." His smile fades into a sigh. "Humans and their machines . . . those are the real dangers."

After dinner, Mom and Nieves insist on washing the dishes, while Leo and Isa offer to lead Gali back to his hut to rest. "You coming, Coco?" Leo asks.

I let out a big, exaggerated yawn. "I'm tired. I'm going straight to bed."

It's dark, just the three light bulbs in the volunteer huts. The moon hasn't risen yet. Once the others are out of sight, lost in the shadows, I slide on the boots, grab a flashlight, and head out in the other direction, the direction of the ceiba, alone, into the night forest.

The Night Forest

The jungle at night sounds like a zillion heartbeats pounding in their own rhythms. You know how intricate the world looks in the daytime, all the shapes and colors and movements and textures and patterns? Imagine all of that stuff transformed into sound. Imagine sculptures and paintings and designs made of chirps and calls and songs.

And I'm smack in the middle of it all. Darkness and music.

My flashlight casts a weak beam before me. I head in the direction of the ceiba, which isn't easy because I can't see the treetops well. My beam only reaches a few feet in front of me. I pass through the groves of cacao, their pods shining in the faint pool of light. Everywhere, pinprick pairs of spiders' eyes glow like stars.

I struggle to remember exactly where I followed Leo earlier today. Once I enter the dense forest, it's nothing but mammoth leaves and branches and trunks all around me. I remember following him out to a clearing by the river and noticing that rough path toward the ceiba. But now I can't even figure out which direction the river's in.

I feel so tiny all of a sudden. Practically microscopic, like a beneficial bacterium swallowed in a giant's spoonful of yogurt.

It occurs to me I could get lost; after all, I'm not on a trail, and I don't have a GPS. But I'm getting closer to the tree, I have to be. Creatures dart in and out of my flashlight beam. Silvery webs with spiders the size of my palm. Bugs that look like massive cockroaches. Lizards skittering here and there. Lightning bugs flashing. And there are rustlings near my feet as I pass, rustlings that make me jump, but when I shine the beam on them, they're gone. Hopefully not snakes. Just in case, I'm glad I wore the clunky rubber boots.

Noises come from above, too, from shadowy creatures creeping in the branches. When I shine the light at them, I see a pair of big golden eyes staring down at me. A monkey? One of those tree rodents whose name I forgot? The eyes stare at me, unblinking.

A ribbon of sweat trickles down my cheek. I glance back to see if the light of the volunteer huts is still visible. No, it's been eaten by the jungle. I'm crazy, I realize. I'm walking around alone in the Amazon looking for a treasure. A treasure I heard about *in a dream*. I'm completely crazy.

My hands are shaking with thrill and fear, and every nerve ending is alert. I remind myself that fate has a treasure in store for me. I remind myself that I'm protected, that my dream prophecy is like invisible armor. I remind myself my motives are noble: I'm not doing this for myself; I'm doing it for Mom, too, and El Corazón, and our precious life that is hanging in the balance in Heartbeat Springs. I'm not a lost girl alone in the jungle . . . I'm a knight on a quest.

How much time has passed? Am I walking in circles? Haven't I already passed that enormous spider?

And then my flashlight flickers and fades.

Nooo! I shake it. Nothing. I shake it some more. I whack it against my leg. Nothing.

I am in absolute darkness, just a few fireflies lighting up here and there.

I could scream *HELP!* at the top of my lungs. But I'm far enough into the jungle, no one back at the huts would hear me over the racket of frogs and insects. Anyway, if I screamed, I'd have to explain what I was doing out here alone. I'd have to admit defeat. I shove the useless flashlight into my pocket.

Everything is black except for the unpredictable yellow blink of lightning bugs. One flies right by my head. I reach out and try to catch it. Got it. A flutter against my fingers, a tickle on my palm.

I go after some more . . . maybe if I can collect enough . . .

It's not easy. They only light up for a couple of seconds, and right when I lunge for one, it vanishes into the darkness. And I keep tripping and running into plants I can't see. But these bugs are my only hope for finding my way out of here on my own.

After a while, I've managed to capture four lightning bugs that make the tiny spaces between my fingers glow. I hold up my cupped hands like a lantern. The glow is faint, but my eyes have adjusted to the blackness, so even this hint of light is enough to make out shapes of my surroundings.

I take a few steps forward through the brush and find myself in front of a root taller than me. And another. And another.

They're like tidal waves, these roots, towering over me. I press my cheek against the wood, as if greeting an animal, a friendly one I've met before. Tingles shoot through my cheek, my neck, my spine.

The ceiba.

Within my roots a treasure awaits. This will take some time. Her roots form separate chambers, about five or six, around the trunk, walls that taper toward the ground at the end of the curving, spoking walls.

I step back, holding up my firefly lantern, and try to take in the whole tree at once. Impossible; it's too enormous and my light source is too weak. I can only take in pieces of her at a time, a bit of the truck, a cluster of branches, a couple ceiling-high roots. Scanning the ground, I see nothing that looks like a treasure. I walk outward from her trunk and into the next root chamber. Nothing. What was I expecting? A golden chest? A pile of emeralds? A check made out to El Corazón?

Bits of my mind and gut are aware that by now probably Mom is worried, maybe even frantic, and I wonder if she's calling for me, but the crickets are so loud, they'd drown out the calls. I strain to listen for any human voices, but hear only insects and owls and a few animal cries here and there.

I'll just hurry up and finish as fast as I can. I move on to her final chamber. No treasure here, at least nothing obvious. Maybe this isn't my dream tree after all . . .

I'm just trying to listen for some message from my tree, when I hear a noise from above. I look upward, to the top of her buttress roots, holding out my firefly lantern. The glow is reflected by two yellow eyes.

This time the creature is close enough to see clearly, maybe ten feet away. And it's not a monkey or a tree-climbing rodent.

It's a giant feline. Black as the night. Small round ears. Thick skull and jaw. Flat nose. Whiskers fanned at the sides. Enormous paws. Under hooded lids, those eyes staring right at me.

A jaguar.

Part of my mind, the brain stem, the cave girl part, is flashing red lights, screaming alarms. *You're being stalked! By the most deadly creature of the forest! Run! Hide! Fight!*

But there's the dream part of my mind that stares right back, transfixed. It's a calm part of my mind that recognizes some magic, some connection, something happening beyond words and fear.

The jaguar stares at me.

I stare back.

"Coco! Coco! Coco!"

Someone's calling my name. It's faint at first, then louder and closer. It's echoing through the jungle, soaring over the insect chirps. Many voices calling for me at once.

"I'm here!" I shout. "By the ceiba!"

Within seconds, there's a sound to my right, the underbrush being trampled, a machete whacking through vines and branches. It's Isa, stumbling toward me, pointing her flashlight at the ground. I look at her, then back up at the jaguar, but it's gone.

Sweat trickles from her temples, beads on her upper lip. "Coco! Are you all right?"

I nod, still stunned, still holding the fireflies.

Isa calls out, "I found her!" She's breathing hard. "I saw your tracks," she gasps. "But then I saw the prints of a jaguar. Fresh prints." She shines her flashlight around in the trees, nervously.

"Don't kill it," I say.

"Of course not. We'd never kill a jaguar."

"Why not?"

"It could be someone's ancestor, the spirit of a loved one."

I want to ask her more about this, but now Leo's appeared, breathing hard. "You okay, Coco?" he asks, moving his flashlight beam over me.

"Fine."

Now Alma is rushing through the branches with her own machete, followed by Mom and Nieves.

Mom throws herself onto me like a football tackle. I wrap my arms around her, letting the lightning bugs fly free. She hugs me for a full minute. "Are you okay?" Her face is streaked with tears. Red scratches cover her arms and legs. The ruffles on her flowered Indian cotton blouse are torn.

"Yeah," I say, suddenly ashamed. What was I thinking? "I'm sorry, Mom. I'm really sorry."

"What on earth were you doing out here?"

I shrug. "Nothing. Just—just exploring."

Leo is staring at me. I can feel it: He knows I'm lying. And there's more. It's dawned on him that I had the dream, too.

Now his gaze has shifted to the tree. He's running his hand over the ceiba's roots and peering deeply into the spaces between her roots, just as I did. Only he has a working flashlight, which is much more effective. And in the bright beam, I can understand just how gargantuan this mother tree is. Her trunk looks about ten feet in diameter—that's two of me, lying down, head to toe. It's wide enough that, if it were hollow, you could make a little house inside it.

He shines his beam slowly and methodically, revealing dozens of different kinds of insects and mosses and tiny plants and flowers and frogs and lizards. Little worlds existing right here between the roots.

It's miraculous all right, but there's no actual treasure. The message was clear: *Within my roots a treasure awaits.* This can't be my dream tree. I'll have to keep looking.

Isa is watching both of us curiously. She knows something is up.

Meanwhile, Mom's relief has morphed to anger. "Coco, if I could, I'd take you straight home to Heartbeat Springs after a stunt like this. And the only reason I'm not doing that is because we're stuck here. At least till the plane comes next week."

She clutches my face in her hands, peers into my eyes. "You haven't acted like this since, I don't know, since you were a toddler. What were you thinking?"

I want to tell her the truth: that I did this for us, to protect our life together. But I can't explain that, not now, not without showing my cards to Leo. "I'm really sorry," I mumble.

"Promise me you won't wander off alone again."

"I promise, Mom."

"That goes for you, too, Leo," Nieves says, watching her son scan earth and root and branch and trunk.

As we leave the ceiba, I can almost feel the jaguar's golden eyes watching me go.

Walking past the night shadows of cacao trees, Nieves ticks off all the dangers I could have succumbed to—scorpions, deadly spiders, venomous snakes, boa constrictors. And of course, the jaguar. She's in lawyer mode, building the case that it's a terrible idea to wander alone with a broken flashlight in the jungle.

"I know, I'm sorry," I say for the tenth time. "I promise I won't do it again."

Nieves gives me a hug good night, and Leo gives me a weak wave, then they head to their hut. Alma walks back to her hut to check on the little kids. But embarrassingly, Mom doesn't let go of my hand till we reach our cabin.

Outside on the porch, after Mom goes inside, I pull Isa aside, whisper to her, "Thanks."

I can feel Mom's eyes on me through the screen.

Isa whispers back. "That was smart of you to use the fireflies. We do that, too, when we run out of batteries." She smiles. "Listen, if you want to go somewhere, just ask me. I'll take you there."

I tilt my head, lower my voice even further. "Isa, there are other giant ceiba trees around here, right?"

She nods. "Every community along the Shiripuno River is marked by its own ceiba."

"Could you bring me to them?"

She studies me, surprised. "I could take you out in the canoe tomorrow."

"*Waponi!*" I say with a nod, looking around to make sure Leo is out of earshot. There he is, back in his cabin; I see his silhouette against the yellow light. "And, Isa, can it just be me and you?"

Her expression is muddled. "I have to bring my brothers and sister along."

"But not Leo, okay?"

She pauses. "Then what will he do?"

"Help the moms."

She looks disapproving. She looks suspicious. She looks like maybe she doesn't like me. "Leo seems nice," she says softly. "And he knows a lot about our forest."

"That's because he hogged all the books!"

She shrugs a shoulder. "And he's funny with those magic tricks."

"I can entertain you, too, Isa. I know lots of funny stories about the history of chocolate."

She sighs. "And he cares about you. He was the first who noticed you were missing."

"Really?"

"You should've seen his face. He was almost as upset as your mom." Isa pauses, twists her tooth necklace around her fingers. "What do you have against him?"

I can't tell her we're in competition for the treasure. That I have to find it first to save El Corazón. My voice shakes as I whisper my answer. "Back in Colorado, he abandoned me."

And it's true, maybe Heartbeat Springs Middle School isn't exactly the Amazon jungle, and maybe the dangers aren't on par with boas and scorpions, but it *felt* like he'd abandoned me in the jungle. Like he couldn't have cared less if Caitlyn and her cronies had torn me limb from limb with their words, their laughter, their disdain, and worst of all, their utter lack of interest in me and my world.

Isa considers this. "People make mistakes. Maybe he's changed."

"Well, maybe *I've* changed," I say.

She gives me a long look. "I'm glad you're here to help us. But I'm worried, too."

I wonder if she somehow knows my plan to find the treasure. Cautiously, I ask, "Why?"

"Because you might abandon us."

"What are you talking about, Isa?"

"You'll probably stay for a week and have fun and learn about our life and take things and then go to your home and forget about us. Like the other volunteers have done."

I know that shifty eyes are a telltale sign of lying, so I stare straight into hers, in an almost-psycho way, when I say, "I wouldn't do that." And as my words come out, they leave something behind. A tiny dart. A drop of poison. Shame.

Then I remember something Alma said earlier. "But what did your mom mean about volunteers maybe being scared off?"

Isa drops her gaze. "There were explosions. That's how the *petroleros* decide where to drill."

Explosions? My mouth turns dry and I'm trying to form words, but then she adds, "And there's more. When we tried to make them stop . . . something bad happened."

I want to ask her more, but her chin is trembling. At first I look away because it's horrible to see someone trying so hard not to cry, especially someone you barely know. But then I look back at her and take a step toward her, to hold her hand or comfort her or something.

With a creak, the screen door opens. "Come on, Coco," Mom says, cinching her dragon robe around her waist. "Let's go to bed."

I raise my hand in a wave to Isa. "*Waponi*. For everything."

Back inside, through the screen, I watch her shadow vanish into the night, heading to her home downstream. Isa, protector of the forest.

Soon I'm in bed, surrounded by a million cricket chirps, waves of sounds, drifting through an ocean of insect songs all night long, and somewhere out there is a jaguar who may or may not want to eat me, and somewhere out there is my dream tree, waiting for me.

Waves of dream-questions lap at me like refrains:

How can I take my treasure without betraying anyone, without betraying the jungle?

How can I take my treasure while helping Isa be protector of the forest?

How can I take my treasure without turning Leo into my enemy?

How can I take my treasure without lodging more poison darts in my heart?

The Ceiba Tree

AMAZON RAIN FOREST

Many things have settled into the chambers of my roots over the centuries. Moss and mushrooms, flowers and bones. Mostly bones of small creatures, baby peccaries and otters, the flesh eaten by jaguars, the bones dropping down softly to the earth.

Human bones rest in my roots, too. The skeleton of a human friend, an old healer who tended to the healing herbs and blooms in my skirts. He died not by the teeth of a predator, or the bullet of a gun, but of simple old age. He was the last in a long line of healers, and I knew every one of them for three hundred years. It's been comforting to feel him decaying into the soil beneath the blossoms he once nurtured, his nutrients moving into me, into the forest, ever so slowly.

Still, I miss him. I miss how he and his ancestors gathered my silky fibers for fires, used my leaves for medicine. How deeply they knew the healing vines and plants. How they passed down this knowledge much in the way that I pass down my own knowledge to young trees. I miss the gentle, wise hands of these healers, how they brushed their fingertips over my bark and napped in my buttress roots and dreamt and listened and asked me to protect the treasure.

But now they are gone, the treasure forgotten. Now, all I can do is whisper my truth, and hope it reaches someone who listens.

DNA and the Milky Way

The creatures of this jungle form a gigantic symphony orchestra, so gigantic they need a concert hall stretching for one and a half billion acres. And all night long, different instrument-animals join in the songs with their own rhythms and tempos and solos. Thousands of melodies weave themselves together, in and out, up and down, back and forth. And through it all, like the lightest percussion, the rain drums, sometimes soft and constant, sometimes growing louder, sometimes softer.

That's what nighttime in the rain forest sounds like.

All night long, I drift in and out of questions and dreams and songs, awakened by a frog solo here, a cricket solo there, listening for a bit and drifting off again, and later, awakened by another song.

In my dreams this forest music is not made only by animals and raindrops, but trees and plants and rivers, too. They all have messages for me. And I listen. I can't quite figure out what they're saying. Still, I listen.

One message comes through loud and clear, the message

I know up and down, forward and backward: *Within my roots a treasure awaits.*

But there's more, so much more . . .

When I wake up, I feel oddly rested, ready for my first full day in the rain forest. Through the screen walls, the world looks misty green in the half-light. I lie here, feeling the rhythms of the jungle song sync with my breath.

Mom's still conked out on the twin bed beside me. She actually has a smile on her sleeping face, peaceful and unforced and for herself and no one else. I watch her for a few seconds, then tiptoe to the bathroom and get dressed in a mint-green shirt and tan shorts.

I rebraid my hair, then leave a note on my bed.

Morning, Mom. Foraging for breakfast in the dining hut.

Love you.

Not sure why I add that last part. Maybe because I've woken up here, alive, in this strange and wonder-filled place, and because today will hold an adventure, I feel it in my tree-breath-laced blood. I douse myself with sunscreen and herbal bug spray, slip on my mud-caked boots, and clomp down the path toward the dining hut.

Outside, the river looks mysterious, all silvery with morning fog, and the air feels cool and wet and secret. I run my fingertips over dripping leaves and thick petals. Yes, today my treasure is ready for me.

Isa and her mom and uncle are already there, cooking breakfast—the familiar, homey smell of scrambled eggs. Yum.

"*Waponi*," I say, waving at them through the screen.

"*Waponi*," they call out softly in return.

When I walk through the screened kitchen door, they look happy and kind of relieved, as though they were afraid I'd disappear in the night.

I volunteer to chop the papaya. It's fun. I've missed doing arty stuff with food. I make trapezoid-shaped slices that I arrange carefully, spiraling inward on a plate, just the way I'd display chocolate truffles in El Corazón. A DNA spiral. We share about half of our DNA with trees . . . and out here surrounded by so many trees, I can feel that 50 percent in my bones, these bones that are kind of like branches and trunks and roots.

I would tell Isa this interesting fact but I can't remember how to say DNA in Spanish. Spanish acronyms are usually different from English. It could be AND, NDA, DAN, ADN . . . who knows.

José nods at my handiwork in approval. "That's how we presented fruit in the hotel. Very pretty."

"*Waponi*," I say, pleased.

Isa admires my fruit spirals, too, then dumps a bundle of fresh chamomile into a pot of boiling water. I wonder if I should ask her about the *something bad* that happened after the *petroleros'* explosions, but she seems so chipper this morning, and I don't want to see her chin quiver like that again. Instead, I give her a big, encouraging smile.

She smiles back. She's wearing a soft white T-shirt with one of those gold and red and black Lucky Cats from Japan on it. The kitty's raising a paw in a cheery greeting, and over its ear is the big, sharp, shiny tooth dangling from Isa's red seed necklace. "What did you dream about, Coco?"

I blink, papaya slice in hand, trying to remember the details. "Something about forest music and messages."

She nods, smoothing her dark ponytail.

"How about you?" I ask to be polite, in case this is how people here greet each other in the mornings.

"I dreamed about a tree."

I pause in my papaya spiral, muscles suddenly tense. "What kind?"

"Ceiba," she says, stirring the tea and inhaling the sweet steam.

I drop my gaze, my nerves abuzz with electricity. I try to keep cool, but my pulse is speeding up like crazy. "So what happened in the dream?"

"The tree talked to me," she says matter-of-factly.

Act casual, Coco. "What did she say?"

She looks out the screened window at the river. "That she was not far. That she, too, lived on this river. The Shiripuno. And she was waiting for us."

My knees nearly buckle. With papaya-goo-covered hands, I clutch the wood counter.

"What do you think about my dream?" she asks after a beat.

I swallow hard, avoid her eyes. So she heard the tree, too? Does she know about the treasure? Hopefully not. "No idea. I mean, maybe you just had the dream because yesterday I asked you to take me to some ceibas."

Isa gives a thoughtful smile. "Maybe. Or maybe not."

I clear my throat. My mouth is desert dry. "Why was the tree waiting?" I ask, hoping she won't mention a treasure. The last thing I want to do is fight Isa over this.

"I think the ceiba needed help." She pauses. "It's not the first time I've heard her call."

I think about the parts of my dream I've chosen to ignore. I've focused so much on the treasure, on saving my home, that I've overlooked the ceiba's desperate pleas. I've let them fade to the background, while the shiny, golden treasure looms huge in my imagination, so huge it elbows out the calls for help. "What kind of help?"

Isa's face looks pained as she speaks. "The loggers are coming closer, clearing trees to make roads for oil rigs. They're killing our forest, even our sacred trees. We have to find a way to stop them."

José wipes his hands on a towel and rests them on Isa's shoulders. "You're just like your father. He'd be proud."

No one speaks for a moment. Their eyes shine.

Finally, I say, "Well, it's just a dream."

Isa's mother gathers herself, resumes stirring the eggs. "Oh, dreams are more than that. Here, we talk about our dreams every morning."

"Why?"

"Our dreams tell us things," Isa says. "They know things we don't. They tell us good places to hunt or find plants or fish."

Alma adds, "And sometimes you need to piece together different people's dreams to make sense of it all."

Isa gives me a meaningful look. "That's why we share them."

Who owns a dream? That's what I'm thinking as Mom strolls up the path, arm in arm with Gali at his slug pace. Behind them are Leo and Nieves. *"¡Buenos días!"* the moms call out, coming through the dining hut door, bringing with them the smells of bug spray and sunscreen.

"Mmm . . . eggs?" Nieves guesses, adjusting a black headband over her glossy hair.

"And papaya," I say.

"Yes!" Nieves gets a melty look in her eyes.

"Thanks for your note, sweet bean," Mom says, kissing the top of my head. There's something different about her. No dark circles. And her cheeks look rosy even though she's not wearing makeup. Two braids fall over her shoulders, Pippi Longstocking–style. She's wearing a cotton baby doll dress over leggings; not exactly rain forest attire, but she looks cute and chipper in it.

I help Isa and Alma serve the eggs and toast and tea and papaya. As we eat, thankfully, no one brings up the topic of dreams again. The last thing I need is for Leo to hear about it.

At the moment, Leo's surrounded by Isa's little brothers and sister like they're a gaggle of goslings. He pulls a coin from one of their ears as they giggle. Next he grabs three crayons from his pockets and asks the kids to choose a color, any color.

At the moms' insistence, Gali says he'll rest again today before setting out on his mysterious mission. He tosses out a few early morning secrets to happiness: *Dream with crickets. Wake up to rivers. Converse with trees.* Eyeing my papaya spiral, he adds, "Make art with food."

"And harvest chocolate!" Mom pipes in. She claps her hands together, which are adorned with old turquoise jewelry she must have dug out from the depths of her jewelry box back home. She's wildly excited about gathering the cacao pods today. When Alma shows her the extra machetes she's brought for them, Mom practically starts salivating.

"You kids want to help us with the cacao harvest?" Nieves asks.

"Actually," I say quickly, in English, "Isa's taking me out on the canoe today." I flick my eyes away and, unsure where to look, just stare at my eggs. My insides have turned to lumps of runny, guilty mush.

"*¡Excelente!*" Nieves says. "Doesn't that sound fun, Leo?"

Heat rises to my face. So she assumes he's invited.

Cringing, I glance at him. He's examining his own pile of eggs. He knows what I meant. He knows when he's not invited. It's a basic middle school skill.

I've been there. I spent weeks figuring out what it meant *not* to be invited somewhere. I can still feel the six-month-old sting of realizing that Leo rejected me for Caitlyn and her cronies. Part of me wants him to know what it feels like to be left out. And then there's the practical reason of needing to find the treasure under the ceiba before him. I could ignore his misery, abandon him, and head out on the river with Isa.

Or I could open my mouth and say, *Oh, of course we want you to come with us!*

Instead, I watch him blinking fast, humiliated.

"I'll just stay here and help you guys," he tells Nieves, his voice cracking.

Shame slides over me, primordial blackish-green goo. I've become Caitlyn Bland. But a version of Caitlyn Bland who *knows* how mean she's being, who feels her victim's pain.

I mumble, "You should come."

"What's that, Coco?" Nieves asks.

"Leo should come with us," I say a little more loudly.

He looks at me, his expression a mix of confusion and hurt and pride.

AWK-ward.

With a tiny nod, he forks some more papaya on his plate. Under his breath, he says, "Nice Milky Way."

He must be referring to my papaya spiral. "Actually," I correct him, "it's DNA."

"So you're going microscopic, not astronomical."

Our conversation is a whisper, in English.

"Yeah," I say.

The others are shoveling papaya and eggs into their mouths. No one else has a clue what we're talking about. This is how things used to be. Our secret language. Like that underground tree language he was going on about yesterday.

And now, in our secret language, a quiet apology is passed

back and forth. It's an apology that feels both cosmically big and nearly invisibly small.

As he chews his papaya, the right corner of his mouth turns up.

The left corner of my mouth turns up.

Isa notices. And she approves. Eyes flicking back and forth between us, she beams a straight-on smile.

A rush of affection for Leo and Isa and everyone at this table fills me. I open my mouth to come clean about the tree dreams.

But then I close it again. The force of self-preservation wins out . . . preserving my heart and my home. Still, the poison dart doesn't ache so much.

With a glint in her eye, Isa asks, "Ready to explore?"

The Original Jungle Gym

Downstream we float in the dugout canoe—Leo, me, Isa, and her flock of siblings. She stands majestically at the front with a bamboo pole, navigating the gentle waters. While the little boys goof off, she chats with her sister in Huaorani. Leo and I talk in English, creakily, rustily, as though we're speaking a language we haven't spoken in ages.

"So where're we headed?" Leo asks, swigging some water from his bottle.

I can't see his eyes behind his sunglasses, but his question seems innocent enough. "To see some ceiba trees," I say.

A few beats of silence. I wish I could see his eyes. "Coco," he says finally, "listen."

Oh no, what if he says it first? Claims the treasure? Quickly, I spew out, "Whatever's under the ceiba is mine, Leo."

More silence.

"Sure, okay," he says.

Really? It's that easy? Or is he trying to trick me? Give me a false sense of safety? "I need it to save El Corazón," I say, defensive.

He tilts his head. "What do you mean?"

"If we don't start making lots more money soon, we'll have to close the chocolate shop." I try to control the shaking in my voice. *Don't cry, Coco, please don't cry.* "And move away from Heartbeat Springs."

"What?" He leans forward, puts his fist to his mouth. "You can't move away!"

His vehemence startles me. It's as if he actually cares.

"That's why I need the treasure, Leo."

"Wait," he says. "So you think what's under the ceiba . . . it's like, money or something?"

"Or gold, or jewels, or ancient coins . . ."

"And you want to sell it and use the money for the chocolate shop?"

I wind my crystal necklace around my fingers. "Yeah," I admit.

"Where'd you get this idea?" His voice sounds flat, as if he already knows the answer.

I swallow hard, let the crystal pendant fall back over my chest. "A dream."

He takes off his baseball cap, runs his hands through his hair, puts the hat back on. "I'll help you, Coco."

I stare at him, mystified. Inside me, the dream feels like a creature with a life of its own, intermingling with my blood vessels, growing and pushing and urging me to reveal its truth.

What if my dream is a piece of a puzzle? And Leo's is another piece? What if we're not supposed to work *against* each other but *with* each other?

Just then, Isa points to the right bank and announces, "Ceiba. Want to go ashore and see it?"

How could I have missed it? "Yes, *waponi!*"

Leo hops out first and hoists the little kids onto shore. I let him take my hand and help me balance as I plunk my rubber boot into the mud.

We help Isa drag the canoe up the bank. Then we head up branching trails, in the dappled light, toward the ceiba. Once we're deep inside the foliage, layers of leaf canopy hide the sky and I lose track of the ceiba.

As if she can read my thoughts, Isa says, "Don't worry, I know how to get there."

I have to admit, without Isa we'd never be able to find the tree. Which makes me feel I owe her something, like telling her my dream. Or offering to share the treasure with her. But what if I need the whole thing to save the chocolate shop? That's the reason I came here.

You're not doing anything wrong, I tell myself. But my heart asks, *Then why do I feel like a new dart's stuck in here, a dart oozing slimy goo?*

I twist my crystal necklace back and forth around my fingers. How else am I supposed to save what I love?

As we head toward the ceiba, the little kids show off the forest, their own gigantic backyard jungle gym.

Marcos points to high-up fruit and races up the long, slender trunk to retrieve it. Lily zooms up the tree next to his. It all happens so fast. They're defying gravity. Within twenty seconds, they're fifty feet high in the upper branches, plucking some kind of fruit I've never seen before and dropping it down, calling down something that I guess is *watch out!* in Huaorani.

The fruit plunks beside us, peach-colored with smooth skin, about the size of a big avocado. Inside, it's mostly giant whitish seeds held together with some tart, sweet gluey juice. Isa and little Dany show us how to suck the good stuff off the seeds and spit them out.

If Gali were with us, he'd add, *Trying brand-new, freshly picked fruit that has no name in English* to his secrets to happiness.

Once the kids shimmy down, they teach us their technique in slow-mo. They wrap their arms and hands around the slender trunk, then plant the soles of their bare feet on the trunk and walk upward. Then they hug the trunk with their feet and push themselves straight up, then clutch a higher spot on the trunk, then walk upward a few more steps.

"Now you!" they urge, excited.

Exchanging glances, Leo and I pull off our boots, revealing sweaty bare feet. We only manage to get up a few feet, then fall to the ground laughing. And I'd always prided myself in being a good tree-climber . . . but that's when there are branches for help, not just a long, skinny, trunk. And these kids have trained their feet to clutch the trunk—it's as if they have a second pair of hands. Meanwhile, my feet are just used to walking inside shoes on flat, even surfaces. I bet the sole-of-foot part of their brain has zillions of neural connections, sparking like crazy.

The kids stifle their giggles as Leo and I slide our boots back on in defeat.

"Just keep practicing," Isa says kindly.

"Where'd you learn how to do that?" I ask the kids.

"Our dad taught us," Lily says.

Marcos nods solemnly. "Before he got killed."

My chest squeezes the air right out of me. "Oh. I'm sorry."

"Me too," Leo whispers. His voice crackles, this new, strangely deep voice of his.

Isa puts an arm around Marcos and says, "It happened three years ago."

"How?" I venture, thinking of snakes and jaguars.

"Gunshot to the chest," she says.

Her words from last night come back to me: *Something bad happened.* I want to ask more, but now Lily has found something she wants to show us. "A monkey's comb!" she says, holding up a brown seedpod covered in little spikes. She brushes her hair with it, and offers it to me. "Try it! Monkeys use it, too!"

I unbraid my hair and run the monkey's comb through it.

Apparently the kids have a makeover in mind, because now the boys have found some wet clay and are spreading it on their cheeks. "Now you!"

Leo and I kneel down and let the kids paint stripes on our cheekbones with the sand-colored clay. It feels cool and wet at first, and then starts drying and cracking.

Lily tugs at Isa's woven fiber bag and whispers something in Huaorani that makes her big sister smile. *"Bueno,"* Isa says, and pulls out a small gourd, dumping some red seeds onto her palm. "Achiote seeds," she says, holding them out for us to inspect.

She rubs the seeds together until her hands are covered in

bright orange-red. With careful fingertips, she paints circles around our eyes in a kind of raccoon mask.

"Perfect," she says, laughing, then paints her own face and her siblings' faces. Soon the little kids get ahold of some seeds and are chasing each other around, smearing red all over each other.

Their hollering and giggling replace the heaviness of the conversation about their dad's death. I decide to leave it be, embrace the playful atmosphere. I doubt the tragedy is something Isa would want to talk about in front of the little ones anyway.

We walk a few more minutes, trying to corral the kids, but then they get distracted by a vine in the shape of a swing, hanging from a tree. A "walking palm" is what Isa calls it. At first I thought it was because its trunk is divided and looks like legs, but she explains that it moves to follow the bits of sunlight that make it through the canopy.

We all take turns swinging on the vine. When my turn comes after the little kids', Leo entertains them with three nutshells on a flat stone, moving the shells around and having his audience guess which shell is hiding the red seed. He must have practiced this one a lot. His hands move in a swift blur, yet he always knows which shell the seed is under.

I close my eyes, flying back and forth. Happiness. I make a mental note to tell Gali about a few more secrets to happiness: *swinging on vines, climbing trees barefoot, painting your face.*

I swing, back and forth, back and forth, remembering what Leo said about the forest having its own kind of group brain. Hanging here, I feel like part of the tree, like one of the vines or flowers or fungi that lives in its world. I breathe the humid air in and warm it up and let its oxygen expand my lungs and enter my bloodstream and move through my heart and then, once it's filled with carbon dioxide, I breathe out again. I'm a piece of this jungle and my breath is intermingling with the breath of this tree and what a strange feeling this is.

Leo comes over, gives me a soft push on the vine.

I swing higher. Somehow, feeling part of something as huge as this jungle, and hearing about big problems like a murdered father . . . it makes the gap between me and Leo feel smaller, easier to reach across.

He gives me another push, and I swing higher still. He looks like a completely different person now, with the red eye mask and the clay stripes. Maybe that's what gives him courage to ask me something real, or maybe he's feeling that gap between us shrink, too. Who knows, but he asks, "How's your heart?"

"My heart," I say, "is passing molecules back and forth with this tree."

"Sweet," he says, like he really means it, like this was exactly the kind of answer he was looking for.

"Here, try it," I say, jumping down from the vine.

Once he's swinging, I push him higher, and he closes his red-coated eyelids and takes long deep breaths in and out, and I wonder if his heart feels the molecules, too.

Unlike me, Leo is naturally cool. He exudes coolness, even tromping through the jungle in huge rubber boots with his face painted red. Especially with his face painted red. It's something about the relaxed way he swings his arms, walks in long, loping strides, not swaggering exactly, but just walking through the world with quiet confidence. And it's something about the way his hair effortlessly flops over one eye, and he always has something to do with his hands—brushing the bangs from his face.

Can I trust this boy again? Will he really let me keep the treasure? Or will he betray me?

I'm blindly trusting Isa, there's no question about that. The deeper we go into the jungle, the more I have to trust her. I'd be lost and helpless without her. I'm not quite sure what I'll do if she tries to stop me from taking the treasure. Or claims it for herself. My mind doesn't want to go there.

As we walk, Isa's siblings take out three blowguns from her bag. They're made of bamboo, about two feet long, and the diameter of my wrist. The kids use a stick to stuff some cottony fibers in the end.

"It's silk from ceiba trees," Isa says. "It holds their seeds." She explains that these are child-sized *cerbatanas*. The adult-sized ones are ten feet long and packed with darts whose tips are dipped in a specially prepared poison made from a vine. Luckily, the kids shoot tree seeds not poison darts—at each other. They squeal and laugh and run around like crazy—a jungle version of the water gun fights Leo and I used to have in the courtyard when we were their age.

Marcos offers Leo his *cerbatana*. Grinning, Leo grabs it and tries to blow a seed at me. It flops a few feet in front of my feet.

I laugh. Dany hands me his *cerbatana*. Fumbling, I find a red tree nut on the forest floor, poke it inside the end with some ceiba silk, and aim for Leo.

He watches, amused, through his red achiote mask, as it bounces lightly off his boot. Soon we're screeching and zipping around and whooping battle cries, as the kids run after us.

And that's what we're doing when Isa says, "Here's the tree."

I look up and see a clearing and a circle of enormous roots, like a mountain range, taller even than a tall man, and the thick trunk rising above all the other trees. Far, far above, through layers of other tree canopies, I see bits of her crown, spreading like an umbrella. It's leafless since she's dropped her green for dry season. And growing on her roots and trunk and branches are plants of all kinds—orchids and vines and lichen and mosses, all shapes and sizes and sheens. She's a world within herself.

Plunk. A seed ricochets off my head. It doesn't hurt but I cry, "Ouch!"

I turn to see Leo give a guilty grin beneath his red eye mask.

He lowers his *cerbatana.* "Sorry, Coco. I couldn't miss the chance." Then, in English, he says softly, "So where's this treasure?"

I shrug. "Guess I'll know it when I see it." I feel icky telling secrets in English in front of Isa. We wouldn't even be here without her. She's leaning against one of the massive roots, unraveling some strands of dried palm leaves with agile fingers.

He glances at her, too, looking uncomfortable, then starts searching between the roots opposite her. "Have you told her about it yet?"

I shake my head.

"Shouldn't we tell her?"

I say nothing. Now she's expertly weaving the palm strands.

He pushes. "I mean, it's her forest, right?"

"I guess, but . . ." I'm not sure how to finish my sentence. Keeping my eyes downcast, I scan the base of the tree.

After a moment, Leo says, "We're all in this together, Coco."

The kids notice we're looking for something. They start climbing over the lower tips of the buttress roots, peering in the spaces between the roots, curious.

Leo and I are slowly circling the tree, exploring chamber by chamber. I wish I knew what exactly I'm looking for, what exactly this treasure is. And what exactly is going on with Leo— mainly why he's here with me. The red mask and clay stripes on my face make me bold.

When we're on the far side of the tree from Isa, I ask, "Why'd you want to come here anyway, Leo? Why'd you enter the contest? Why'd you tell me *you thought you had to*?"

He runs his hand through his hair. "One day last month I kind of fell asleep in the cottonwood while I was waiting for my mom to finish up work. And I had a weird dream."

He pauses, reluctant to say more. I urge him, "Go on."

"There was a tree talking to me. I recognized it as a ceiba. Like the one in that old photo hanging in El Corazón. The one that Gali's in."

Gali's the guy in that picture? I want to ask about it, but more than that, I want to hear this dream. I stay quiet and listen.

Leo continues slowly, halting here and there. "Anyway, the ceiba in my dream—you were there with it. You were looking for something. And the tree told me, 'Within my roots a treasure awaits.'" He pauses. "Then a jaguar walked up behind you. I was afraid it would attack. I ran toward you . . . and then I woke up."

My eyes widen. "A jaguar . . . is that how you got the idea for your Home Sweet Home entry?"

He nods. And then, mumbling so low I can barely hear, he adds, "Coco, I wanted to be here with you. *For* you. To protect you. Or whatever."

My hand rises to my chest, clutches the crystal of my necklace. "So you came here . . . *to help me?*"

"Yeah. Sort of. I mean, I wasn't sure how to do it. I knew the only way we'd get to the Amazon was one of us winning the chocolate contest. I figured if I won, I'd bring you along as my guest. And I hoped that if you won, you'd bring me."

Everything is rearranging itself inside my head. "But . . . *Leo*. You told me to *stay away*."

He leans against a giant root that forms an arc above his head. "I'm sorry. I was wrong. I was . . . *mean*. I guess I wanted to try something different. So I started hanging out with those guys . . . but then . . . that didn't feel completely right either. I figured if we made it to the Amazon, everything would work itself out. Like Gali says, *destiny*."

I try to take this in, the galaxy-shaking idea that Leo actually wanted to be here with me all along. I feel like hugging him, but instead I ask, "What did you think the treasure was, Leo?"

He bites his lip and looks at me, unusually awkward. "You."

A moment of shock. *Me?*

"I wanted—I *want*—to be friends again, Coco. I thought coming here with you . . . that it might happen."

176

There are a million things I could ask and say and do. I whittle it down to, "*Waponi, amigo.*"

"*Waponi, amiga,*" he says. And then, looking embarrassed, he starts walking around the other root chambers. "Well, no white flowers here either."

I'm still wrapping my mind around the idea that he thought *I* was the treasure, so I just manage to echo his words. "White flowers?"

"In my dream there were tons of white flowers in the roots. Was it the same in yours?"

I force myself to focus and scan my memory. "I didn't notice them. Or I don't remember."

By now we've made it all the way around the massive trunk, back to our starting point.

Isa has just finished weaving a palm bracelet with a red tree nut in the center. "For you, Coco," she says.

"Oh, you don't need to give me any presents," I protest, heat rising to my face.

But she's already taken my wrist and is double-knotting the bracelet.

"*Waponi,*" I say softly. I don't deserve her kindness or gifts. I swallow hard and venture, "Isa, you know any ceibas with white flowers at the roots?"

She thinks, furrowing her brows. "I don't know. But we can keep looking. Ready?"

Leo nods, looks at the bracelet and then at me. *Tell her,* his eyes are saying. *Tell her.*

As we head back to the canoe, I notice a large animal track that I didn't see before. I let the others go ahead, and linger back to get a better look. The upside-down heart pad with four toes, the size of a saucer. A jaguar's footprint, fresh in the mud.

I jog ahead and keep this to myself.

***

The farther downstream we float, the stranger Isa's been acting.

At noon, she bites her lip and says, "We should turn back now."

We've stopped at two more ceibas, both without white flowers or treasures. But we've been having fun, getting practice walking up trees barefoot and having more impromptu blowgun fights. With each stop, Isa looks more distracted. I wonder if she's guessed that Leo and I are keeping secrets. Or maybe she's worried that the jaguar is stalking us.

Leo studies her face, which is now free of paint and clay. We all took a swim in the river after the second ceiba and washed off our smeared masks. "You okay, Isa?"

She gives an unconvincing nod. She's navigated the canoe to shore, but we all stay seated inside it. She's still at the front of the boat, bamboo pole in hand. "We have to turn around."

"Let's go a little farther," I urge. "Aren't there more ceibas downstream?"

"It's not a good idea." Her voice is oddly firm.

I squint into the distance, see the telltale bare crown of a ceiba that looks less than a mile away. What if this is my ceiba? What if I've come so far, only to turn around when my treasure's just within reach? "Come on, Isa, just a little farther. Please?"

"There are dangers ahead."

I think of all the predators in our midst, toothed and poisonous. I'm willing to risk it. I mean, if I'm gonna die, death by jaguar would be a cool way to go. At least, that's what I tell myself.

"Worried about jaguars?" I ask her.

She shakes her head. "As long we stick together, no jaguar will attack us."

"Then let's keep going, Isa." As I say this, I glance at Leo. His expression says, *Bad idea.* He flicks his gaze to the little kids, and I can tell what he's thinking: *We'd be putting them in danger.*

But I've come so far. And everything depends on me finding the ceiba. What if this one is mine? If it is, and if the treasure is valuable enough that it can pay back El Corazón's debts with some left over, then I'll share it with her. Win-win for everyone, even if she's not aware of it. "Come on, Isa."

She says nothing, her jaw fixed like stone.

"We'll be careful," I assure her. "Please, take us?"

She shakes her head.

I breathe out, exasperated. "Then you guys wait for me here. I'll take the canoe there myself."

Her face tightens. "Fine. We'll take you."

Despite the heat, I shiver. Sensing something is amiss, the little kids huddle together in silence. Leo won't meet my eyes. And as Isa stands at the bow of the canoe, pole in hand, somberly pushing us offshore, she looks like the goddess Styx, leading us down to the Underworld.

What have I gotten us into?

The Ceiba Tree

AMAZON RAIN FOREST

What a strange idea, to own a piece of earth. Or what's above the earth, like a tree. Or what's inside the earth, like oil or rock. It's strange, even, to think of owning one's body, with so many other wee creatures living on it and inside it. It's like trying to own the air, to own a dream.

We are worlds unto ourselves, we trees, you humans. We are webs of living things, and no matter how wise we are, we can never grasp the countless ways we all depend on each other.

We can never truly own anything, can we?

At the moment, a tiny frog is bathing in a bromeliad on one side of my trunk. A hummingbird is pollenating an orchid on the other side. A jaguar is napping on my buttress roots. An elfish monkey is swinging far above him. A parrot is tending to her babies in the upper reaches. Tiny

threads of fungi move nourishment in and out of
the tips of my roots.

Do I own these beings? Do they own me? Or
are we something . . . more . . . to one another?

Carnage

I hear it before I see it. The whir and roar and whine of machinery, both heavy and sharp, like a thousand machetes chopping through the forest music. And as we float farther, the birds and crickets taper off and there are just a few lone melodies surviving in the shadow of harsh motors.

Next comes the stench. A burning odor. Something sickening.

And next comes a bone-deep feeling that something isn't right. It's the noise and smell and something more . . . a feeling of dread, an emptiness, a darkness. Is it too late to ask Isa to turn back?

We turn a bend in the river and see it: carnage.

Trees butchered, strewn like corpses. Sawdust and splintered wood. Crushed bushes and smashed flowers. Dirt marred by tire tracks and plow marks. A huge expanse of destruction, the sky unnaturally visible, the clouds hanging gray and low and ominous.

I think of the worlds within every one of those fallen trees, the thousands of plants and insects and lichen and moss and birds and orchids and vines that made their home within their branches. Now it's a graveyard.

The naked dirt stretches farther than a football field, littered with dead, fallen trees around the edges. In the center, the ground is brownish-red clay and cleared of brush, cleared of any life. A tower looms tall, and at its peak, a fire burns like a giant candle, releasing black smoke into the gray sky. Near it are two giant ditches brimming with murky liquid—one shiny and purple-black, and the other rusty rainbow-orange goo.

A few trucks and bulldozers rumble around, weaving among little corrugated metal shacks and a smattering of pipes and enormous can-shaped tanks. An oil rig pumps up and down like a giant, alien robot.

Men in orange jumpsuits stained oil-black and boots covered in mud are welding one of the pipes that leads into the jungle. Others are standing around watching the pump extract oil. Some wear helmets and goggles and elbow-length rubber gloves . . . everything splattered with sludge.

And there, at the very edge of the field is the ceiba tree, towering high, but not as high as the oil rig or the flaming flare. Inside the jungle, ceibas look majestic and indestructible. But this one here looks exposed and vulnerable. A truck is idling near it, too close.

Isa has guided the canoe to shore. But she doesn't get out. Voice shaking, she says, "Now that you've seen it, let's go back."

I glance over at Leo. He's shell-shocked, his eyes glassy. He covers his face, as if it's an unbearably sad or scary part of a movie. "Yeah," he says, his voice breaking, "let's go back."

And I feel like throwing up or crying, too, but what if this is my ceiba? Are there white flowers at the base? I need to go closer to see. "I'm going to check it out."

"Coco, no," Isa says, "it's too dangerous."

"Then you guys stay here."

Before they respond, I scramble up the bank, through a patch of crushed underbrush and scraggly palms. Beneath my feet is shiny, gooey liquid that isn't mud or river water. It's sludge, oily and reddish-brown and black with a hint of petroleum purple. It's coating the forest floor. I clomp through it in my boots, feeling my stomach turn.

The air presses on me, heavy and hot and damp. I'm sweating, adrenaline pumping. My breath is jagged, my blood rushing loud in my ears.

Soon I leave behind the scant protection of the jungle's edge and race into the middle of the field. The Underworld. That's where we are. If the rain forest was a kind of lush, musical paradise, this is the opposite. This is the barren wasteland full of corpses and carnage at the end of the river Styx. The Land of the Dead.

It steals my breath to feel so exposed in the field of debris. The equipment and machines dwarf me. The sun burns my skin, blazing and relentless without canopies of leaves to filter it. And the air is thick with gas fumes, chemical odors, truck exhaust, oil smoke. Coughing and gagging, I cover my mouth with the neck of my T-shirt and forge ahead. I break into a fullout run toward the ceiba, tripping over crushed water bottles and beer cans and plastic bags.

Once I'm about a hundred feet away, I see that a worker is ramming one of the mountainous roots with a chainsaw. It looks ridiculous, like he's fighting a hopeless battle, since the tree's diameter is wider than the man is tall. Her roots alone are taller than the man. Still, he pushes on the chain saw, making a gash that looks like a paper cut compared to the size of the tree. It seems impossible to kill something this magnificently massive.

But as I climb over the mounds of dead, broken trees, I realize that although it could take a while, this ceiba will be felled just like the rest of them.

Growing closer, I struggle to see around the equipment and trucks to make out the base of the tree. Within its monumental roots are piles of brown and green plant debris. I wipe the sweat from my eyes, squint harder, shield my eyes from the sun.

And there, poking up through the sawdust and litter, are flashes of white.

White petals.

White flowers.

This must be my dream tree.

Instinct takes over. I race toward the man, screaming, "No! *¡Basta! ¡Deténgase!*" I'm yelling at the top of my lungs, but it's all drowned out by the machinery and truck engine and chainsaw motor. I'm nothing more than a mosquito buzzing around.

But the driver leaning against the truck cab door notices me. His face screws up in alarm.

"What are you doing here?" he yells in a raspy voice. He's stocky and wide, with plenty of heft.

I'm shaking and sweating and can't find the right words in Spanish. I spew out, "He can't do that. She's a ceiba. A mother tree. Make him stop!"

The man looks at me like I'm crazy. "Where'd you come from?"

"Colorado. The United States."

He gives me a strange look, with a touch of fear, as though I'm a ghost. Then he reaches through the open window, pulls a radio from his truck dashboard, and mumbles something into it.

I keep my eyes on the ceiba. The gash in the root is growing deeper. "Stop!" I yell.

The man continues sawing, oblivious.

I can practically hear the ceiba crying. Practically hear the remaining few insects and birds slowing their songs into one of mourning. "Stop!" I shriek, louder still.

"Quiet," the driver says, putting away his radio. He moves closer to me. "Get in the truck."

There's no way I'm getting into the truck. Maybe he intends to drive me somewhere safe . . . or maybe he has less noble plans in mind. Either way, I have to get away and save the ceiba.

I take a deep breath and dash toward the tree, fast approaching the man with the chainsaw. He still can't hear me shouting because of his ear protection and the motor roar, which is so loud it rattles my brain. Flinching, I tap him on the shoulder. When he turns toward me, I jump back, away from the whirring chainsaw.

He gapes at me. Turns off the machine. "You must leave, girl," he says. "It's dangerous." He speaks Spanish with an accent similar to Isa's, and I get the feeling he's indigenous—maybe Huaorani, maybe from another group. He has the same diagonal scars on his cheeks as Isa's uncle José, and wears the same round earrings I've seen on some of her other uncles.

There is kind concern in his eyes behind the fear. "Please, go," he says. "These men . . ."

Thick hands clamp my upper arms. Two men have grabbed me, one on each side. They must have come in the second truck now parked by the other one. They're middle-aged, dark hair flecked with strands of gray. Their grips are iron-tight, and their breaths reek of liquor.

"Let me go!" I shout, panicked.

No response. They lead me back toward the trucks, where the driver stands beside a young man. He must have just arrived. As we grow closer, I see that he's holding a black pistol in his right hand.

With all my might, I try to wrench my arms away, with no luck. I look back at the kind man with the chainsaw, hoping he'll help. But he has revved up the chainsaw engine and put his ear protection back on.

I'm trapped.

***

"What're you doing?" the gunman shouts in my face. He smells of onions and beer. "Trying to get yourself killed?"

I'm not sure if he means by chainsaw or gunshot. I register how young he is, twenty years old at most. He sports buzzed hair and an expression so brash it makes my legs feel like they might buckle. Who knows if he's an official security guard or just some guy with a gun.

I force my voice to stay steady. "Trying to save that tree."

From behind me, Isa and Leo appear. Thank goodness. They're holding the hands of the little kids, whose eyes are wide and petrified.

The gunman turns to the rest of my ragtag group. "Who're you?"

Leo's voice comes out strangely confident, as if he's performing onstage. "A magician, as a matter of fact," he says, extending his hand for a shake.

Caught off guard, the gunman returns the shake with his free hand.

Leo turns to the older men at my side. They release their grip on me to meet his handshake.

I rub my arms and step away as Leo shakes hands with the driver, too.

Good thinking, Leo. We've used this technique with grumpy customers at the chocolate shop before. It's what we call the change-the-story technique. As in, if you don't like the way the story's going, change it. When things are going badly— like little kids fighting while their dad's choosing truffles—all you have to do is (1) surprise the kids with something totally unexpected, like throwing chocolate hearts at them, and (2) take control of the situation yourself, like by getting them to play catch-the-chocolate-hearts.

Leo moves on to step two. I suck in a breath. The stakes are so much higher than little-kid sibling rivalry. There's a *gun* involved.

He pulls a deck of cards from his pocket and does some fancy shuffling. "Pick a card, any card," he says in Spanish.

There's nothing mumbly or crackly about his voice now. It's brazen and commanding.

The men blink at each other. It's probably bizarre enough for them to encounter two American kids out here . . . and even more bizarre to have one of them doing card tricks out of the blue.

But that's how you change the story. You take a risk.

I bite the inside of my cheek, hoping they don't shoot us. Isa's father was shot dead. Under circumstances like this?

After a moment, the driver chuckles, shrugs, and picks a card. "Why not?" he says under his breath. Hiding the card from us, he passes it around to the other men.

Leo does more fancy shuffling, then tells the gunman, "Put the card back in the deck, *señor*, anywhere you like."

Tucking his gun back in the holster, the man obeys. I breathe out, relieved that the weapon is no longer in his hand. Leo smiles and shuffles some more. He looks oddly calm except for the trickle of sweat trailing from his temple to cheek to neck. I have the urge to wipe it away.

All four men are watching him intently, as if they can't figure him out but they're willing to go along for the ride. Their expressions are a mix of curiosity, suspicion, and amusement. Maybe they've been bored doing soulless work out here, without Internet or texting or movies or restaurants. Maybe they've been craving something new, something different. And maybe Leo just tapped into this unspoken need. Maybe, secretly, these men *want* their story changed.

"Now," Leo says, completely in control, "if I pick your card, you let us go with a friendly good-bye."

The men look at each other, their gold teeth shining. "Okay," the driver says. His voice is gruff, but softer now, with a morsel of tenderness. Leo has managed to tap into this man's humanity. He's uncovered the pieces of them that are fathers or brothers or kids.

Leo cuts the deck. "Now pick the top card."

The driver picks it up, his fingers creased with oil and grime.

Leo offers a humble yet confident smile . . . that cool smile that makes everyone like him. Charisma, that's what he has. I notice it with customers—some people come and go and you can't recall their faces ten minutes later. But the ones with charisma—you recognize them when they pop in again next year.

"Is that your card, gentlemen?" Leo asks.

I pray it's the right card . . . if not, what would we get instead of a friendly good-bye?

A grin spreads over the men's faces as they peer at the card. Even the gunman looks impressed, but I can't shake the feeling that he's still dangerous. Unpredictable. The weapon is black and shiny in its holster, like a napping panther.

"Hey," he says, "how'd you do that?"

"A magician never reveals his tricks," Leo says with a wink. He's ready to bolt. Most people couldn't tell, but I can from the way he holds his shoulders and the position of his feet. Another river of sweat snakes down the side of his face. Beside him, Isa and the kids are slowly backing away toward the river.

Leo reaches out to shake the men's hands again. This time they slap him on the back, the way guys do when they're showing affection . . . but a little harder than necessary. The gunman's pat nearly knocks Leo off his feet. Time to leave.

I take a few steps toward Isa. She grabs my hand and clutches it tight. The stench of burning oil fills my nose, flips my stomach.

All smiles, Leo waves and says, "Nice meeting you." He walks away as Isa and the kids and I join him. I can tell by the set of his jaw that he knows the risk he's just taken and he knows what could happen next if the men have a change of heart.

Isa and the kids and I follow, not daring to look back. My muscles stay tense though.

No meaty hands grab my arms, but a rough voice behind us calls out, "You got five minutes to get out of here." And then, a deafening round of automatic gunfire. I jump and cover my ears. A bunch of birds fly from the treetops in a panic. Marcos starts crying. So much for a friendly good-bye.

I dare to glance back. The gunman's pointing his pistol high, angled toward the jungle. He lets out a whoop as the other men curse and tell him to calm down. Ignoring them, he laughs again and shouts after us, "Five minutes!"

Panting and gasping, we run toward the cover of the forest, at top speed. Little Dany trips, sprawling in the mud. Leo picks him up and runs, carrying him like a football under his arm.

We're nearly to the river when another earsplitting spray of gunfire rips through the jungle. I duck my head and look around in a panic. No bullets have reached us.

Once in the shadows of the forest, I slip on the oily sludge. I lose my footing and fall into it, coating myself with the ooze. I can't stop shaking enough to get out.

Isa reaches her hand to my sludge-covered one.

And as she does, my gaze rests on a giant paw print in the slimy mud. "A jaguar?"

She nods. "He's nearby," she says quickly. "Those tracks weren't there ten minutes ago. I saw his tracks earlier today, too."

"The same jaguar?"

"Yes. Yesterday and today." She yanks me up. "Part of the little toe on his front left paw is missing."

The jaguar stalking us seems less scary than these *petroleros*.

Another round of gunfire.

Isa tugs on my arm, breaks into a run. "Hurry!"

I try to keep my panic at bay. These men have no reason to kill us. And they don't seem evil, just an unsettling combination of bored and . . . *explosive*. The young gunman, especially. This is probably just his idea of goofing off.

Still, I run like my life depends on it.

When the riverbank comes into sight, I hurl myself down toward the shore, gasping for breath.

And there, sitting in our canoe, are a teenage boy and little girl. When the boy catches sight of us racing toward the boat, he clutches the child close and presses her head against his chest.

She looks about three or four years old. She's wearing a stained Thomas the Tank Engine T-shirt that's frayed at the hem and neck. Her hair is shoulder-length and wild, and her limbs thin as toothpicks.

"Come on," Isa says, while Leo quickly hoists her siblings inside. Then we both climb in, and Isa takes off upstream, pushing hard with her bamboo pole. She doesn't greet the strangers; there's no time for questions.

The boy picks up the second pole and stands at the back, helping Isa propel forward and steer the boat against the current. He looks about fourteen, and his arms are lean and muscled beneath a black T-shirt featuring a picture of Justin Bieber.

We're heading upstream now, and although the current is slow, it takes much more effort. A steady drizzle has started, and I'm soaked with sweat and mud and rain, but none of that matters. My ears are still throbbing from the thunder of gunfire and machinery and chainsaws. I only want to get away from that Underworld.

Leo comforts the little boys while I put an arm around Lily on one side, and the new girl on the other. Her eyes are wide and glassy, her chin quivering, barely holding back tears. Up close, I notice a rash covering her skin—red, angry-looking bumps that she scratches every so often.

Isa and the guy are pushing the bamboo poles so fast and hard they're breathless. I'd volunteer, but this is hardly the time to learn a new skill. And now her siblings are crying, and Leo and I are trying to calm them down.

This is my fault. They could've been shot. We all could've been shot.

We don't slow down until we're far enough from the oil field that we don't hear any machinery. Until we're safely out of the Underworld. The music of insects and birds surrounds us. My whole body sighs in relief. The leaves, the branches, the vines, all are intact and green and alive . . . it's welcoming, comforting, like a mother's hug.

But it suddenly all feels very, very fragile.

I glance back at the teenage boy at the back of the canoe. Rain is dripping down his cheeks, collecting on his eyelashes. "What's your name?" I ask, struggling to keep my voice from shaking.

"I'm Antonio." He nods at the little girl. "And this is my sister, Susy."

Once we introduce ourselves, he asks quietly, "Where are you from?"

"Colorado, USA." I'm not sure how normal it is to just show up in someone else's canoe without a word of explanation. And I'm not sure how to make small talk after being shot at. "How about you?"

With his chin, he gestures behind us, toward the wasteland. "That's our home."

"Oh," I say, gravely, because what do you say to someone who lives in the most horrifying place you've ever seen? "Where are you going now?" I ask.

"Susy has a rash from the oil spilling in our part of the river. We're going to the waterfall to heal her." He nods with his chin. "It's a little ways upstream."

He glances at the slick sludge on my skin and clothes. "You should wash that off, too. Or else it might give you a rash."

Isa nods. "We'll go with them to the waterfall. To clean up all that ugliness."

Leo turns to Antonio. "Was your home always like that?"

"When I was little, it was a good place. Like it is here, farther upstream. But every year, the oil drilling and logging gets worse. The pollution is making us sick. We get stomachaches. We get dizzy and nauseous. We have no clean water to drink or cook with or wash with. People are getting cancer. The plants and fish and animals are dying. We have little food to eat."

Thinking about this sends a wave of nausea over me.

Antonio pulls a small notebook from his shorts pocket. It's wrapped in a plastic bag. He passes it to Leo, who opens it up and leans forward to share it with me.

The notebook is filled with colored pencil–drawn comic strips. Only they're not funny comics, but sad ones, terribly sad. As Leo and I flip through, I realize it's the story of the boy's home, slowly dying. The first pages are green and lush, the people happy, healthy. Then come the pictures of the river's surface covered in dead fish. The banks littered with dead animals. The women washing white clothes that turn black in the water. Sick, crying children sprawled on mats.

"Did you make this?" I ask in a quavery voice.

He nods. "I want people to know what's happening to my home. I want people to help us stop the *petroleros*."

Leo sniffs, wipes his eyes. His voice comes out in a low creak. "If it's your territory, can't you make them leave?"

Antonio takes a long breath, searching for words. His gaze lands on Isa. "You're the daughter of the famous Roberto, aren't you?" He speaks with reverence.

She nods. "Yes, I'm Isa, his oldest."

Antonio looks back at me and Leo. "Her father was a brave man who tried to make them leave. He formed a group to protect our land. The *petroleros* told him to stop. He didn't . . ."

Antonio's voice fades out, and Isa finishes. "So they shot him."

A moment of shock. The rain pattering on the river, the leaves, our skin. The water rushing by. The hush of insects. A bird calling.

"I'm so sorry," Leo says. And then, quietly, "Have you contacted the police?"

"The police do nothing," Isa says. "They're friends with these men. The *petroleros* and loggers give them money."

I breathe in and out and in and out. The air feels empty. I stare at the sludge coating my clothes and skin. I try rubbing it off, but that only spreads it around. I've never felt so helpless.

I think of this boy's family back in the wasteland. I think of the few remaining plants and animals and trees. I wonder how long it will take for the loggers to kill my ceiba. What a slow and painful death. Is there some way to save my dream tree? Is there some way to help Antonio's community?

My chest aches, my whole body aches, as if there's a chainsaw inside, butchering my own branching vessels. As if, all along, there was a chamber for this tree, for this entire rain forest, and all its people and creatures, inside my heart.

And here, in this soft drizzle, listening to the quiet song of insects and trees, I wonder if my heart isn't what I thought it was. I wonder if it's not a contained little world with its four little chambers. I wonder if it extends into vessels like roots that stretch past the bounds of my body and into the earth and mingle with roots of these trees.

I can feel it, the scream of the ceiba in my blood. In this boy's notebook, I can feel the screams of his people. I can feel the screams of the entire forest echoing in my arteries and veins, all the way into the rooms of my heart.

Antonio and Susy lost their home. And Isa's home is in danger, too. Why is my home any more important than theirs? Why is my heart more important? What if we all share one big heart with countless chambers, countless branches and roots?

Tears pour down my face, for the ceiba, for this brother and sister whose home has been poisoned and destroyed, for the entire forest. Who knows what treasure the ceiba hid. The tree herself was priceless. And I failed to save her.

"I'm sorry," I whisper to no one in particular. I stare into the forest as I say it, over and over and over. *"Lo siento, lo siento, lo siento."*

And because I have to do something, I wipe my tears, open my daypack, and pull out a vanilla milk chocolate bar from the insulated bag. I break off a piece for Susy. She licks it tentatively, and her eyes light up, and yes, for this one moment in time, chocolate is making things better.

I pass pieces of chocolate all around and the mood in the canoe lifts, just a bit, just enough for me to wonder if maybe there is some way. Maybe if we listen closely enough . . . maybe we can hear the jungle whisper the answer . . . and if we can't find any magic, maybe we can make our own.

The Ceiba Tree

AMAZON RAIN FOREST

Oh, brave human saplings! Saplings who walk, who talk, who listen. We are singing our stories to you. Do you hear them?

There are still a few humans left who share our tales. Tales of the mother spirit of the ceiba who created our forest. When she fell, her body formed the Amazon River, her buttress roots formed the delta, and her branches formed the tributaries like the one where I live.

Once upon a time, the ceiba was the humble creator of our world.

And now, blade by blade, we, her descendants, are being destroyed.

Do you see this ancient creator inside us? Do you see the heart we share?

If you truly listen, and if you truly see, then you will find a way to save us.

The Waterfall

About an hour's ride upstream, Isa and Antonio direct the canoe to the right-hand shore, where a dense wall of leaves and vines rises.

"Here we are," Isa says, eyeing her siblings with concern. The chocolate has made them happier, but their faces still hold traces of fear.

We drag the canoe up the bank, then climb a steep hillside path, and walk along a ridge. On the way, Isa kneels down and plucks a thick-leaved plant from the stem, holding out the clear, gooey, sap-filled interior for me to see. "Shampoo and soap."

"Cool." Soon I spot a monkey's comb and put it in my pocket to add to our natural toiletries collection.

I wonder if to Isa and her family, the jungle is like a giant supermarket, stocked with nearly everything you need . . . if you know where to look. I've only gotten a one-day glimpse so far, but this is her world, and she understands its hidden inner workings.

A wave of embarrassment washes over me. I thought I could

teach her about cacao and DNA . . . but if I pay attention, maybe she can teach me about a whole new world.

Meanwhile, Isa's brothers and sister are shaking off their shock, zipping up and down the trees, gathering fruit to share with their new little friend. They seem to sense her sickness and sorrow, and have taken on a protective role.

Antonio runs his hand over his closely cropped hair. "Isa, I left my comic book in the canoe. It's my gift to you in honor of your father."

"*Waponi,*" she says softly.

"He sacrificed his life to protect us," Antonio says.

Isa nods. "I'm going to continue his work. Whatever it takes."

A mountain of emotion blocks my throat. I rack my mind for some way to help them with their mission. I come up with nothing. When I glance at Leo, his eyes are brimming with the same sad frustration that's flooding me.

We're quiet for most of the hike. Finally, after a half hour, I find myself at the end of the path, peering down at a giant valley below. Across the valley, a waterfall pours a hundred feet into a natural pool. The edges of the valley are draped in moss and vines and leaves like a flowy dress with a white lace cascade of water. The sun has come out, casting sequins of light on the water, the leaves, the wet rocks.

Isa and Antonio show us how to descend the steep green cliff, using vines to keep from slipping. I focus all my energy on finding footholds and hanging on with my hands. It takes ages to get to the bottom, and my arms and palms grow sore, but in a good way.

Somehow, the little kids reach the bottom first. They wait at the edge until Antonio catches up and grabs a long stick that he pokes around the bottom of the pool.

I'm about to ask what's going on when Isa says, "Caiman check."

Right. Caimans. In the alligator family. I try not to look too freaked out.

"They like hanging out here," Isa adds.

"Who wouldn't," Leo says.

"All clear," Antonio announces, tossing aside the stick and wading in.

Isa and the kids climb over the rocks at the shore, and test the water with their toes.

Without hesitation, Leo pulls off his shirt and heads into the pool, hands tucked under opposite arms. He used to have a pudgy ring around his waist that hung a little over his swimsuit, but that's gone now. His back makes a V, wide at the shoulders, and tapering to his waist. You can even see some muscles moving beneath the skin as he walks.

He drops to his neck in the water, then turns to me. "Come on in, Coco!"

I weigh the risk of encountering a caiman. But if we can handle *petroleros*, we can handle caimans, right? I stand up, kick off my rubber boots, and enter the water's edge in my shorts and top. It's cold, but I force myself onward. Antonio was right—the sludge on my skin is already starting to itch and burn. I have to wash it off.

The water makes me gasp as I dunk myself under. For the first few minutes, my muscles are tense, wary of caiman teeth.

We stand near the spray and Isa hands us the soap and shampoo plants and shows us how to create foam by rubbing the torn edges with water. We lather it in our hair and all over our skin, making thousands of little bubbles. The oil and sludge wash off, downstream. This worries me—am I polluting the clean water now? But Antonio assures me it's not enough to contaminate the river, that the important thing is to get it off my skin before it hurts me.

Once we're all shiny clean, Isa says, "Now we go under the spray for a *limpia*."

Limpia. Cleaning. I try to figure out what I'm missing. "But aren't we already clean?"

"To clean our insides," she says. "Our hearts." She motions to Susy. "And to heal her pain."

Isa takes my hand and leads me beneath the waterfall. I clench my eyes shut as it rushes over me, pounds against my back, my neck, my head. The force of it creates great gusts and blows clouds of mist. It's so powerful I can feel the sludge on my insides washed and blown away. This reminds me of the melanger stage of chocolate-making, when all the stone grinding releases the sharp volatile chemicals and leaves the mellow, smooth chocolate behind.

I open my eyes. Through the mist floats a brilliant blue butterfly, iridescent and fluttering in the sunshine, from petal to leaf to petal again.

"A blue morpho," Leo says.

I'm just remembering that *morpho* means *change*, and wondering why the butterflies are called morphos, when Leo answers my unasked question. "Morpho because it looks like they're changing shape as they fly."

Together, we watch the morpho, until Isa yells into my ear over the rushing. "Now give thanks!"

"*Waponi!*" I shout. I'm not sure if I'm thanking the waterfall or the jungle or the tree or Isa or the whole universe or the infinitesimal atoms that make us all up . . . but I can say that every bit of my cleaned-out heart feels alive and grateful.

Beside me, a soaking wet Leo is saying his own thanks. His dark hair is plastered to his cheeks and his arms are spread open to the pounding water and his lips are moving. There's still something little-boyish about his earnestness, but then there's something impossibly old about him, too, his knowingness. And then there's something new about him, something in his triangle torso, his visible muscles, his strong jawbone—but here, now, it's all being smoothed out together. It's like the tempering machine, heating and stirring the chocolate so that its separate parts—the white cocoa butter and the deep brown cocoa— ultimately cool into a perfect crystalline structure.

As the spray pounds me, I watch that sapphire butterfly. It feels like it rose up from inside me, from inside all of us, now flying free.

When we climb out from the water onto the warm rocks, I squeeze out my clothes and run the monkey comb over my hair and lean back, letting the sun dry me. Isa sits on one side, and Leo on the other.

I watch Antonio tenderly position Susy beneath the gentle outside spray. The waterfall cleaning might ease her spirit, but the only way to truly fix her is to stop the oil drilling and remove the pollution. There has to be some way to make this happen.

After they emerge from the water, we say our good-byes. They plan to catch a ride downstream with the next canoe that passes. But I can't let them leave without doing *something*.

"Antonio," I say, "your comic book—is it okay if we show it to our moms? And maybe take pictures of it to share with other people?"

"Of course." He looks energized by the idea. "The more people who know, the better. My email address is on the last page."

"How often can you check it?" I ask, remembering how rarely Isa and her family have Internet access.

"My aunt goes to town every month and she can check my email. There's an Internet café next to the clinic where she goes for cancer treatments."

"I'll write to you," I tell him, wishing I could do something more.

As they head toward the leaf-covered cliff, their steps are lighter than before, their strength renewed.

I watch Dany and Marcos and Lily play on the wet stones at the water's edge, laughing together. Hopefully, the waterfall *limpia* removed any last shreds of trauma from them. I'm relieved they weren't hurt back at the oil field. We survived. But my dream tree will probably be dead by the end of the day. Antonio and Susy's home will continue to be poisoned and destroyed. And who knows when the drilling and logging will spread to Isa's home?

I can't ignore it all. Now that I know, now that I care, I have to work with them to make things better.

I look at Isa, watching her brothers and sister in the waterfall spray. Sunshine illuminates her cheekbones, her nose, her forehead, the drops of water on her eyelashes. Her face is powerful, glowing with her own quiet charisma. She is protector of the forest. She's determined to carry on her father's work. But she can't do it alone.

And as I watch the butterfly dance through the bright mist, it's clear to me: Even though my ceiba is nearly gone, and my home will soon be gone . . . there's still hope.

I press my palm over the crystal at my chest. "Isa, somehow, I'll help you save your forest."

At the edge of the waterfall pool, as the blue morpho flits and glitters around us, I tell Isa everything—about my own dream of the ceiba and hoping to use the treasure to save El Corazón.

"I'm sorry I couldn't protect the ceiba in the oil field, Isa. Because if I could, I would have given the treasure to you, to save your home. The treasure should have been yours all along."

Isa takes my hands in hers, squeezes. *"Waponi."*

Leo, on the stones beside us, says, "Maybe the treasure's still there. Maybe we could sneak back and get it, at night or something."

Isa shakes her head quickly. "Too dangerous. If there's anything valuable, the *petroleros* will take it for themselves."

For a moment, we're quiet, and then, suddenly determined,

I say, "Then we'll figure out some other way to protect the forest."

Leo nods. "All of us. We're in this together."

Isa's hand feels warm and strong in mine. "We each have something to offer," she says.

I look at our hands, interlinked. "We each have a part to play."

And as we go on exchanging ideas, something shifts in the droplet-laced air. Isa is no longer a stranger guiding us. She's a friend. She's a partner. She's a treasure herself. And as her face lights up, I feel mine lighting up and see Leo's lighting up, too.

Hope. That's what's sparking like shooting stars in the space between us.

On the way back to the canoe, Isa helps us climb up the steep cliff, which leaves us breathless, adrenaline rushing anew whenever we look down. Eventually, we make it to the top. While Leo and I catch our breath, looking at the waterfall sparkle across the valley, Isa runs ahead with her siblings.

There's still something I need to say. "I'm sorry, Leo."

"For what?"

I run my fingers through my ponytail. Where to begin? "For being selfish."

"You're not selfish, Coco. You've been protecting what you care about."

I say nothing. He's being too generous. I've lied. I've put my own life before anyone else's. "What you said the day of our chocolate fight. That all I cared about was my own weird world. You were right."

He stares down into the deep green canyon. "The thing about you, Coco, is that you're so . . ."

I press my lips together, bracing myself. Whatever he says, I probably deserve.

"So *strong*. It's like you're the nucleus of an atom and everyone else around you is an electron." He pauses, shifts his gaze to meet mine. "I think that's why I acted how I did this year. I wanted to see what would happen if I broke that orbit. To see who I was without you."

I raise an eyebrow. "Since when do you use microscopic metaphors?"

"Well, if you want to get astronomical, you were the sun and I was a comet." He clears his throat. The low crackles in his voice make him sound vulnerable. "And my whole idea of coming here to the jungle with you . . . I wanted us to be friends again, but in a different way."

"And we are. I think we're both rogue comets now."

He laughs, just as a scarlet macaw whooshes by, calling out above our heads. After it disappears into the upper canopy, he says, "It was really brave how you stood up to those loggers. Maybe kinda stupid, but also brave."

"Your magic saved the day, you know." A corner of my mouth turns up. "Without you, I might be shot dead at the bottom of a sludge pit right now."

"Yuck."

A screech from above shatters the cricket sounds. We glance up to see two lanky spider monkeys high in the branches, each hanging by a nimble tail and arm. They're staring at us with curious expressions in their masked eyes. We watch them swinging and chattering for a while, until I ask, "So, Leo, who are you outside the orbit?"

It takes him a moment to understand my question. Then he says, "Still someone who likes carving chocolate. But who likes doing magic, too." He offers a crooked grin. "And someone who . . . *appreciates* . . . people who find existence fascinating."

My right atrium—the Leo chamber—feels warm and full again.

But there are other changes in my heart. It's no longer a fist-sized organ. It's morphed into a giant symphony hall, as big as this forest, as big as a galaxy, and it's near bursting with music of trees and stars, and the closer I listen, the more glimpses I get of how it all fits together. We're made of bits of exploding stars, our molecules of carbon and iron and oxygen, all of us—Isa and Leo and me and the ceiba and the jungle and the *petroleros* and loggers—bursts of creation born from destruction.

Maybe I'm starting to understand the messages in the forest music.

The cluster of huts of the Cooperativa Felicidad comes into sight in the early evening, when our shadows stretch long and the river's turned golden. Isa has taught me and Leo how to pole the canoe, which made us go in slow zigzags at first, but by the time we round the bend to the co-op, we're getting the hang of it.

At the sight of the dining hut, my stomach is rumbling. We

never had lunch, only chocolate along with fruit plucked from trees.

After we pull the canoe to shore, we climb up the muddy embankment and search for the moms. They're in the first place we look—by the cacao trees, along with Isa's uncle José and some other people from their community, mostly cousins, uncles, and aunts. The forest floor is covered in colorful, split-open pods, and the cacao beans are now fermenting in heaps on mats. Mom and Alma are covering them with giant leaves— probably banana and plantain from the looks of them.

My insides do a happy jig. I've never seen this process in real life before, never witnessed the yeasts and microorganisms starting the chemical reactions that give cacao its unique chocolate taste. It's strange that what we consider "germs" are actually key to the heavenly flavor of the Food of the Gods.

As we approach, I try to explain fermentation to Isa, but I have no idea how to translate ethanol, oxidize, aerate, enzyme, not to mention acetic, lactic, and amino acids. But she's taught me so much already, I want to offer her something. So I do my best, summing it up with, "You let things rot and get eaten by icky, tiny bugs, and in the end, it's healthier and more delicious than before."

At first, her face wrinkles up in confusion. And then you can practically see the light bulb over her head. "Oh, I get it. We ferment yuca. To make *chicha*."

"Cool. Can I try some?"

"Tomorrow," she says, delighted.

Just behind us, Leo catches up, slowed by the little kids hanging on to him adoringly and begging for more magic tricks.

"And listen, Isa," I add. "I'll find you a book in Spanish on fermentation so you know all the microorganisms involved. Next time we come."

"Next time?" she asks hopefully. "The *petroleros* haven't scared you away?"

"No! They made me want to come again. Soon, to help you protect your forest."

Leo nods, as Marcos sits, grinning, on his shoulders and Lily and Dany swing his hands. "We'll be back, Isa. Like I said, we're in this together now."

From the pile of rotting beans, Mom catches my eye. She looks ragged and streaked with dirt, but happy. "Coco!" she calls out, waving. "Look, sweetie! Fermentation!"

We head toward the moms and let them hug us. Nieves ruffles Leo's hair, looking amused at the little kids attached to him.

Since it's the first day of fermentation, the beans aren't too smelly yet. But by the end, they'll have a sour scent. That's how they smell once we open the newly arrived sacks of dried cacao at El Corazón.

After the moms recap today's cacao successes, Mom and Nieves gush about everything they've learned from Isa's mom in the forest. "Did you know Alma can smell an animal's scent from, like, a hundred feet away?" Mom looks at her with admiration. "And she even knows what kind of animal it is! Her nose is supersensitive—perfect for chocolate-making!"

Guessing Mom's meaning from gestures, Alma gives a modest shrug.

Nieves pipes in, speaking Spanish. "And she can tell you about every single part of every single plant in this forest—fruit, leaves, roots, bark—and then tell you all the animals that depend on it. And even tell you a story behind it!"

Eventually, Mom asks us, "How was your day?"

We recap the highs and lows as we help the moms cover the still-exposed beans with giant leaves. When we get to the part about the gun, Mom freezes. She drops the leaves and gives me a near-strangulation-grip hug. Once she calms down, and we move on to the card trick, Nieves kisses Leo's head proudly.

Alma is relieved to hear that we cleaned our bodies and spirits in the waterfall afterward. When Isa takes Antonio's notebook out from the plastic bag and flips through it, tears fill Alma's eyes. She passes it to the other moms, and we tell them about Antonio and Susy.

Mom's response, too, is sadness.

But Nieves's is something else altogether. First, her eyes fill with tears and, by the time she finishes the book, with fire. "We will not let this happen! We will join forces to make the oil company leave and fix this mess!"

Her voice rises into a war cry. Now she's in passionate lawyer mode, raising her fist and spouting legal stuff about remediation and compensation. Her face flushes bright as the bromeliads behind her. "This is why I got into law in the first place! To work together for true justice!"

Leo's staring at her, wonderstruck. "Mamá, I haven't seen you so excited about a case since . . . well, since ever."

She ruffles his hair again, which is funny since he's her same height now. "Oh, *mijo*, I used to do cases like this in my twenties, and I'd stay up all night working on them, I cared so much. Then your father gambled away all our savings and I had to start over from scratch. I was a single mother. I had to take the cases that made money. But now we have enough of a nest egg that I can afford to focus on a case I care about. Do some pro bono work that really matters."

As Nieves talks, the rest of us cover the fermenting beans with giant leaves. And by the time all the beans are covered, Nieves has planned out the next steps in the lawsuit and her eyes are two blazing coals. And some of those sparks jump off and catch me, and the hope inside me starts flaming. With Nieves's legal magic—along with Isa's dedication and Antonio's storytelling and Leo's creativity and the dream tree's guidance—maybe we can find a way to protect this forest together.

While Leo and Isa help her uncle José make dinner, and the moms get cleaned up, I walk to Gali's hut. Mom warned me that he wasn't doing well—he's stayed in his hammock all day and refused the offer of lunch. It's drizzling lightly, but I'm so used to being constantly damp—either from river or rain or sweat— that it doesn't bother me.

I step onto his porch, under the cover of the roof. He's swinging gently, eyes closed.

"Hi, Gali," I whisper, to gauge if he's sleeping.

"Coco, dear," he says with a tired smile.

I swallow. His cheeks were always two rosy apples, and now they're sunken and pale. "How's your heart?"

He sighs. "Still searching for that last secret to happiness. The one that can heal me." He gives me a tender look. "And did you find what you were looking for? It was beneath a ceiba tree if I remember correctly."

I give him a half smile. "It's not exactly turning out how I thought." He doesn't seem awake or strong enough to hear the whole crazy story of my day.

I perch on the wood railing beside him. "Gali, have you ever wondered if happiness is kind of a process . . . like turning cacao into chocolate?"

He pushes himself up to sitting, slowly swings his feet to touch the porch floor. "Tell me more, dear Coco."

"Whatever bad thing you did, maybe it was like fermentation. Maybe it makes you feel germy and icky, but maybe that was part of the process that made you who you are."

"Go on."

I bite my lip, trying to find the right words. "Gali, fermentation is the most important part of chocolate-making. It brings out over six hundred different flavor compounds! Without fermentation, chocolate wouldn't have its magic."

I watch him hopefully. He's nodding to himself, and his gaze is far-off, past the twilit river, over the silhouetted treetops. And finally his gaze rests back on me. "*Waponi*, Coco."

He sniffs the air. Scents of fried chicken and yuca and plantain are drifting out from the screened-in kitchen window. "Let's eat, my dear!"

I help him shuffle in his rubber boots to the candlelit dining hut just as Leo and Isa are serving the meal.

Food never tasted so good. I realize halfway through that the chicken we're eating was possibly our traveling companion in the little plane, but I'm so ravenous I don't care. I probably would've eaten boa constrictor if that had been on the menu.

Gali makes an effort at eating, and drinks his entire *agua de limón*. The rest of us are on to seconds while he's still picking at his half-full plate. My chest tightens in concern.

Afterward, Mom breezes into the kitchen and returns with a handful of baggies of our chocolate samples. She's radiant in the candlelight, her hair in a crown-braid, along with a 1970s pink-and-orange sundress that clashes with her red hair in a good way. "A taster flight!" she announces. "To thank our lovely hosts!"

The chocolate is in perfect shape, not a bit melted. Each piece is an anatomically correct heart the size of a quarter, made with a different cacao bean cultivar—criollo, forastero, trinitario, or Nacional—from equatorial countries all around the world.

A bittersweet feeling sweeps over me. This might be one of the last times we do a chocolate tasting, now that El Corazón will be lost.

Next Mom pulls out the description cards I made for each one. This is the art part of chocolate-making. Most of it's science, but how you create and describe the mix of flavors is pure art. I keep a thesaurus on hand to do justice to those six hundred flavor compounds. I need words like *gossamer, ethereal, nuanced* . . .

Isa and her mom and uncle examine the chocolate hearts in their hands, marveling at the tiny vessels.

Mom looks about to explode with excitement. Even her red

tendrils seem to be boinging out of her updo with a life of their own. She tells Alma and the others, "Now, to fully appreciate your cacao beans that are fermenting you need to taste the full potential of the final product."

We take turns sampling each variety of chocolate heart. I never get tired of tasting them, and now, here, in the middle of the Amazon jungle, in the wake of good news, they taste better than ever. They've come home to the place where they originated millennia ago, and they know it, and they're putting on a dazzling show for us.

Everyone takes this very seriously, even the little kids, closing their eyes to get the full impact of the taste.

Mom can't contain how thrilled she is. Neither can her cut-glass earrings, swinging and flashing in the candlelight. "Translate your descriptions, Coco bean!"

As everyone tastes, I go through, card by card, adding instructions. "Move the chocolate around in your mouth and touch it with all parts of your tongue."

Around the table, happy faces twist around as the chocolate hearts tour their mouths.

I look at Isa and her mom and uncle and brothers and sister. After all the things they've taught us about the forest, I'm happy to have something to offer in return. "We'll teach you how to recognize all the subtle flavors. That way, you can become chocolate connoisseurs yourselves. You'll take pride in the cacao and bring out all its potential. Its *exquisite* potential," I add.

"Exquisite indeed," Gali marvels, and I'm glad that even with his weak appetite, he's eating all the tasters.

The others nod, moving the chocolate around their tongues, deeply focused.

I've seen over and over how the chocolate sampler creates warm, happy feelings among customers, and I'm savoring this feeling now, in this candlelit hut, with these strangers who are new friends and, in a way, partners. As we turn the hearts over in our mouths, feeling their arteries and veins melt on our tongues, our brains are releasing neurotransmitters, sending us floating up past the tree canopies.

After the last taster has dissolved in everyone's mouths, and they're on to seconds, I announce shyly, "I want to give one last description. It's a description of my new friend." I glance at Leo and Isa. "*Our* new friend. Here goes."

Isa, of the Ecuadorian Amazonian cultivar.
Graceful, generous, and skilled. Originating from
the pulsing heart of the birthplace of cacao itself.
A mellow softness overlays the majestic, wise core.
Layers of floral sweetness, lush foliage, rich earth,
golden river. The aged aroma of ancient trees.
Slightly bitter undercurrents of sorrow and fear,
with stronger notes of forest music. A shining,
bright finish of hope and determination that
lingers.

Isa smiles at me from across the table. I flush a little, because doesn't everyone do that when they reveal the contents of their heart? But I hope she knows that this is sealing my promise. We're in this together.

We all help ourselves to more chocolate, picking out our favorites from the samples. Everyone's face has a light smile on it, and Gali's is now the brightest of all, as if the chocolate was the remedy he needed. I can almost see the theobromine entering his bloodstream, flowing through his brain and heart, adding a little pink to his cheeks.

Unexpectedly, he speaks. "My dear friends . . ." His voice is humble, yet dignified. He speaks in Spanish, very slowly, maybe so Mom will understand, or maybe he's just choosing every word carefully.

I'm expecting he'll deliver a new secret to happiness, or make a speech to thank everyone, but instead he says, "It's time you know: I was once a millionaire and a murderer."

Gali's Secret

My left ventricle—Gali's spot—is caving in on itself. An earthquake has struck my heart, shaken its foundations, sent the chamber walls crashing down. I press my hand over the crystal dangling from my necklace, squeeze it tight.

Gali's words echo in my brain. *A millionaire and a murderer.* My neurons are zinging like crazy, trying to make sense of this. How can the man who tosses joy around like confetti be a killer?

There's silence around the table. Even outside the screens, the creatures are holding their breaths. The entire night is still and stunned. I've stopped the chocolate mid-movement inside my mouth and everyone else appears to have done the same. We are still except for a facial twitch here and there. I've never stuck a fork in a socket and never plan to, but this must be how it feels. When he'd said he'd done something bad, I'd never imagined . . . *murder.*

We're all staring at Gali, his white hair pulled back in a ponytail, a few strands escaped. I take in his familiar, gentle face, marked deeply with laugh lines around his mouth and eyes. His hands are folded on the table. He looks down at them, then draws in a long, deep breath and speaks.

"My dears, many years ago, when I was a young, brazen man back in Spain, my grandfather, Gregorio Gallo, left me some inheritance. Since my grandfather owned a jewelry business—Joyería Gallo—and I was a bit sentimental, I invested the money in gold mining companies. I thought gold was timeless and classic, a perfect way to honor my grandfather. My stock investment happened to be at the right time, just before the value of gold skyrocketed for a while. Soon I found myself a multimillionaire."

Nieves is whispering to Mom as Gali speaks, translating from Spanish to English. Gali pauses to let her catch up before he continues. "I decided to take a trip to South America, to have an adventure, to see the gold mines that were bringing me such wealth. I don't know what I thought I'd find. Oh, I had such romantic notions of hidden treasure in the great Amazon, all sparkling gold in mysterious jungles.

"When I arrived, I felt I'd been hit by a train. There was nothing dazzling about it, my dears. An enormous patch of forest had been destroyed. It looked like an asteroid had hit, crushing and burning the trees, forming an enormous crater. And the people working there—Indians, we called them at the time, though I suppose now you'd say indigenous," he adds with a respectful nod to Isa and her family. "They toiled like slaves—men, women, children. And the children, oh the children!"

He looks at Lily and Dany and Marcos, who are now happily sprawled on the floor, playing with the tiny robot Gali gifted them. "Most of the children were sick, poisoned from the mercury dumped in the river with the gold extraction."

His voice cracks, fades. He pulls a yellow bandanna from his safari suit pocket, wipes his eyes, then blows his nose.

I think about the sludge and oil that coated me earlier today, the rash on Susy, her sick family and friends, their poisoned water and food. I glance at Isa and Leo, and I can feel their chests tightening the way mine is.

With great effort, Gali continues, his voice shaking. "Children were dying and it was my fault. It was my money driving the operations. My money that started this chain of terrible events that destroyed the forest and the creatures and humans inside it."

I stare at the candle flame on the table, flickering in the night breeze. How can Gali be a bad guy? My gaze moves to Mom with her hand over her mouth, her brows furrowed. Nieves is pressing her hand to her forehead, distressed as she murmurs the translation. Leo's looking down at his lap—he's let his bangs fall over his face, hiding his eyes. Isa and her family are listening intently, their faces still as statues, unreadable.

I don't know what my own face looks like, but my insides are reeling. I try to focus on breathing. I'm the one who told Gali that the bad stuff is part of the happiness journey. I'm the one who sparked him to tell the truth tonight. So I just listen and try to remember this story is the fermentation part of his journey, before he became who he is now.

"My heart felt poisoned," he whispers, barely audible over the insect songs outside. "I grew very sick myself, nearly died in the Amazon, but the local people took care of me, brought me on a three-day canoe journey to a powerful healer. He gave me some special tea and told me that my problem wasn't malaria or parasites or toxic chemicals, no, it was my shame that sickened me. He was compassionate enough to heal me, though he claimed I was the one healing myself.

"When I returned home to Spain, I wanted to cast off my old life. I wanted a new start. One night I spun the globe and my finger landed in the center of North America, in the Rocky Mountains. I found a map and read the names of all the small towns where I could hide away like a hermit. I settled on Heartbeat Springs. I liked the sound of it. I thought maybe that place could clean up my heart, put it back in working order.

"I sold my house, said good-bye to my old life. Sold all my gold stocks and donated the money to nature conservation groups. I moved to Heartbeat Springs and bought a place there. I rented out space so I had money to live on. I made art, heart art, to try and heal mine. I wanted nothing to do with gold. I buried that shameful past."

In our little yellow candlelit dining hut, in the middle of the vast, dark rain forest, we huddle beneath a blanket of quiet. Outside, the crickets and frogs continue their music. But inside this thick silence, there is no sound but our breathing, our heartbeats, the occasional flutter of moth wings.

Gali sniffles, wipes his tears with his sleeve, blows his nose into the bandanna.

I lean over and pat his shoulder awkwardly. Leo pats his other shoulder.

Mom speaks first. "You're not a murderer. You didn't know. You didn't poison anyone on purpose."

"Ignorance is no excuse," he says. "*No one* directly fed those children poison. Together, our actions killed them. I take my share of responsibility. I still haven't forgiven myself."

I swallow hard, wonder what I've done without knowing, what I need to take responsibility for.

"There in the barren crater," he says, "I learned the first secret to happiness: True happiness never comes at the cost of another's happiness." He pauses. "So I made little robots. Tried to make children smile. And adults, too. I've tried to bring more happiness to make up for the suffering I caused. I became a scholar of happiness. And I've tried to share these secrets to happiness. I've tried to grow my own heart back."

Another beat of silence. "Yet it's not enough. I have to do more . . . but I don't know what."

"So this is why you're really here," I say.

Slowly, he nods, taps his chest. "As you can tell, I'm sick once again. Heart disease. The doctors say I'm too frail for surgery. There's nothing else they can do."

A lump comes to my throat. Hot tears to my eyes. It shouldn't come as a shock, not with his weakness, the way he's been talking about death. But I've never been close to anyone who's died before. Who's *dying.*

"Oh, Gali," Mom says, her eyes welling up. "I'm so sorry."

"Thank you, my dear."

"Is there anything we can do?" Nieves asks between sniffles. She's probably thinking along the lines of bringing him casseroles or going to doctor's appointments with him.

"You're all here with me, and that's brought me more happiness than you can imagine. My life could end any day now. First I must make amends."

"How?" I ask.

"That's what I need to figure it out." From his safari pants pocket, he pulls out an old, yellowed folded piece of paper. It looks torn from a notebook or journal. He passes it to me.

I unfold it carefully. It's a hand-drawn map, with coordinates, latitude and longitude. There's a network of rivers. And there's an X that reads *Casa de Bai*.

I pass it to Leo, who looks at it and then passes it around to the others.

"Who's Bai?" As I say the name, I notice Isa and her mom give each other meaningful looks.

Gali doesn't notice. "The one who can tell me how to fix my crimes. How to fix my heart. He's the shaman who helped me decades ago. But he told me that the cure could only last for so long. That I would need to return one day to complete it. Now, as an old man, I understand there are things I still must do to right my wrongs. My heart will continue to crumble until I do."

After I translate, Mom's brow wrinkles. "I don't get it. What exactly do you need to do, Gali?"

"Bai will help me figure that out. I believe his home is not too far from here, perhaps within a day's travel by foot or canoe."

Gali pulls out a GPS from his other pocket and taps something in, then passes it around. I'm not sure how to decipher the numbers, but from the digital map, it looks like the beeline distance is twenty miles. It would probably be much longer by trails and rivers. I can't imagine Gali making that journey in his condition.

"Is that why you brought us to this spot?" Leo asks. "This co-op?"

Gali nods. "I knew the coordinates, and the librarian helped me find this place online. Happiness Cacao Co-op. The name felt like a sign. It wasn't far from an airstrip. It was the closest inhabited area to Bai's house. Plus, it had accommodations of some sort for visitors. And perfect for chocolatiers such as yourselves. Destiny, I decided."

"So you were behind the contest?" Nieves says, barking out a laugh.

Mom turns to me and Leo, noting our lack of surprise. "You both knew?"

I nod, relieved the moms seem more bewildered than angry. Leo nods, too, looking slightly guilty.

Meanwhile, Isa and her mom and uncle are simply watching, with curious expressions, as our drama plays out. They don't know the whole story, but they listen carefully, soaking it all in, filling in the pieces little by little.

"Forgive me, my dears," Gali says, "but I knew you'd never let me pay your way. I knew you'd say I was too frail. I'd already asked some friends from the DBA, and that was their response."

Nieves and Mom exchange glances. With dawning realization, Mom murmurs, "But you thought if our kids won a contest, we couldn't refuse the trip."

He nods sheepishly. "I decided to make my own magic. So I set up the contest. I tossed the possibility out to the cosmos. Oh, I knew all kinds of things could go wrong with my plan. I knew someone else might win. I knew you might not come for some other reason. But I'm old and sick and have nothing to lose. I figured that if the stars happen to align . . ."

His voice drifts off and comes back stronger. "That's a secret to happiness, you know. Taking a wild risk to give destiny a nudge."

The moms blink, trying to absorb this.

Gali gazes at Leo and me like we're shooting stars. "You're grandchildren to me. And I sensed both of you were . . . *restless*." His gaze shifts to Mom and Nieves. "And you two ladies, as well. I felt you all—*we* all—needed a change. A purpose. I hoped it would be win-win for all of us."

Mom rubs her chin. "But at first there was only going to be one winner . . . until you decided there could be two."

Gali smiles at Leo and me. "At first I assumed that whoever won would bring along the other as a guest, but then I realized that you two were, shall we say, *on the rocks*."

My face flushes. I shift my gaze to see Leo's cheeks redden, too.

Gali continues. "So I decided to allow for a tie—two winners with guests. Of course, it also occurred me that your mothers wouldn't let you go without them."

"You got that right." Mom's eyes are wide, processing all this. Shaking her head, she sighs. "Well, Gali, I wish you'd been honest from the beginning." She lays her ring-bedecked hand over his age-spotted one. "But yes, we're happy to be here with you. And yes, I needed this."

"Me too," Nieves admits, then studies him with concern. "So you think this Bai guy can cure your heart disease?" she asks, not hiding the doubt in her voice.

"Who knows. Perhaps he will help me find redemption, strengthen my heart. The doctors say if I get stronger, I can survive the surgery."

Isa and her mom and uncle José have been quiet. For them, I realize, this is so much more personal, but their faces don't reveal their feelings. Anger? Betrayal? Their neighbors and relatives have suffered from the kind of business Gali funded. Their homes are threatened. Isn't oil called black gold? Gold and oil . . . they're not much different in the end. Extracting mineral resources and killing the forest for money.

The three of them converse for a minute in Huaorani. "We will take you to Bai's place," Isa says. "We will help you make up for what you did. And heal your heart."

"*Waponi,*" Gali says, and a new round of tears slip from his eyes.

Isa gives him an even look. "Bai comes from a long line of powerful shamans. Our grandparents and great-grandparents went to him with the worst sicknesses." She pauses, glances at her mother. "But for the past ten years, no one has seen him."

Leo asks the question we're all wondering. "Is he alive?"

Isa clutches the tooth on her necklace. "Let's go find out."

As we walk back toward the huts, our flashlight beams make yellow circles over the jungle, illuminating moths and bats. Softly, we make plans to bring Gali to see Bai tomorrow. The moms say they'll come, too, since the beans will need a few days to ferment. The cacao will just sit there, heating up and letting the microorganisms work their magic. The beans will need to be stirred here and there, but José has volunteered to do that.

"Sound good, Gali?" I ask, turning to look back at him.

He's lagging behind, arm in arm with Leo, who's supporting

him in the shadows. When my flashlight beam lands on Gali's face, it's twisted in pain.

"Gali?" I move closer, see he's dripping sweat.

His cane falls to the ground. He moves his hand over his chest, and then up to his neck, tugging at the skin. And now he's gasping for air, making choking sounds.

"What's wrong?" Leo asks, tightening his grip around Gali.

I run to his other side.

And then Gali collapses.

A split second of chaos and gasps.

Leo and I manage to keep him from free-falling. He's suddenly a heavy, dead weight at the mercy of gravity. We lower him all the way to lie on the ground, carefully lay down his head. The others gather around him, shining flashlights on his sprawled-out body.

He's motionless, eyes closed.

My heart stops. Is he dead?

Mom drops to her knees, rests her hand on his damp forehead. "Gali?" she whispers. And then, louder, more urgently, "Gali?"

He doesn't respond. There's just the hum of crickets and insects and birds.

Nieves presses her ear to his chest as the rest of us hold our breaths.

Then, a flutter of his eyelashes. He rubs his head and looks around, blinking. "What happened?"

"You collapsed," Mom says, her eyebrows knit.

"Oh dear." He looks confused, presses his hand over his chest.

"Just rest," Nieves says, gently pushing him down when he tries to get up.

We pat his shoulder, hold his hand, stroke his arms, trying to comfort him.

"Does your chest hurt?" Mom asks.

"I'll be fine, Mara," he says, wincing.

Nieves sucks in a breath. "You should be in a hospital."

He speaks with great effort. "I knew I might die here in the jungle, Nieves dear. And that's my choice. Perhaps my destiny. I'm only sorry that it upsets you, my dear. I'm so sorry to you all."

The moms confer in panicked whispers as Leo and Isa and I try to soothe Gali's pain.

After a few moments, he says, "All right. Help me up before a fer-de-lance comes our way. I need to rest tonight for our big trip."

The moms look at each other. Firmly, Nieves says, "Rest for a few days, then we'll see if you're well enough to go."

"But—"

"No buts," she says. "I won't have you dying in the middle of the jungle."

Gali opens his mouth to protest, then sighs and offers a weak nod.

At the pace of an invalid snail, he lets us lead him to his hut.

All night, I slip in and out of strange dreams of trees. There is our ceiba, alive and magnificent, towering over so many layers of leaves. This time I see the white flowers—they're like snow-fall between enormous, deep folds of skirts.

"Do not give up hope," says the tree. "The treasure still awaits."

I wake up early, leap out of bed, eager to share my dream. After I get dressed, I tiptoe by Gali's hut and peek through the screen walls. His chest is rising and falling, evenly, peacefully. I breathe out in relief. There's still hope for him, too.

As I head to the dining hut, I see Isa and Leo are walking there from different directions. All the moms must have slept in, tired from their long day of harvesting and fermenting. At home, Mom always wakes up in the middle of the night with insomnia and patters restlessly around the house. But here, she sleeps softly, like moss, all night long.

Isa and Leo and I sit on the wooden steps of the dining hut in a light drizzle, facing the river. It's all blue-green shadows, wrapped in white mist.

After morning greetings, I jump in. "So what did you guys dream about?"

Isa lights up. "A ceiba! With white flowers in her roots! She said, 'Come to me.'"

Leo speaks next, matching her excitement. "The ceiba was in my dream, too. She said, 'Be brave.'"

I'm practically flying now. "I saw her, too! She said, 'Don't give up hope.' You think she's still alive? That they didn't cut her down after all?"

"Maybe," Isa says doubtfully. "Or maybe the dream ceiba isn't the one from the oil field. Maybe she's a different one we haven't gone to yet."

"But that one had white flowers."

Isa nods. "But there could be other ceibas with white flowers. And in my dream there was no oil field, just jungle surrounding her. And her roots were perfect, no chainsaw marks."

"Same with my dream," Leo says.

Now that I think about it, mine too. I rest my bony elbows on my even bonier knees and look at Isa. "If we find our dream tree, whatever's in her roots is yours," I say. "Yours to use to protect your forest."

"Thank you." She holds my gaze and smiles.

"Any idea where our tree could be?" Leo asks, scratching a mosquito bite on his arm.

"We went downstream yesterday," Isa says. "So let's try upstream today. And remember my other dream? The tree's not far, somewhere on this Shiripuno River."

I peer upstream, into the morning fog covering the water, a veil of mystery.

Come to me. Be brave. Do not give up hope.

For five days Leo and Isa and her siblings and I take the canoe out each morning and pole it upstream, stopping at giant mother ceibas along the way. Every one is magnificent, yet none has flowers in her roots. Each evening we come back, mud-caked and sweat-covered and rain-soaked, and check on Gali first thing. And each evening, he's dozing in his hammock.

When we ask whether he feels ready to visit Bai yet, Gali says, "Maybe tomorrow," as the moms exchange skeptical looks. His chest is no longer tight and hurting, but he's exhausted.

Mom and Nieves are convinced he had a mild heart attack that night, and they don't want it to happen again, especially so far from a hospital.

Over our days waiting for Gali to recover, we explore upstream, meeting people from different indigenous groups—Shuar, Eastern Quichua, and more Huaorani. In the past they had conflicts among each other, sometimes involving spears, but now they have more in common than not. Now they have a shared goal: to protect their home.

Leo delights them with magic tricks and in turn, they invite us into their homes.

Most of the homes are triangular, like giant tents, only with walls and a roof of dried palm fronds. The floors are packed dirt, and there's hardly any furniture—just some hammocks, a fire pit, hooks, and a couple of shelves holding cooking equipment and hunting tools. Some of the older women wear handmade clothes made of dried palm and leather, woven and stitched into skirts and halters.

In each home, people offer us *chicha*, which I've wanted to taste ever since Isa told me it was fermented.

At the first home, Leo and I sip it, curious. It's milky white and tastes both sweet and sour, with undercurrents of cider.

Leo licks his lips. "Not bad. How's it made?"

Isa explains that women boil and mash yuca root—our starchy white side dish for dinner every night. But instead of frying it up, like José does for our meals, the women chew it up and spit it back out into big wood containers.

"Wait," Leo says, suddenly looking green. "Chew up and spit out?"

"Saliva has enzymes that convert starch to sugar," I explain. "Food for the bacteria and wild yeast." I take another sip, relishing the complex flavors that come with fermentation. "Anyway," I assure him in English, "all that lactic acid bacteria is so good for you it probably cancels out any gross stuff in the spit."

"Hmm." Leo doesn't look convinced.

So I herald the wonders of fermentation. "Dude, it's basically delicious, hygienic rot. Same with chocolate. Minus the spit."

I grin at him, kind of in teasing mode, but mostly in happy-we're-friends mode. A warmth comes over me, and I'm not sure if it's the *chicha* or the feeling that someday, we'll look back on this moment and laugh together like a new-and-improved version of old times. Leo and I have passed through the fermentation and winnowing and grinding and now our friendship is something with a bright, surprising flavor.

He narrows his eyes at me, in that joking way he does when he's thinking, *I'll get you for this!* Trying not to wince, he takes another sip, then turns to our hosts and forces a polite smile. *"Waponi."*

We get into a rhythm over these five days, meeting new people, sipping *chicha*, poling upstream through patches of sunshine and drizzle and sunshine again.

We spot all manner of animals on the shores and in the trees—sloths, caimans, peccaries, anteaters, monkeys.

We don't see the jaguar himself, but we notice his distinct tracks, always nearby.

We recount stories about our lives.

We tell each other our dreams.

We tell tales of our homes.

We joke, we laugh, we swim, we have water fights.

We become best friends . . . all three of us . . . Isa, Leo, and me. My friendship with Leo has taken on the same shiny feeling as my friendship with Isa. I let go of any last bits of jealousy I had about Leo and Isa being friends. Isa is the just-right ingredient in this brand-new, bigger friendship . . . like the three of us are cacao and sugar and cream all blended together to form a perfectly balanced flavor.

And each time we approach a new ceiba, I feel the anticipation of making another new friend, an arboreal one. We run our hands over each one's enormous roots as we look for white flowers. Meeting tree after tree, we see hundreds of insects and plants and lichens living on the bark, but no white flowers within the buttresses.

Still, it's good to bond with these mothers, to know these trees are alive and towering and spreading out wisdom. It's good to know that they're safe—for the moment—from oil rigs and chainsaws.

Every day after lunch—leftovers from dinner the nights before—we doze, leaning against the comfortable roots. In that dreamy state, I try to send a message of my own to our dream ceiba: *Hang on. We're coming.*

My quest has transformed, too, undergone its own kind of fermentation, complete with a dose of ickiness along the way, and resulting in something new and sweet. My whole journey . . . it's not about the treasure awaiting. It's the miracle of the dream tree talking to me in the first place. And me, figuring out how to listen. How to work together with my friends to save her.

Best of all, she's still alive. She urges us on in our dreams every night. Now whenever I close my eyes and listen carefully to the forest music, I hear her calling.

These five days are good and full of hope, and there's only a little room for fear.

At least, at first.

With every day closer to our departure, our fear grows, taking up more room inside us and elbowing out the hope.

When we have only three days left, we confide our worries in whispers: *What if Gali doesn't recover? What if we don't find our ceiba in time? What if one day that jaguar with the half-missing toe stops stalking and starts attacking?*

On our seventh day in the jungle, Gali shows up at breakfast with his backpack. He sets his GPS on the table. "Today's the day we find Bai," he announces.

"Oh, I don't know," Nieves says, twisting her earring. "How's your heart? I mean, literally, how is it, Gali? Strong enough?"

"It's now or never!" His voice does sound stronger, more like the old Gali's. And the spark has returned to his eyes. "The plane's coming for us the day after tomorrow. This is the only chance for me."

Mom looks distraught. "But today's the last day of fermentation for the cacao. I have to show everyone how to spread out the beans and dry them. We have to build a palm shelter to keep any rain off. And I need Nieves here to translate for me. It has to be today. If we overferment, the flavor will turn bad."

"You and Nieves don't need to come," I tell her, scooping a forkful of eggs into my mouth. "Isa can bring me and Leo. We've spent all week exploring up and down the river. And Gali has a GPS. We can do it ourselves."

Nieves shakes her head. "It's pretty far. It might require an overnight stay somewhere." Her face tightens. "There aren't any oil operations in that area, are there?"

Alma shakes her head. "They're downstream."

"Don't more predators come out at night?" Mom asks, anxiety creeping in.

I'm about to protest, when Isa says, "I'll keep us safe."

"Yes, she will," Alma says, looking so completely confident in her daughter's survival skills, no one can argue with her.

Leo's mom and mine discuss the risks in low voices, until finally, reluctantly, Nieves tells us, "All right. But if Gali shows any symptoms again, no matter how small, you turn around and come right back."

"Promise," Leo and I say in unison.

"Jinx, you owe me a truffle," he says.

I wrinkle my face at him in a frown-smile.

"And you can't be gone more than two days," Mom adds. "Even if you don't find Bai, you have to come back by then. Promise?"

"Promise," Leo and I say together.

"Jinx, you owe me a truffle," I say at lightning speed.

"Guess we're even," he says with a half smile.

"For now."

Isa watches our banter, stifling a laugh.

After breakfast, we pack small bags with clothes, food, and hammocks, then help Gali into the canoe. We hug the moms good-bye, repeating our promise to be safe and return on time. I let Mom hug me extra long. And when I finally pull away, I have a weird feeling. I see my mother for the first time as someone separate from me, someone who existed before me. Mara Hidden. A hopeful human being on her own happiness journey.

I see that on this trip, especially at this cacao co-op, Mom's been transforming, too. I see it in the crazy, unsuitable vintage dresses she's been wearing, the turquoise necklaces and rhinestone earrings, the elaborate braids, the lightness in her step, the exuberant smiles. She's *happy*.

As I'm climbing in the canoe, I look down and catch my breath. In the mud, there's a clear imprint of the jaguar paw, its little toe half missing. I exchange looks with Isa and Leo, gesturing to the track with my chin.

Leo steps into the dugout next, making a point to casually stomp out the paw print on the way. I nod at him in thanks. No need to worry the moms. No need for them to envision us alone in the jungle at night with a nocturnal predator waiting for the right time to attack. Let them focus on the chocolate in progress and be happy.

With a little ache in my chest, I blow Mom a kiss.

Then we push off into the mist, three new friends and a dying old man.

The Ceiba Tree

AMAZON RAIN FOREST

One thing I've learned over the centuries is that there is no such thing as good and bad. There is happiness and there is suffering. There is balance and imbalance. There are tiny hearts and big hearts. And it's all changing, growing and decaying and growing again, all the time. That is the story of life.

But those of us who are wise, or perhaps simply old—we have learned how to let our hearts open wide enough for happiness. And we have learned that sometimes, the very creature who has caused suffering can cause joy.

So I've sent out my call, over and over . . . not only to the humans and trees, but to whatever creature, whatever spirit, will listen.

Jaguars included. Jaguars can kill a human with a single pounce, a single bite to the neck.

I have witnessed their predatory grace. But I also know that they have an intriguing bond with human souls.

Jaguars have a special talent for reaching humans in the realm of dreams and spirits. And since jaguars love lazing around on my roots, and stashing their prey in the limbs of my shorter neighbors, these felines have an interest in keeping us trees alive. True, they've been known to kill humans, but they've also been known to help them.

One jaguar in particular.

Bai

As Isa, Leo, and I take turns partnering to push our dugout upstream with bamboo poles, Gali sits there like an old-time royal explorer with his safari clothing—all khaki, but not the kind of high-tech fabric you'd find at an outdoors store. If it were shades of sepia, you could believe he walked right out of an old photo of an Amazon adventurer... kind of like the one hanging in El Corazón.

From time to time, he pulls an ancient leather-bound note-book from his front shirt pocket. It's sealed in a plastic bag, which he carefully opens and closes. He takes out his pair of old-fashioned spectacles from his other pocket, and peruses the worn, yellowed pages.

Poling this boat upstream feels like running a marathon in a sauna, and I'm gasping for breath. But my curiosity wins out and I use my remaining breath to ask, "What's that?"

"My journal from a half century ago, my dear. I have detailed maps and notes that might help us locate Bai."

"Good," Isa says, relieved. She doesn't trust the electronic GPS. Number coordinates mean nothing to her and batteries can fail . . . but drawings of her forest she can relate to. "A couple more hours till the fork in the river," she says. "Then we'll take a break."

A couple more hours? My muscles just want to melt into a puddle.

All of our clothes are soaked in sweat and rain from on-and-off drizzles. Isa's lavender Smurfette shirt is clinging to her. She seems to alternate the Smurfette shirt with the Lucky Cat shirt, wearing one while the other one is washed and dried on a line. Those might be the only shirts she owns, but at least they're cool ones.

Over the next exhausting hours, we briefly stop at two ceibas, not far from shore. Isa hops off and looks for white flowers at their bases, while Leo and I rest with Gali, too tired to tackle the climb up the riverbank. "Nothing," she reports, looking glum.

After what feels like an eternity of poling—definitely more than two hours—the river forks. Isa points out some banana trees at the shore. My mouth immediately starts watering. "Snack time?" I ask hopefully.

"Sure," she says, guiding the canoe to shore.

I'm scared to ask her how much farther we have to go after this fork.

Climbing out, Leo takes a long look at Gali. "How's your heart?" As in, *Is it going to conk out any time soon?*

"Oh, never better," Gali says, tapping his chest. "We're giving it just what it needs."

I can imagine what Nieves would say to this: that 98 percent humidity and ninety-degree heat and a jungle boat ride hundreds of miles from the nearest hospital is the opposite of what his heart needs . . . but I see his point.

My joints creak as I climb out after Leo and Isa. I stretch my sore arms, splash water on my face. Leo and Isa do the same. Walking stiffly to the trees, we pluck and devour banana after banana.

Gali has stayed seated in the canoe, so I deliver him a bunch of bananas. He's dripping sweat and red-faced, but then again, we all are, so it's hard to tell if it's another impending heart attack or just part of adventuring in the jungle.

"Sure you're okay?" Leo asks him.

"Just fine, son." He pulls his reading glasses from his left shirt pocket, then reaches into the right pocket and pulls out his journal. Carefully, he removes it from the plastic bag and flips through till he lands on a page about halfway through. He smooths the paper and hands the book to Leo.

He takes it gently, as though it's a baby bird.

"The two-page map spread should help," Gali says.

As Isa and Leo and I munch on bananas, we huddle together over the journal. I want to read it all, but it's a diary after all, probably full of personal stuff, so I restrain myself.

The map is warped and water-stained, just barely readable. It's similar to the map Gali passed around after our chocolate-tasting, only more of a close-up of Bai's home and surrounding jungle, with landmarks like giant trees and river bends.

I can't orient myself, but thankfully Isa can. With her fingertip, she traces the lines of river that fork here and there and eventually lead to a spot marked X. *Casa de Bai.*

"We're about here now," she says, pointing to the river

curving at the edge of the page. "And we have to get here," she says, following the river up and letting her finger land on the X.

"How much longer?" I ask, wary. My arms have turned into rubbery noodles.

"A couple more hours," Isa estimates, closing the book and resealing it in the bag.

That's what she said last time, and it ended up being an eternity. My shoulder and back shout in protest, but I climb back in the boat for the next round.

Over the next two hours, we see a peccary—sort of a wild pig—a giant river otter, a tapir—also piglike but with a flexible snout—four people fishing, five thatched huts, and three more ceibas . . . none of them graced with flowers at their roots.

Just when I can barely hold the pole, when every last ounce of energy has been spent, when my bones have practically dissolved in the wet heat, Isa points a finger. "There."

Gali's eyes light up.

Through the foliage, I glimpse the thatched roof of a hut. A wave of energy ripples through me.

"Bai's place," Isa says, satisfied.

With renewed enthusiasm, Leo and I pole to the shore, jump out, and drag the canoe partway onto the beach. We wade into the river to help Gali out, each of us holding an elbow. Shakily, he steps to shore. He's breathing hard, and I can imagine his heart feels like it's a boat struggling against a current . . . but his eyes are bright.

We shuffle up the embankment with him, slipping in the mud and stopping every few paces so he can rest. I try to think of something encouraging to say, and settle on, "Your heart will be happy soon."

Isa looks worried, though. I remember that Bai hasn't been heard from for years. *Please be there,* I whisper under my breath.

It's hard to tell if there was once a trail. If so, it's completely overgrown now. Not a good sign. Can Gali's limping-along heart stand the blow of disappointment? The last time he felt intense emotion—the night he told us his story—he ended up with a mild heart attack. I get the feeling his heart has just been hanging in there, barely pumping, just long enough to reach Bai and find peace. So if Bai isn't here . . . then what?

We shuffle along, heading toward the hut, pulling vines and branches out of Gali's way. Pulse pounding, I swipe aside a final giant leaf.

There, ahead, is the hut in full view.

And it's falling apart. The palm frond roof has torn off, leaving a gaping hole. One of the walls has caved in. Debris from the broken-down hut scatters the ground in various states of decay.

In an unexpected burst of strength, Gali moves toward the door in a lopsided half jog, tripping along in those rubber boots.

"Bai?" he calls into the shadows. "My old friend? Are you there?"

Inside, the hut is so dark it takes a moment for my eyes to adjust. Narrow ribbons of sunshine find their way through gaps in the palm fronds. A golden rectangle of light pours through the doorway, illuminating a patch of dirt floor. Insects flit in and out of the beams. Its earthy, damp smell wraps around us.

I shiver. This place is full of ghosts and memories.

Leo and I take hold of Gali's elbows to support him. As the emptiness sinks into him, he leans heavily on us.

I scan the large room, just in case I've missed something, some living thing. The basic layout is similar to the huts where we drank *chicha* earlier in the week—packed dirt floor, fire ring, hooks on the walls and beams, no furniture except for the essentials. There are the same kinds of tools and utensils as we've seen in the other huts—long bamboo blowguns, an iron pot, charcoal-filled fire pit, gourds of all sizes, a worn *chicha* holder, fiber bags, wooden spears—but these are scattered around, broken and forlorn. A woven hammock hangs in shreds from two wooden support poles.

Gali sinks to the ground. "Oh, Bai."

Isa lowers her head. "Your friend must have passed away. I'm sorry."

Tears slip down Gali's cheeks. He presses his forehead to the dirt. It's as if he's given up resisting gravity altogether, wants to let it pull him right into the earth's core.

This cannot be good for his heart. This shock and sorrow. He's done so much for me all these years, cheered me up so many times. Shared with me so many secrets of happiness, just when I needed them the most. But I don't know what to do for him. I kneel beside him, pat his shoulder. Leo does the same.

After a while, I say, "You mentioned a special tea that Bai gave you. Maybe we can make it ourselves. Remember what was in it?"

He shakes his head. "It was so long ago, my dear."

Dead end. I keep patting his shoulder with Leo. Meanwhile, Isa is walking around inside, reverently inspecting the decay.

She circles back to us, by the muddy entrance. "Look," she whispers.

She's pointing to the ground, to a paw track. A big pad and four toes at the front. Recognizing the print, I murmur, "Our jaguar."

Leo and I follow her outside, searching for more prints. Now that we're looking, I can see them in the mud all around the hut. Inside, Gali pushes himself to sitting. "Is it really a jaguar?"

Isa nods, returning to help him stand. "And the tracks are very fresh."

"We've been seeing his prints all over the place this past week," Leo tells Gali. "It's strange, almost like he's been tracking us."

"Or guiding us," Isa says thoughtfully.

I take in her words, take in the music of the insects and birds and frogs, take in the underground messages humming beneath it all. And understanding dawns over me, like an actual sun rising into the half-light and making everything clear.

"Gali," I say, my excitement building by the second, "did you know that Isa's people believe that when a person dies, his soul becomes a wild cat? And that the most powerful ones become jaguars?"

Hope fills Gali's face. "You think . . . you think this jaguar could be Bai's soul?"

"It would make sense," says Isa.

"Maybe he can still heal you," I say, full of hope.

If Gali was a dying fire, this idea is a fresh new log, setting him ablaze. "Or help me heal myself."

Leo gives Gali a tender pat on the shoulder. "Let's see where Bai leads us."

With courage and fear and hope all swirling together, we nod, silently agreeing to follow the jaguar into the unknown.

Leo and I wrap our arms around Gali's waist, and Isa walks a little ways ahead. The prints lead us around the back of the house, into the thick jungle. Isa is able to follow the tracks even when they disappear, sensing signs in a crushed branch or a torn leaf. I wouldn't be surprised if she could smell the jaguar, too.

Again, awe sweeps over me. There's so much she knows about the forest . . . and so much I have to learn.

For several minutes we follow the tracks through dense forest, pausing often to move tangles of vines and branches out of the way.

Now Gali is gasping for breath, and sweat is pouring down his temples, and I'm not sure how much farther he can go. What if he has another heart attack out here—a not-so-mild one?

Just when I'm about to suggest we let him rest, the forest opens up into a kind of clearing. Before us are the tallest roots I've ever seen, taller even than the roots of the other ceibas we've met. They're over twice our height and they curve and arch and swirl out from the massive trunk at the center, like a seashell, a snowflake, a galaxy.

And filling them are heaps of white petals, as delicate and

elegant as swan feathers. I stretch my neck back, squint through layers of canopy toward the top of the ceiba, glimpse only the tiniest patches of its crown far in the sky. This is a tower, a cathedral, a pathway to the heavens.

I look back down to my feet, imagine the ceiba's underground roots spreading beneath the earth, sending out her call, all the way to Heartbeat Springs.

We stand for a moment, soaking in this discovery. And when I tear my gaze away to glance at Leo and Isa, I can tell they feel it, too—a sense of recognition.

Leo breaks the silence. "Look! The jaguar tracks." He points to the path they make right into the mountainous roots.

Bai's jaguar-spirit has led us here. Was he in cahoots with the tree all along? Following us, leading us, keeping us safe? My first night in the jungle, when I snuck off to that first ceiba in the darkness . . . was Bai's spirit watching me through those golden feline eyes, protecting me, hoping I'd eventually make it to the dream tree? And the jaguar in Leo's dream . . . was it Bai, joining forces with the ceiba?

I pull off my boots, toss them aside, and barefoot, I move toward the ceiba, trying not to step on any white flowers . . . but there are so many! I lean down, brush my fingertips over the petals. There must be a hundred petals on each bloom, and they're so iridescent white they're nearly glowing. The blooms are the size of an apple, resting atop leafy, foot–high stems. I've never seen anything quite like them before, but their starry, round shape makes me think of mums or water lilies.

I kneel down, let my nose rest in their softness. They have the most delicate scent, sweet and honeyed, like layers of lace or silk, a touch of oldness, notes of ancient secrets . . . while the core is fresh, like waterfall spray, cool and new and bright in beams of sunlight.

I reach forward, run my hand along the smooth curves of the roots.

And something moves from the tree into my palms, through my skin and vessels and blood, into my center. I listen to the insects and birds and breeze through leaves, and there it is, a whisper beneath it all, the music of the dream tree's breath. It's like talking to an old friend.

I glance at Leo and Isa and see that they, too, are barefoot and listening, touching the tree with their own wonderstruck hands.

Our eyes meet. *Yes, this is our tree.*

Slowly, in a kind of reverent dance, we circle the massive trunk, peering into all its chambers. We tiptoe lightly, barefoot, on the patches of soft moss among the flowers. The fragrance wraps around us, soothing, healing. We take in the tree's breathing song, mesmerized.

It's not till I fully circle the tree that I remember my original reason for wanting to find her: a treasure at her roots.

But now I can see that the tree herself is the treasure.

The tree and all the plants and creatures living in her world.

Isa and Leo are brushing their hands over the flowers, peering between the petals, maybe searching for an ancient chest of gold. And I hope they find one. It would be in good hands with Isa, protector of the forest.

"She's a grandmother tree," Isa says with reverence, "older and bigger than any other ceiba I've seen."

I glance at Gali, whose gaze is moving up and down the roots and trunk and branches in awe. "Coco, dear, have you found what you're looking for?"

I smile, glad that even though his body is weak, his mind is sharp and his heart kind. "Yeah." And then, because he's looking a little woozy, I ask, "Want to sit down?"

He nods, and I help him settle in a patch of moss by the flowers and lean against the tree root.

"I'm sorry about Bai," I say, sitting cross-legged beside him.

"He was extraordinary." Gali pulls out his journal and passes it to me. "I don't know what I did with my glasses, dear, so would you mind reading me the part about Bai?"

Quickly, I flip through the pages. They're packed with tiny, neat writing in Spanish, and plenty of drawings, diagrams, and maps. I turn back to the beginning, where young Gali's words are bursting with his thrill of planning the trip, lists of what he'll bring, plenty of exclamation points. Then there's his arrival in Quito and the edge of the jungle. Here the words are practically floating on the page with the excitement of a new place, the anticipation of what's to come.

And then comes a nearly blank page with a single sentence, written hard in black ink and gone over and over and over till it pierces through to the other side.

Oh, what have I done?

The next pages are filled with drawings of the gold mining site, not much different from the barren logging and oil-drilling site downstream. The sketches remind me of Antonio's, sending another wave of sadness over me. There are pictures of children, sickened and thin, with distended bellies and heart-crushed expressions. These pages are wavy, as if they've been dampened by tears. I swallow hard, try to hold back my own, remind myself I'm looking for the part about Bai.

I flip forward a few dozen pages, past the map of our location. Now here are pictures of Bai's house, looking neat and well maintained and intact, inside and out. A tidy A-frame of wood draped with palm. And here's a picture of Bai sporting shorts, chest bared, wearing a palm fiber crown and a woven-fiber-and-nut necklace with a large tooth dangling at the center of his chest. There's a proud look on his face, which is painted with red achiote—actual red achiote that Gali used to embellish the black-and-white pen drawing. And beneath the picture, Bai's words, in quotations: *You will come back again, my friend.*

I clear my throat and read the sentence aloud.

Gali nods, staring at a large jaguar paw print. "And I have come back, my friend."

I glance at Isa and Leo, who apparently haven't found a chest of gold. They've settled in the same huge root chamber with Gali and me, but they don't look disappointed. It's impossible to feel disappointed when we're sitting in a cloud of white flowers that smell like . . . *hope.*

And I can't shake the feeling that Gali's little journal might hold a clue, some message from Bai across time. There has to be a reason his spirit jaguar led us here. "Mind if I read more, Gali?"

"Feel free, Coco dear."

Carefully turning the delicate pages, I skim over his labeled sketches of birds and insects. The paper is yellowed and rippled with old water spots. Some of the pages are stuck together, and I have to slide my finger between the pages to separate them.

I admire a butterfly sketch and turn the next page. Tiny white petals fall out from the center seam . . . a crumbling, pressed flower that must have been stuck between those pages for decades. Tenderly, I collect the petals and cradle them in my palm, then return my attention to the journal.

Now I'm staring at the unstuck pages showing a huge, close-up sketch of a flower with about a hundred petals. The same flower in pieces in my hand. The same flower growing beneath the tree. On the opposite page, *STAR FLOWER* is written in huge letters, surrounded by little stars. In tidy script below, there's a simple recipe.

"Star flower," I read, wonderstruck. Comets zip around inside my chest.

Gali takes the book, mouth open in disbelief.

Leo and Isa move to crouch beside him and peer over his shoulder.

"The pages were stuck together," I explain, and pour the pressed petals into Gali's hand. "These were inside."

"Star flower," he muses. "Yes, that's the tea Bai gave me. How could I have forgotten such a lovely name?"

Leo's eyes grow wide. "Gali, we're surrounded by star flowers . . . and Bai led us straight here!"

Gali beams, and laughter bubbles up. "Why, yes he did."

"Look!" Isa points to the recipe. "We can even prepare it ourselves."

I have to squint to read the tiny, blurred letters. *Hot water and ten petals per cup. Honey for added sweetness.*

 251

Leo rolls back on his heels. "How did Bai serve it, Gali? I mean, was there some kind of ritual?"

Gali closes his eyes, searching his memory. "We talked and sipped the tea. Oh, it had the most exquisite taste. He told me to think about how to heal myself. And by the time I drank the last drop, the answer was clear. As bright as stars on a night with no clouds or moon." He smiles. "I knew I needed to donate my gold money. To make heart art."

"So the flower tea isn't, like, actual medicine?" I ask, trying to understand. "Like aspirin or antibiotics or cough syrup or something?"

Gali leans over and takes a deep whiff of a flower beside him. "You know how chocolate makes you feel happy? And chamomile makes you feel calm? And mint makes you feel refreshed? Well, the star flower tea made me feel . . . *clear.*"

Leo and Isa nod, and I think I get what Gali's saying, but there's no time to waste. I pluck some petals for him and stick them into my pocket, silently thanking the flower and the tree.

Watching me gather the petals, Isa says, "Let's boil water in the hut. I'll rinse the pot and gourds in the river."

And off she runs as Leo and I help Gali to his feet.

By the time Leo and Gali and I reach the hut—following the jaguar tracks backward at our sloth's pace—Isa has already returned from the river with a pot of water. She's kneeling beside a piece of wood riddled with holes. Sweat beads on her face as she pulls a wisp of ceiba silk from her fiber bag and positions it by a hole. She puts a straight stick the size of a pencil into the hole, tucking the ceiba silk beside it, and rolls the stick fast between her palms.

"What're you doing?" asks Leo.

"Making fire."

"We have matches in the first aid kit," I say.

But as I speak, sparks are already leaping off the wood and singeing the ceiba silk. The friction between the stick and the hole-punched wood must be burning hot.

Leo leans close, blowing lightly on the baby flame to encourage it.

By the time they've gotten a good fire going, I've gathered twigs and dry debris from around the hut to keep it burning. We set the heavy pot on the stone hearth and wait. Soft sounds fill the minutes—the flicker of the fire, the occasional hiss, the crickets and birds outside, Gali's soft snoring as he dozes.

And then, almost as if it's coming from the ground, a low rumble. Thunder? The jaguar?

I blink my eyes for a long moment, concentrating. "Hear that?"

Leo tilts his head. "What is it?"

Isa's hand flies to her mouth. A wave of panic spreads over her.

Gali's eyes open. He must have sensed the alarm in our words.

"Wait here," Isa tells Gali. "Keep an eye on the fire."

She gestures to me and Leo to follow her outside. My stomach tightens; it's rare to see Isa so upset. Without another word, we obey.

Outside, the noise is louder.

The rumble is growing closer.

It's a motor.

Star Flower

"No!" Isa cries, and takes off running through the trees toward the noise. Her legs are like a deer's, stretching long and soaring over the underbrush.

I grab my bag, slip on my boots, and run after her, trying to keep up. Leo follows, right at my heels. But we're not as agile, especially in our clunky rubber boots. As I run, twigs scrape at my face and arms, and I nearly smack my head into a low branch, ducking at the last second.

"No, no, no!" she yells ahead.

The rumble is growing louder, so loud I want to put my hands over my ears. It thunders and screeches, like an eighteen-wheeler engine and a lawn mower and weed whacker and leaf blower all in one.

We pass through another clump of palm, and come face-to-face with a killing machine. It's a cross between a giant tractor and a truck, a dangerous heap of steel painted dark green and yellow and black. An enormous claw at the front is grabbing and ripping down trees in its path. It's an evil robot. A weapon of mass destruction. It does not belong here.

Isa and Leo fall behind, but I keep running toward it, my bag bouncing.

"Stop!" I shout, but the engine noise drowns out my words. The driver is wearing ear-protecting mufflers, oblivious.

Ahead, right in its path, is a slender young palm, not much more than a sapling. I dash in front of it, putting myself between the machine and the tree.

The driver finally sees me. He bolts up, alarmed. After a moment of shock, he starts fumbling with the levers and wheel and buttons on the dashboard. But the killing machine keeps going, with momentum of its own.

"Coco!" Isa screams, running toward me.

My feet refuse to move.

At the last second, Isa and Leo grab me and pull me out of the vehicle's path just as the claws tear down the young palm where I stood moments ago. Suddenly, I start shaking all over. When Isa offers her hand, I hold it, tight.

The man cuts his engine and jumps out of the machine. He removes his ear protection and takes off his baseball cap, running his hand over short hair peppered with silver. His white button-down short-sleeve shirt is stained with oil and mud and sweat, littered with sawdust and wood chips and plant debris.

Dazed, he walks toward us. "What's wrong? You lost? You need help?"

I command my knees to stop wobbling. Standing tall and throwing back my shoulders, I try to make myself look bigger and braver than I feel. "You have to stop!"

He takes in my words, surprised. Slowly, he says, "The

company I work for owns logging rights here. Oil rights, too, *señorita*."

I feel like shouting, but Leo asks the man calmly, "What exactly are you doing, *señor*?"

The man wipes sweat from his forehead with a rag. "Building an access road for more logging and drilling."

Our dream tree is close, just a five-minute walk from here. Jaw tense, I ask, "How much farther are you going?"

"Another kilometer or so that way, all the way to the river."

Isa and Leo and I exchange glances. That would mean razing our ceiba.

I stand up straighter, lift my chin. "Well, we'd like to talk with your manager."

Leo gives me a look like I'm crazy.

The man laughs. "Why?"

"We . . . we have important information for him." I'll figure out what that information is later. Maybe some of Leo's statistics about the rain forest. The important thing is to stall.

The man looks at Isa with sympathy. "Your family lives over there?"

She freezes for a moment, then says, "Something like that."

"Well, my work day's nearly over anyway. I'll stop here for now." His voice softens. "I'll give you this afternoon to move out. We'll wait for tomorrow to plow through."

I bite the inside of my cheek. "We'd like to officially invite your boss over for a cup of chocolate at our hut tomorrow."

The man shakes his head. "He won't waste his time on this kind of thing."

From my pocket, I pull out a half-melted mango truffle,

made with our finest Madagascar trinitario. Then I pick the white petals from my other pocket and plaster them onto the chocolate. They stick to the melted exterior. Maybe they can help this man see clearly.

I'm not following Bai's tea instructions, and the presentation is lacking—none of my usual artistic flair—but it'll have to do. I hand it to the man. "Chocolate makes everything better, *señor*."

He takes it, examines it, sniffs it. "A bribe?" he says, laughing, and pops it into his mouth. He licks the chocolate from his fingers and wipes it from the corners of his mouth. "Good. Thanks."

Then he takes a bucket of paint and a brush from the back of his machine. He dips the brush into bright red paint and marks the thick trunk of an enormous palm. The slash looks like a bleeding wound.

"What're you doing?" I ask, horrified.

"Marking the trees that are too big for my machine to rip out. These need to be sawed down. We'll bring that equipment tomorrow."

Isa is watching him, her fists and jaw clenched.

The man moves from large tree to tree, slopping on paint. I have the urge to erase it, or somehow camouflage it with gray-brown paint. For a while he works without speaking, as we watch him like hawks.

"So what are you two?" he asks eventually, motioning with his chin to Leo and me. "American?"

"Yeah." I brush some gnats away from my face.

"What are you doing in the jungle?"

"Protecting it," says Leo.

"Well, good luck, kids."

I can't tell if he's being sarcastic. He's headed toward the ceiba—it's just through this patch of vegetation.

"Why don't you go over there instead?" I ask, urging him away from our tree.

"Supposed to go this way, right to the river." He points with his lips. "Later we'll be dredging and straightening the river for transporting logs."

I'm not sure what *dredging* involves but it doesn't sound good.

He continues painting bloodred slashes on the trunks of the big trees, marking them for death.

And now we've reached the ceiba.

Her roots rise high above us in majestic curves. She's queenly, and enormous, and so old. So essential.

The man pauses, his brush hovering over the bucket, dripping red. He lets out a long, low whistle. "Big one."

I stand in front of our tree. "Not her. You can't mark her."

"She's a mother," Leo says. "She helps the other trees, sends them nutrients and knowledge."

The man laughs, shakes his head as if Leo's either joking or crazy. He raises the paintbrush like an ax. Then he pauses, staring at the tree, as if trying to decide where to mark it. The roots arc taller than him, so in order to reach the trunk he'd have to climb up them.

Slowly, he puts the brush back into the can, sets it on the ground. "A mother?" he repeats. Now he's looking at the ceiba as if she's a *mother*, not a thing. Something's shifting inside him. Maybe it's the dopamine and serotonin released by the chocolate making him see the tree through joy-tinted glasses. Maybe the star flower is sparking other possibilities in his mind like bright constellations.

"Here." I extend another truffle to him. "Have more."

He hesitates, but I can practically see his mouth watering. I know that look from the ladies who come into the shop and make a nibbly little show of resisting the deliciousness, then toss their diets to the wind and devour an entire bar . . . and wash it all down with a mug of French hot chocolate. Not that this man is on a diet, but he's supposed to be working, not snacking and talking with a bunch of strange kids. "Thanks," he says finally, popping it into his mouth whole.

"Now, Leo," I whisper. "Tell him some Amazon tree facts."

Leo spills them out, lingering on the mycelia, those thin threads of fungus connecting the trees' roots. The neural synapses in the underground brain. The capillaries in the hidden heart. He moves on to the precious ecosystems that can be destroyed if even one part is taken away. Bats and flowers and pollination and on and on . . .

And the man listens to it all intently, his mouth full of chocolate.

When Leo slows down with the fact-spewing, Isa motions to the white blooms at our feet. "These star flowers are rare, *señor*. The flowers were used by a powerful shaman, and the shamans before him. They might be the only ones left."

The man swallows the last of the chocolate, but I'm ready with another truffle. I hand it over before he can refuse, and observe him taking a thoughtful bite.

A macaw flies past us, a blur of blue and yellow, and rests above us on a walking palm. I watch the man watching the bird and munching on the chocolate. Something is changing in his eyes. They're clearer somehow, more alive, more *here*.

He moves his gaze to us. Extending his hand, he says, "We never introduced ourselves. I'm Paulo."

We shake, tell him our names.

It could be the chocolate, or the star flower, or good luck, or Leo's factoids . . . or maybe just the human connection we've made with Paulo. Whatever it is, I have the feeling that he wants to help us.

"Paulo," I begin with a long breath, "we understand you're just doing what you're told. Following orders. But we need to talk to the person in charge. The person with the power to save this piece of forest."

He lets out a long sigh. "I'll see what I can do. But don't get your hopes up." He bends down to look at a flower. "May I?" he asks Isa.

She nods, looking a bit nervous, a bit hopeful, twisting her tooth necklace back and forth on her finger.

Paulo plucks the bloom, tucks it into his shirt pocket. "Good luck, kids," he says with a sigh. This time I know he's not being sarcastic. He trudges back to his killing machine, turning to take a long look back at the ceiba.

"Here," I say, running after him. From my bag, I take out a bar of Chantilly cream chocolate and hand it to him. "Give this to your boss. Tell him there's more waiting for him if he comes to see us."

Paulo gives a nod and a wave, and settles into the seat of his vehicle. Soon the roar of the machine fades in the distance.

For a moment, we're quiet, listening to the jungle music around us, now free of the engine noise. I hear the ceiba's wise voice that's more a dream than a sound. *Within my roots a treasure awaits.* I kneel down before the flowers, peer closely at their iridescent white petals. I listen.

After a moment, I look back at Isa and Leo. "Maybe the star flowers are the key."

Leo pushes his bangs from his eyes. "They might help us find a solution."

Isa nods. "A way to save this tree."

"And this forest," I add.

"And Isa's home," Leo says.

With tender hands, Isa plucks some petals. "Ten for each of us," she says.

Petals in hand, we head back through the leafy green light and into the cool shadows of the hut.

Gali is sitting by the boiling water. He looks up, concerned. "What's going on, my dears?"

I hope he's strong enough to handle the latest bad news.

"They're logging this part of the jungle now," Leo says, as if a loved one has been diagnosed with a terminal illness. "For oil drilling."

Gali's face falls.

Isa pats his shoulder. "They plan to take down the ceiba."

"That would break Bai's heart," Gali whispers.

Isa nods, her expression a mix of sorrow and anger. "And if they open it up to drilling, that means the pollution will be just upstream of my home. It means my community could get as sick as Antonio and Susy's."

"We won't let it happen." My voice comes out surprisingly fierce. "Together, we'll find a way."

I have no idea what that way might be. Even if Paulo returns with his boss, what then? The oil companies are huge and rich and powerful. They're a thousand killing machines put together, all over the world. We've just caught a glimpse of this one. Even if we can change the minds of one or two workers, how can we change an entire enormous company?

I try to let go of my doubts and focus on the rise and fall of insects and frogs.

Isa drops the petals into the pot. Down they float like fluff from a cottonwood in the springtime, settling on the surface. Slowly, with a long wooden spoon, she stirs and swirls the petals.

After the tea brews for a while, we scoop the clear, steaming liquid into our gourds. I take a tentative sip. Hot. I blow on it, take another sip. The taste is as delicate as the smell, a cousin to jasmine or honeysuckle. But it's missing something.

Creating recipes is my specialty, and I've fine-tuned my taste buds over the years to know precisely what flavor will fill the gap. In Gali's journal, he mentioned honey for sweetness. But I can do even better. I pull out a few pieces of chocolate— pure, dark Peruvian Nacional—and hand them out.

I drop mine into the hot tea, let it dissolve, stir it with a stick. Sip again. Yes. That's what was missing. I feel myself brighten.

"Chocolate makes everything better," Leo says, stirring it in his tea. "Especially chocolate with flowers," he adds, glancing at me.

"A true secret to happiness," Gali says, patting his hand softly over his chest.

"Delicious," Isa says, offering a smile of approval.

Together, we bring our drinks out to our ceiba, sit cradled in its roots, and raise our star flower hot chocolate in a toast.

Before we sip, Gali says, with a twinkle in his eye, "Here's where we make our own magic."

The Ceiba Tree

AMAZON RAIN FOREST

You have found the treasure!

These star flowers are the last patch in the forest. They grow only in the lap of mother ceibas. They live only in this piece of jungle, with the particular web of creatures and plants that we cradle.

I am the home of this treasure. And who knows how much longer I will stand.

But there is hope. You are hope.

You have listened. You have journeyed here. You have earned wisdom. You have discovered something precious beyond measure.

How will you use this treasure? You know that something priceless teeters on the edge of existence. Now use your human mind and heart and soul.

After three centuries, this might be my last

moon, last stars, last sweet song with my forest. And yes, I am sad, but my underground heart is happy with you nestled in my roots, the treasure blooming around you, our thoughts intertwined.

Thank you for your company.

Thank you for sharing your breath, your beating heart, your sparking mind.

Even if I am felled, I trust you will save my world.

The Jaguar

Sipping the star flower chocolate is like sipping the Milky Way.

Not only is the taste exquisite, but it makes every one of my neurons twinkle. I imagine a vast, starry sky inside my brain—a hundred trillion connections illuminated. Then I imagine the connections sparking in the forest's underground mind. A whole constellation of them. And it's clear to me: If we put our minds together—arboreal and human and feline—then we can find a way to save our worlds.

Leo speaks first. "Isa, remember what you said about how rare these star flowers are? You think they might be officially endangered?"

"Maybe." She takes another sip of chocolate, moving it around in her mouth to maximize taste bud contact before she swallows. "I've never seen these flowers before. And I know most of the plants here as well as my own brothers and sister."

Gali is tapping his chin thoughtfully. "You know, I remember talking about this to Permelia from the flower shop years ago. I even showed her the flower I'd pressed in the journal.

Back then, the pages weren't yet stuck together, I suppose. As I recall, she did some research and couldn't identify the flower. If memory serves me correctly, she suspected it could be an undiscovered species."

The light of the cosmos fills me. "If it's a newly discovered species, and it's on the verge of extinction, then these last flowers have to be saved!"

"Indeed," Gali says, looking sprightlier than he has in ages. "The rain forest groups I've donated to—they do this kind of conservation work. They partner with scientists to find rare species and protect them."

A blue morpho flutters between us, hovers there like a candle flicker, then flies away. After we watch it vanish, Isa says, "You think this whole part of the jungle could be protected?"

"It's a good possibility, my dear," Gali says, moving his hand over his chest. "And helping you save your forest . . . well, it just might fix my heart."

"Win-win," Leo says, slipping a quarter from one hand to another, practicing his magic between sips of tea.

For a moment, Isa beams, and then she glances at me and a cloud passes over her face. "Coco, what about your home? Your chocolate shop? Is there some way to save it?"

Thinking, I take another small sip of the star-touched chocolate. The flavor is so new and different, it makes me think of the zillions of other new and different things waiting for Mom and me. The thought of moving away from Heartbeat Springs is still scary . . . but no longer horrible. Finally, I say, "I don't think we'll save the shop."

And with these words, I close my eyes and let it go—my

small version of the world. I say a silent good-bye to my home, good-bye to El Corazón, good-bye to Heartbeat Springs, good-bye to the cottonwood, good-bye to Permelia and Gooey Marshmallow and Gali. The hardest is saying good-bye to Leo, even in my head, because we've just become friends again, and now I'll be moving away.

It hurts—it hurts in my chest, in my bones, in my blood. But it hurts in the way the pounding waterfall hurt . . . it hurts in a clean, pure, good way. As if the old is making way for something new.

"Coco," Isa says, her voice clear as a toucan's call. "Why don't you and your mother move here?"

I open my eyes and blink. *Here?*

She smiles, her eyes wide. "You could help us sell the cacao. You understand the chocolate business. You could connect us with people to buy our beans. And that would help save our forest, too."

"But . . ." I try to finish the sentence.

But . . . there *are* no buts. I love it here. Mom loves it here. If I suggest it—once she gets over the shock—I have a feeling she'll be on board. Everything she's said has been pointing to this— how she needs to get outside our own little world, do something meaningful. And she's come alive here. She's left behind that trudging mechanical robot mode and entered flying wild macaw mode.

Isa's face glows with determination. "And I can teach you more about the forest. There's so much left to show you."

I look to Leo, to see if he thinks this idea is too zany.

He drains his last drop of chocolate and wipes his mouth with the back of his hand. Then he announces, "Yes!"

I take a deep breath. "Yes?"

"You should live here, Coco," Leo says, without a doubt in his voice. "We'll visit you during school breaks."

"Another secret to happiness," Gali says, his voice strong, "make room in your heart for the wildest of ideas."

I finish my last drop of tea, lick the starlight from my lips, and say, "Isa, your idea feels . . . strangely . . . exactly . . . perfectly . . . *right*."

For a while, we toss up our words and let them intermingle, feel more ideas crystallize like tempered chocolate. Then we sort through them, holding each wild one up to the light to examine it.

Here's the only problem we can't see a clear way around: It will take time to get nature conservation groups involved in protecting the star flower . . . assuming it *is* endangered and it *is* a new species. But tomorrow Paulo and his crew plan to cut down our ceiba. How do we protect her?

"Hopefully his boss will come," I say. "We'll convince him."

"But how?" asks Isa.

Out of the blue, Leo raises his hand and pulls a rainbow silk scarf from the air. "We make more magic."

When night falls, the four of us lie in hammocks strung to trees beneath the ceiba's canopy. It feels surprisingly comfortable, swinging here gently. We're wearing enough bug spray to

269

keep the mosquitos away, and although it's misty, there's no rain falling.

Our bellies are pleasantly full of the hard-boiled eggs and fried yuca the moms packed for us. We supplemented dinner with some freshly caught piranha, cooked over Bai's hearth fire. And cardamom truffles for dessert.

The moms might not approve of us sleeping outside with a jaguar nearby, but if this happens to be the ceiba's last night on earth, we want to be here with her.

Isa's hammock is just an arm's length from mine. I sense her watching me play with the bracelet she made for me, the woven palm with the smooth, shiny red nut. On an impulse, I take off my crystal necklace—the one I've faithfully worn most of my life—and hand it to her. "For you, Isa."

"I'm glad we're friends," she says, letting the silver strand of the crystal necklace settle beside the fibers of her tooth necklace.

"Me too." And I realize she's the first close friend my own age I've had besides Leo. It feels good. Especially good knowing that if we give destiny a nudge, we might end up being neighbors, too.

She settles back into the hammock and closes her eyes, half smiling and holding the crystal and tooth pendants over her chest. Gali is already snoring gently a few feet away.

I don't feel tired yet, so I stay awake, letting the forest sounds mesmerize me.

From the corner of my eye, I see a flash. A red spark is leaping through the air above Leo's hammock. He tosses the spark from one hand to another. I have no clue what trick is behind this magic, but I like it. I like that Leo de la Cueva has transformed into this mysterious, spark-throwing person.

"Don't let it get to your head, Leo . . . but this new you . . . it's not too shabby."

He gives an embarrassed smile. I bet I'd see him blushing if it wasn't dark. "I missed you, Coco."

I feel strong enough, finally, to free him from the small right atrium of my heart, let him have his own space to stretch and grow, let his own vessels branch out.

"Hey, Leo, when we get back home, you should be whoever you want to be, be friends with whoever you want. And if I move to the Amazon, I hope we stay friends, too."

Back and forth the red spark flies, between Leo's hands. "Always, Coco."

He smiles and pops the red spark in his mouth so his whole face is aglow. Then he makes a big gulping sound and swallows it whole.

A moment later, there's a long, loud burp.

A moment later, my laughter mingles with his, and then melts into sighs, and then we fall into dreams.

I wake at dawn, when the black shadows of night are morphing into the blue-green shadows of morning. The songs of insects and birds are shifting to daytime rhythms. A tiny drizzle starts, a little more than a fog moving through the forest.

I close my eyes again, trying to stay in the bubbling currents of dreams I've been swimming in and out of all night. In my dreams, this forest was my new home. And every creature in the forest welcomed me.

Memorizing as many details as I can, I prop myself onto my elbow and see that the others are waking up, too. Before their dreams can escape, I ask in a sleep-crackled voice, "What were your dreams?"

Isa rubs her eyes. "A plane." Her voice is scratchy, too, but laced with wonder. "I dreamed we were in a plane delivering bags of cacao. Cacao from our co-op."

I press my lips together in excitement and wait for Leo to go next.

He lets out a big yawn and stretches his arms over his head. "In my dream, I was back in Heartbeat Springs. A bunch of students were selling hot chocolate in the hall before school started. The profits were going to help this forest."

I feel wide-awake by now and can't resist jumping in before Gali. "I dreamed I lived here!"

Isa looks ready to do a happy dance with me. She turns to Gali and asks, "What about you?"

A long pause. He smooths his rumpled safari clothes, adjusts the cuffs. "My dream . . ." Shaking his head slowly, he whispers, "I forget my dream."

I give him a long look. "Well, maybe it'll come to you later."

———

Once we stretch out our creakiness, we head to the river to wash up and collect water for hot chocolate. Creamy milk would be the ideal liquid to mix with it, but thankfully our chocolate's divine enough for water alone.

Leo helps Gali lower to his knees before the river. In a flash, Gali dunks his whole head in the current, like some kind of baptism. With a shiver, he rubs his face and squeezes out his ponytail.

Laughing, Leo dunks his head, too, then shakes out his hair, wet-dog style.

Isa and I give each other amused looks, then splash cool river on our faces.

When I open my eyes, there, across the river, wrapped in mist, is a huge, black, shining creature.

The jaguar.

The animal looks like he just stepped out of a dream. He's standing at the bank, lapping water with a big pink tongue. In this early morning light, I can make out black spots gleaming on a backdrop of smooth black fur.

"Look!" I whisper hoarsely.

Motionless, we watch him.

He licks the water from his dripping jowls and regards us from the opposite shore. His eyes glow, two spoonfuls of honey beaming sunlight. His small triangle ears stand alert over long whiskers and powerful jaws. Every part of him is gigantic, from his wide head to his massive paws to his thick shoulders. Muscles ripple beneath luminous fur.

Gingerly, Gali raises his hand in a salutation.

The jaguar's gaze fixes on his. It's as if they're having a silent conversation. It's as if the creature is speaking with his golden eyes. There's something wild and wise in this gaze, something terrifying and beautiful.

After a long moment, Gali gives a nod, as if agreeing to a promise. Softly, he says, "*Waponi,* my friend."

With a flick of the long tail, the jaguar turns and saunters into the foliage. He leaves an airy grace in his wake, like a comet's trail.

For a moment, we four humans stand there blinking, dripping with river water, in pulse-pounding silence. I can almost feel bits of the jaguar's stardust floating in the air, across the river, into my breath, my skin.

Gali pats his face dry with his bandanna, then hangs it to dry on a branch. "My dream. I remember it now, my dears. This very jaguar was in it. Bai's spirit. He led me to a tree . . . a cottonwood . . . the very same one in our courtyard in Heartbeat Springs. He looked at me and pawed at the ground and looked at me again."

Gali pauses, smoothing his rumpled safari clothes.

I'm not sure if he's finished, so I ask, "What do you think it means?"

No hesitation. "That a treasure awaits beneath the tree."

"Beneath our cottonwood?" I sputter.

Leo runs a hand through his damp hair, looking skeptical. "Seriously, Gali?"

Gali nods. "I know it's there."

"How?" I ask.

"Why, I buried it myself."

Leo balks. "What?"

"I buried it one moonlit night . . . along with my shame. Oh, it's been buried for so long, I forgot it existed, my dears. I wanted to forget. Until now."

Something wells up inside me. "I bet the dream was a reminder from your unconscious."

"Perhaps," Gali says. "I think you and Leo must bring the treasure into the light. Transform it from something shameful . . . into something useful." He looks at Isa. "Something that might help you save this forest, my dear. Something that is rightfully yours."

Isa's face lights up. "Really?"

I try not to let myself get too ecstatic. I'm still not sure whether he's talking in metaphors. "Is it a real treasure, Gali? Like, worth money?"

He raises a white caterpillar eyebrow. "Indeed it is. Quite a bit, in fact."

"What *is* it?" asks Leo, running his hand through his hair, looking impatient.

Gali chuckles under his breath. His cheeks are turning pink. The heavy circles are gone, and his eyes shine brighter. It's as if his heart has found some new enthusiasm for moving blood around his circulatory system.

"Let's just say . . . if saving this forest is our destiny, then this will give it quite a nudge. Leo and Coco, why don't you two unbury the treasure when we get home? Then Isa and her family can decide how to use it."

"*Waponi,*" Isa tells him, her eyes sparkling.

A brand-new leaf of hope unfurls inside me. "We'll do it the second we get home, Isa."

Leo's about to jump out of his skin with curiosity. "Can't you just tell us what it is now, Gali?"

Gali smiles mysteriously. "You know another secret to happiness? Embracing the unknown."

Leo screws up his face, ready to argue.

"We can wait," I say, elbowing him. "Right?"

After a moment, he gives a reluctant shrug. "Okay." He stands up, extends his hand to help Gali. "How about some hot chocolate?"

We head back toward the hut, me carrying the pot of water, while Leo keeps hold of Gali's elbow up the overgrown path. Along the way, Isa cuts pieces of toothpaste plants for toothbrushing later.

As we walk, I listen to the song of birdcalls and insect chirps and running water and dripping leaves . . . and one message comes through clear as wind chimes. Saving the forest depends on all of us working together—Gali and Leo and Isa and me and our moms and Bai and the jaguar and the ceiba. We've each had to listen and dream and risk and trust and share and hope. Only by joining forces could we get this far.

And we still have a long way to go. Together. Starting with saving our ceiba today.

That's what I'm thinking when a distant rumble plows through the forest music.

The Gambler

Alarmed, I turn to the others. Their eyes tell me they've heard the roar, too. We hurry back toward the hut, half dragging Gali along, splashing water from the pot.

As we move closer, I can tell it's the noise of an engine, but without the violent whir of the killing machine yesterday.

Just as the hut comes into sight, a red ATV pulls up, its tires huge and deeply treaded. Paulo is in the passenger seat and another man is in the driver's seat. He's large, fair-skinned, with a sunburnt nose and a brazen expression. His clothes look new and crisp—high-tech camping garb—as if he's just stepped out of the dressing room in an outdoor store. He wears wraparound sunglasses with mirrored lenses.

"Tom Weed," he booms, extending his hand. "Supervising this operation."

He pumps our hands hard enough to extract some minerals.

We introduce ourselves and greet Paulo.

Tom speaks in English with an American accent, a slight Southern twang, and the volume turned way up. "Fancy meetin' y'all out here!"

His voice thunders through the jungle, nearly as loud as the ATV. "My buddy Paulo here said you wanted to talk." Nodding to Gali, he adds, "Didn't mention this gentleman."

Gali has been hanging back, breathing hard after the exertion of half running here. But now he steps forward, stands up straight, and offers his hand. "Galileo Gallo," he says with a formal nod.

I translate everything quickly for Isa, noting that Tom doesn't seem scary or cruel. Just surprisingly well-mannered and *loud*.

"Thanks for coming," Leo tells Tom.

"No problem. And I gotta say, you've got me curious about what you're doing all the way out here. Good chocolate by the way. Couldn't resist your invitation for more." He winks. "Though it's more like chocolate ice cream weather out here if you ask me."

We stay by his ATV and do small talk—which I'm not bad at, with grown-ups at least, thanks to my customer service skills at El Corazón.

Meanwhile, Isa slips inside, murmuring in Spanish that she's going to prepare the star flower hot chocolate. Maybe it will give him that feeling it gave us . . . like you're gazing at the night sky and possibilities are popping out at you like stars that were there all along, just waiting for you to notice. Maybe one of those possibilities will be *not killing our ceiba*.

Tom mostly talks. He tells us he's just started working for this oil company—turns out it's the same one doing the operation downstream in Antonio's community. This sends chills through me, but I remember our immediate goal of saving our ceiba, so I refrain from yelling at Tom. Permelia from the flower shop always says you catch more flies with honey. *And chocolate,* I add.

Tom goes on for a while about how sorry he is to wreck this house but it looks like it's falling apart anyway. He plucks a bill from a black leather wallet. Handing it to Gali, he says, "Pass this along to the girl's family for their trouble, will you?"

When I see it's a hundred-dollar bill, I can barely keep my eyes from popping out. Who carries around a hundred-dollar bill in the jungle?

Gali hands the money directly to Isa, who examines Ben Franklin's face for a moment, then tucks it into her fiber bag beside the ceiba silk.

When Tom finds out we're from Colorado, he gets extra sweaty and red-faced with excitement. "I worked on some rigs there! Good fishing and casinos."

We keep him chatting until Isa comes out with a gourd of hot chocolate with ten flower petals floating in it. He sniffs, takes a sip, then gulps the rest of it down as if he's chugging a beer. He wipes his mouth with the back of a hairy hand. "Good stuff."

He keeps talking, the dam let loose on a raging river of words. He's probably glad for English-speaking company to listen. We try to get a few comments in edgewise—tell him about the cacao co-op, toss in some astounding rain forest facts—but he goes on and on about his family back home and his two kids, who are also in middle school. I can't help thinking they must be kind of relieved when he goes away on trips so they can hear themselves think.

"Now, my wife, she's what you call a chocoholic! I'm not that bad, but I've been known to scarf down a Hershey's bar or two for an afternoon pick-me-up." He guffaws. "Used to drink and smoke, but now chocolate's my only vice. Well, that and casinos, my wife would tell you, but now I only gamble on vacations."

After a while, he straightens up, stretches, and says, "Well, this was nice. Thank you kindly for that delicious cocoa. Best I've had. Wish my wife was here to have some. Now I've got to get back to the ol' grindstone."

Tom starts climbing back in the ATV beside Paulo.

"Wait, Mr. Weed!" I sputter.

He turns to me. "Yeah?"

I'm still trying to figure out what to say, when Leo announces, "We'd like you to stop logging and drilling in this part of the forest."

"Excuse me, son?"

Leo repeats his request, now in a stronger voice.

Tom chuckles. "Sorry, no can do. We've already invested loads of time and energy and money."

Leo speaks earnestly. "The flower in your hot chocolate—it has medicinal value. We think it's an undiscovered species, and endangered, maybe even the last patch of its kind. It's growing beneath an ancient ceiba nearby."

Tom wrinkles his forehead, rubs his chin. "An ancient *what*?"

"Come here, *señor*," Isa says in Spanish, motioning to Tom, and leading him in the direction of the ceiba.

Tom glances at a large watch around his freckled wrist. "I've got ten minutes, honey." He follows her, and Paulo walks silently beside him.

At the ceiba, Isa says in Spanish, "Please, at least spare this tree. And these flowers."

Tom doesn't seem to understand, so I translate.

He nods appreciatively. "I'm no tree hugger, but I'll admit, it's a beauty." He runs his hands over the roots, and I wince as he crushes the flowers underfoot with his hiking boots. "Tell ya what. We'll see if we can work around it. But I can't promise anything."

It's hopeful to think he might spare her . . . Still, I imagine how lonely the ceiba would feel, standing there with no other trees nearby to chat with, no forest music to hear.

I glance back at Tom, who has fallen shockingly silent. He's staring at the jungle around him, up and down the tree, noticing the flowers at his feet, the moss and lichens on the roots, the orchids and vines on the trunk. He peers into a shiny red bromeliad, smiles when a tiny frog hops out of it.

Now's our chance. I nod to Leo—my signal for him to bombard Tom with tree factoids.

Instead, Leo pulls out a little pouch from his pocket. He kneels at a flat stone. Then he puts the brown nutshells and a shiny red tree seed on the smooth surface. He looks at Tom. "How about we make a bet?"

"A bet?"

Leo holds out the seed in his palm. "I'll put this seed under one of the shells and mix them up while you watch. If you can guess what shell it's under, then you can go ahead and clear the area around the ceiba for your road. But if you don't guess right, and I do, then you redirect the road access. You don't touch the ceiba or a few hundred feet around her."

Tom guffaws, slaps his knee. "Y'all are entertaining, I'll give you that. So why on earth would I make a bet like that when there's nothing in it for me?"

Quickly, I say, "If you win, your wife gets a lifetime supply of chocolate. A box of El Corazón's finest bean-to-bar truffles, prepared by award-winning chocolate makers and mailed to your home once a month." I'm not sure what I'll do when El Corazón closes . . . but I'll cross that bridge if I come to it. For now, I have to be the world's most convincing chocolate seller. "It'll be like Valentine's Day every month for her. You'll be the best husband on the planet."

Again, Tom laughs. "Now that is tempting. Might make up for me being gone all the time." He pauses. "Oh, kids, I respect what you're doing. I can see y'all have good solid hearts. I can see this place is special. I can see you're protecting it like you would family. But fact is, business is business."

"Look," I say, undaunted. "You're probably doing hundreds of acres of logging. You can save this one little piece, can't you? It won't hurt your company to reroute the road a little, will it?"

Tom gazes around the jungle, at the tree, the flowers, the insects, the mushrooms, even the lichen.

"A lifetime supply of chocolate," Leo says. "What would your wife say? And your kids? You'd be their hero."

I think of what Leo's told me about his gambling-addict dad. He can never resist. His brain's reward system is out of whack. He craves the neurotransmitters like dopamine that are released when he gambles. Once Leo told me that his dad's addiction to gambling was on par with cocaine or morphine.

Tom's a gambler. He loves casinos. He gets that thrill from making a bet, that fleeting rush of happiness, that floating, warm feeling. He loves his wife and kids. He isn't a bad guy. He's a man who's worked hard and been friendly and gotten lucky. And he's lonely.

Gali speaks next. And even though he's an old, stooped, white-haired man, something about him looks tall now. Majestic as a giant ceiba imparting wisdom. "Years ago, my friend, I came to the jungle, just like you. Gold mining operations. But then I saw what it was doing to the forest and the people in it."

Gali pats Tom's shoulder with a wrinkled, age-spotted hand. "And I need to tell you this, son, because I can tell you're trying to be a decent man. If you cut down this tree, if you destroy the precious flowers at its roots, well, one day you won't be able to live with yourself. Now's your chance to do something good. Something important. Something that would make your own kids proud."

Tom lets out a sigh. "Let's see." He takes a GPS from his pocket, pulls up a map and studies it, zooming in and out, making inadvertently funny faces.

He must be deciding how he could reroute the road. I bite my lip hopefully. *Please, please find a way.*

Finally, stroking the stubble at his chin, he says, "All right, then. I win, my wife gets bucketloads of chocolate. You win, I reroute the access road farther upstream. Won't come within five hundred feet of the tree. Or near anyone's homes."

"Promise?" Leo says, reaching out his hand.

Tom offers his fleshy hand to Leo. And they shake. Then, for good measure, the rest of us shake Tom's hand, wincing at his iron grasp. There's no going back on this handshake, that's for sure.

"Ready to play?" Leo asks with a smile.

"Yep." Tom's eager, almost bouncing around.

Leo once told me that even the anticipation of gambling gives addicts a rush. Maybe that's why Tom has taken him up on the deal. Or maybe it's that we remind Tom of his own kids. Or that he's bored with his job. Or that he thinks the shell game would be fun. Or that he hears the ceiba's whispers. Or that the star flower tea has opened up possibilities. Or that the chocolate has made him happy. Or maybe it's a mix of all these things, a unique magical recipe.

"Hold on." Leo turns to Gali, looking very professional. "May I take a couple of blank pages from your journal?"

Gali obliges, and Leo starts writing swiftly.

I peer over his shoulder. It's a contract packed with legalese spelling out our agreement with Tom. Leo shakes out his tired hand, then copies it onto a second blank page while I translate for Isa.

"Oh, come on, bud. We shook hands already."

"I'm a lawyer's son, what can I say?"

"Sign and date on the lines marked with an X," Leo tells Tom. "And initial each page."

With an amused sigh, Tom obeys.

Leo signs and initials as well, and the rest of us sign as witnesses.

Next, Leo holds out a blank paper to Tom, all business.

"Could you write down your contact information and home address?"

Tom takes the paper and scribbles the words and numbers. Handing it back, he says, "I respect your gumption, kid." He looks like he's having the time of his life. Rubbing his hands together, he says, "All right, lifetime supply of chocolate, here we come!"

Farewell

Leo draws in a deep breath, shows Tom the red seed, and places it under the center shell. Then he slides the shells over the smooth stone. It's not a bad makeshift tabletop. In fact, I wonder if Bai might have used it for grinding seeds and nuts.

Leo starts slowly, working his way faster. For a while, I try keeping track, but soon give up. The hum of the forest becomes a soundtrack to the strange, magical dance Leo's hands are doing.

Tom has taken off his shades, and now he's leaning forward, intent on tracking the shells. Sweat drips from his face onto the stone surface. Leo's hands quicken, forming a whirlwind, swirling and spiraling the shells. And then they stop.

Grinning, Tom points to the shell on the far right.

Leo taps his finger on it. "Is this your choice?"

Tom nods. You can tell that he's enjoying this, the way his whole body is zinging with anticipation. It's as if he's a little kid and we're at a stuffed-animal-packed booth at the county fair.

"Lift it up," Leo says, giving nothing away with his expression.

Isa and I join hands and hold our breaths.

Tom picks up the shell.

Nothing.

Big, beautiful nothing.

Tom's face turns red, and he squeezes his hairy fists . . . and then he melts into a pile of laughter.

I let out a breath, unclench my hand from Isa's. Now, can Leo pick the shell with the seed under it?

He reaches forward slowly, rests his hand on the one in the middle, lifts it up. There's the seed, sitting pretty.

Tom laughs for a full minute. Even though he lost the bet, the dopamine is still flooding his body. "Well, now this was a fun way to spend a morning!"

He reaches out to shake Leo's hand. "And that was some mighty fine handiwork, son."

Leo regards him cautiously. "Will you honor our agreement?"

"Of course! I'm a man of my word!" With his vise grip, he shakes hands with the rest of us.

As I thank him, I feel so generous, I might just mail his family a dozen surprise truffles when we get back to Heartbeat Springs.

When Tom climbs into the ATV, beside him, Paulo gives us an impressed nod and says, *"Felicidades."* Congratulations. Or, it occurs to me now, with a literal translation: *Happinesses.*

And that's how I feel . . . as if all Gali's keys to happiness have come together in one big heap of *happinesses.*

After the men roar off on the red ATV, I head to our ceiba with Gali and Leo and Isa one last time. I press myself against her roots in a kind of embrace. "*Waponi*," I whisper. "Good-bye." Hopefully a temporary good-bye, assuming I'm able to convince Mom to let us move here. I let my lips touch the bark of the tree, a farewell, a wispy kiss.

In other root chambers, Leo and Isa and Gali are probably doing some version of the same.

Before we leave, we carefully gather some star flower blossoms for botanists to examine back home.

Then we pack up and take off in the canoe.

The trip downstream is much shorter than the trip here since the currents are with us. No brute strength is necessary, just gentle guiding around logs and rocks.

As we float down the river, worry replaces my happiness at our victory. Worry for the forest around me. If Tom's company keeps polluting this region, it could be sickened and destroyed . . . except for an oasis of plants around our ceiba. It's a relief we've saved her, but if the other mother trees upstream are butchered, the creatures within them would be left homeless, the fungi's mycelia killed, the underground heart torn apart.

I cradle the star flower in my palm, this precious thing that might save the forest. I hold tight to the hope that once scientists and conservation groups know about the star flower, it will make a difference.

I wonder what Gali's treasure is, and if it will really help. Strange, isn't it, that we had to journey all the way to the remote Amazon to discover a treasure in our own backyard?

When we finally turn out of the last bend to the co-op in the early evening, the moms skid down the muddy embankment to smother us with hugs. At least, Leo's and my mom do. Alma just slings an arm lovingly around her daughter, never having doubted her survival skills.

"Okay," Mom says, "I admit I was a tad worried when you didn't come back last night."

"More like frantic, Mara," says Nieves.

"Hey! So were you!" Mom counters.

Leo slides out of his mom's grasp and rearranges his hair. "Mamá, you knew we'd probably spend the night there."

"I know, but still. You were out in the middle of the jungle!"

Mom gives Gali a gentle hug, as if he might break. "You're looking good, Gali." Over his shoulder, she gives me a relieved look, as if to say, *Thanks for keeping him alive.*

The moms usher us up the embankment and into the dining hut, which is already full of the mouthwatering scent of piranha frying. José greets us warmly and pours us each freshly squeezed orange juice.

"Now tell us everything!" Nieves demands.

And we do. We sip our tart, sweet juice and tell them about the tree dreams that Leo and Isa and I had—and the jaguar, which makes Mom's hand fly to her chest and Nieves's eyes widen twice their size. We tell them about the star flower, and how it might be key to saving this forest.

When we recount Leo's shell game and show them the legal

contract with Tom, a fierce pride flares in Nieves's face. "That's my boy," she says, ruffling his hair.

As the others talk, I shift my focus to the chirps of insects and birds, and beneath their song, the deeper song of the underground heart. I hear it loud and clear, the message of hope.

Now I just have to get Mom on board with moving to the Amazon.

At night, by the faint light of the bare bulb, Mom and I pack our bags. We have to leave for the airstrip tomorrow morning. I'm waiting for just the right time to suggest moving here.

She's bouncing around our cabin in a sleeveless blue Hawaiian-themed 1950s dress, chatting about how smoothly the fermentation went, how cooperative the weather's been, how she's learned to make a shelter with palm fronds. "The beans are drying as we speak!" she says triumphantly.

She tells me how earlier today, she showed Alma how to spread the fermented cacao out on woven mats under the new palm shelter, and gave instructions for how often to turn the beans, and how to know they're ready to pack up. The plan is that we'll pay the pilot ahead of time to pick up the sacks of cacao next week. We'll arrange to have them delivered by truck, then ship, then truck again all the way to Heartbeat Springs. Probably the last batch of chocolate we make in El Corazón.

"What about after that?" I ask, laying the groundwork for my plan. "Who will pick up the cacao for future shipments?"

Mom sighs, folding a flowery skirt. "I told Alma I'd try to

find a cacao trader for them to work with, but I'll admit, it'll be hard. They're so remote here."

For a moment, I watch the moths flutter by the light above us, wings aglow. Then I muster up my courage and say, "*We* could be the cacao traders, Mom."

My words hang in the air like crystals holding hidden colors.

And then, "Oh, Coco!" Mom laughs and shakes out a pair of polka-dotted leggings. "Wait, you're serious?"

I nod. "Why not, Mom?"

"For starters, Heartbeat Springs is too far away. Their cacao trader would need to live nearby."

I wedge my water sandals into the gaps between folded clothes in my bag. "We'll probably have to move away from Heartbeat Springs anyway, Mom. Why not move here?"

"*Here?*" Mom drops the leggings she was folding. She looks around the hut, maybe imagining what it would be like to be wrapped in thrumming green every day. She peers past the screen wall, into the night, alive with the songs of hidden creatures.

I try to keep my voice as velvety smooth as chocolate fresh from the melanger machine. "We could rent a place in Quito or Baños to use as an office and warehouse." I zip my bag and set it calmly on the floor. I had the whole canoe ride back to think this through, to plan how to make it seem not totally crazy. "We could split our time between here and the city. I bet rent's cheaper than in Heartbeat Springs."

For a while, Mom's quiet, dazed, biting her lip and staring into the tree shadows. "I'll admit I love this idea, Coco. I mean, really, really, really love it. But . . ."

I cross my fingers, hoping she won't be able to find a *but*.

"But . . . we'd need enough funds to start it up. When we sell El Corazón, most of the money will go to paying back debts. And our little mobile home isn't worth much either, with all the repairs it needs. Maybe if we found someone to partner with . . ." Her voice drifts off.

I pull a pillow onto my lap, hug it tight. "What if Isa and her family became our partners?"

Mom perches on the bed, smooths her hair into three sections, and starts weaving a side braid over her shoulder. "Oh, Coco bean, I adore them, but Alma says they have no cash to invest at this point, only big hopes for the cacao harvest."

"What if they suddenly *did* have money?"

Mom tosses me a quizzical look.

I take a breath and tell her about Gali's mysterious treasure buried right in our backyard beneath the cotton tree. I try to make it sound as sane as possible.

Still, she laughs so hard she cries, and then, wiping the tears away, says, "I suppose anything's possible with Gali in the mix. So tell me more about your crazy plan."

We talk as we brush our teeth and wash our faces, tossing out question after question, idea after idea, back and forth. We keep talking after she crawls into her bed, and me into mine. In the spaces between our words, I can hear Leo and Nieves in their hut, talking in animated voices about helping the downstream community bring a lawsuit against the oil company. I catch phrases here and there: endangered species, public campaigns, unethical corporations, protected habitat, indigenous rights.

And finally, when I'm nearly talked out, and feeling lulled into dreams by insect rhythms, Mom says sleepily, "This is wild, Coco . . . but maybe it's exactly what we've needed all along."

I whisper back, "We just didn't know it."

The next morning, after a breakfast of fried eggs and plantains and *agua de papaya,* we exchange gifts. Isa and her family give the moms delicate palm strand necklaces woven with smooth red-and-gray nuts. To Leo, they give a necklace dangling a piranha jaw pendant—complete with dozens of sharp, tiny teeth. To me, they give a peccary tooth necklace hanging from a strand of red seeds, just like Isa's. It matches the bracelet she gave me a week earlier, before we'd become best friends. The little kids hand us two blowguns, complete with woven palm pouches of wooden darts and ceiba silk.

In return, I give Isa most of the clothes I've brought—the mocha-latte lace shirt and all the rest of my usual standbys. Now she'll triple her wardrobe size from the Smurfette and the Lucky Cat tops, and she'll remember me when she wears them. When she hugs me in thanks, I whisper, "I'll bring more when we come back . . . to be your neighbors."

Mom hasn't agreed to my plan yet, but it was the first thing she talked about when she woke up. And over breakfast, she ran the idea by Alma, who looked ecstatic at the possibility, and insisted we could live in the same hut we stayed in this past week.

Mom gives Alma a bunch of retro sixties bangles and some turquoise earrings, and Nieves gives her rubber hair bands—apparently in great demand here—along with our first aid kit. Leo gives José his brand-new water shoes, which happen to be the right size. To the adults, Gali gives a cute little robot with an old mint tin as a torso and a rusty tea strainer as a head. When Alma opens the tin, she finds a wad of bills, which she tries to hand back to Gali, but he insists that it's gratitude for the excellent food and lodging. And finally, to the little kids, we offer most of our remaining stash of chocolate and truffles along with the insulated bags.

Afterward, we head out in the dugout canoe with Isa's entire family. It's like a floating farewell party in here. It's tough going upstream with so much weight, but there are more of us to take turns poling.

I remember how strange the jungle felt when we first entered it a week and a half ago. Now it's a familiar friend, and maybe a near-future home. Now I speak its language, hear its heartbeat.

This last river ride passes quickly, too quickly. It seems like just moments later that we're dragging the canoe ashore and trekking through the thick foliage toward the airstrip. On the way, I hear the rush of a plane engine overhead, growing louder and closer. I breathe in deeply the smell of green and earth and bark and decay and growth, trying to make it part of me.

Soon, we're standing at the edge of the clearing, watching the little plane skid to a stop on the wet grass. The pilot waves. It's the same man we had on our way here. He looks pleased and maybe a little surprised to find all of us intact. "You made it, *amigos*," he says with a congratulatory grin.

As he loads our bags into the back, we hug Isa and her family good-bye.

Tears fill Isa's eyes, and she holds my hand in hers, not willing to let it go. We both know she can't just text me, or email me, or call me, or hop on a bike to see me.

I squeeze her hand, tell her in my most confident voice, "We'll see you again soon. Somehow I'll convince my mom. I promise."

Leo adds, "We'll find your treasure under the cottonwood. We'll make sure you get it."

And once we're inside the plane, we can't stop waving goodbye to Isa, protector of the forest, even when we're too far away for her to see us.

On the flight back, I'm a different person than the one who came out here ten days ago. The treetops below are no longer broccoli, but friends, trying to protect their pulsing, breathing, singing worlds. My eyes zero in on the few-and-far-between ceiba crowns, rising majestically over the mounds of green.

And when we fly over patches of barren dirt and killing machines and oil rigs, the roots of my heart wince.

Our last plane arrives in Heartbeat Springs at midnight.

At one a.m., Leo and I are shivering in the courtyard of El Corazón, inspecting the cottonwood's roots in the dim light from the back porch. It's cold outside, which is a shock to my system, but I'm bundled up in a jacket and hat and scarf and gloves. At least the snow has thawed into mud. And the steam from the hot springs warms me a little.

I missed this familiar *thump thump thump* of the springs beneath the ground. The steam makes everything look mysterious, magical. The cottonwood's bare branches and limbs stretch out to greet us like arms. A mother tree. I've never called her that, but of course that's what she is, huge and old and wise. I brush my hands over the familiar bark of her trunk and silently thank her for guarding this treasure.

It's strange to be out here, awake, when everyone else in Heartbeat Springs is in dreamland. The moms are asleep inside—Nieves on the couch in her office, and Mom on the sofa bed in the back room of El Corazón. Thankfully, they were too tired to argue with Leo's and my plan, and said they'd just spend the night in the Roost while we searched. Gali dozed most of the way home, exhausted after a packed day of travel, from hot jungle to cold mountains. Now he's asleep in his home next to the chocolate shop. He doesn't know we're out here, that we couldn't wait till morning.

Leo and I circle the cottonwood like some bizarre ritual. We were bleary-eyed when we got off the last plane, but the sharp, cold air has given us a second wind.

He hugs his arms, rocking back and forth on his heels, trying to warm up. "Wish I knew what exactly we were looking for."

There's nothing but mud and a few scraggly weeds under here, no indication where the treasure might be buried. "Let's pick a spot and dig," I say, and grab a couple of shovels from the tool shed. On its roof, the rooster weather vane spins back and forth in gusts from the north and west, as if it can't make up its mind.

Luckily, the ground is so soft with melted snow that our shovels enter easily. "Not too close to the roots," I caution. "We don't want to hurt her."

Randomly, we dig in shallow holes here and there.

By three in the morning, my arms feel as rubbery as they did poling upstream. And that second wind of mine is rapidly fading. After so much work, we've come up with nothing but mud and stones. By now we're sweating, our coats and scarves and hats flung aside.

Leo wipes his forehead and leans on his shovel. "Maybe we should just do this tomorrow so Gali can tell us where to dig."

"I'll never get to sleep knowing it's out here." I shake out my stiff hands.

"Yeah, you're right." He raises the shovel overhead to stretch his back. "Let's just take a break."

We set down our shovels and climb into the tree nook, the place where all four main limbs branch out, leaving a space the size of a small sofa in the center.

Leo settles in his spot and I settle in mine. It feels different to be in this space with him again. We're not touching except for our boots. No words come from our mouths, just steamy breath intermingling in the cold night air.

I close my eyes, let the cottonwood hold me, and listen to the music of Heartbeat Springs. There's the underground thump, an owl *whooo*-ing, a dog howling. It's pretty stark here in wintertime compared to the Amazon. More like a three-person a cappella group than a football-field-sized symphony orchestra.

Talk to me, I silently ask the tree.

I squinch my eyes shut, focus all my energy on listening.

And I hear my name.

"Coco!" It's a whisper-shout. And then, "Leo!"

My eyes fly opened, stunned. It sounds so real. Leo and I look at each other. He's heard it, too.

297

"Couldn't wait till morning, could you?" Another whisper-shout, but the voice is familiar now. As is the happy chuckle that follows it.

We sit up, look toward the sound. It's Gali, peering out his window in a bathrobe. His head is silhouetted against golden lamplight, loose hair flying around his face.

"You've been making quite a racket out here." He leans farther out the window, pointing. "Check under that rock, my dears."

A bunch of blue morphos flit around in my belly, all glitter and hope.

"Which rock?" Leo asks with renewed enthusiasm.

Gali leans out the window and points. "There, on the west side of the tree."

Leo and I exchange looks of wonderment and circle to the other side. My gaze lands on a rock the size of a watermelon. Of course I recognize it. I've stepped on it thousands of times climbing in and out of the tree. "This one, Gali?"

"Yes!"

We try heaving the stone with our hands, but it's too heavy and stuck in the mud. Then Leo grabs his shovel and starts prying. Meanwhile, I push on the cold stone with all my might. Creakily, it rolls out of the way.

He digs with renewed vigor, spewing dirt everywhere. After a few minutes, when he starts slowing down, I take over. My arms feel strong from all that canoe poling, and I relish the smell of damp, fresh earth.

Finally, I see something. "Look, Leo!"

A patch of white is showing through the dirt. Leo brushes away the soil, his eyes like sparklers. "Want me to take over?"

With exhausted arms, I hand him the shovel. Carefully, he wedges it beneath the possible treasure and starts pushing. Judging by the muscles and tendons nearly popping out of his neck, it must be heavy. With a final, loud grunt, he heaves it up, nearly falling over backward with the effort.

It's wrapped in plastic grocery bags stuffed with newspaper. Not exactly what I'd imagined. Still breathing hard, Leo raises a skeptical eyebrow, as if to say, *We stayed up all night digging in the freezing cold . . . for this?*

And now there's the creak and clang of Gali coming down the outdoor metal stairs in an overcoat wrapped around his bathrobe. Wooly slippers poke out from beneath the hem. He's wearing a thick plaid scarf and an enormous fur hat, something you'd expect to see in Siberia. His cane clicks on the stone path as he makes his way toward us. I jump up to help him walk the rest of the way.

Once we reach the tree, he leans against the trunk, panting, and gestures to the newspaper-stuffed grocery bags. "Here it is, my dears. The moment we've all been waiting for."

The Ceiba Tree

AMAZON RAIN FOREST

Every moment is magical when you stop to notice it. And there are certain moments even more magical than the rest. Moments when the impossible becomes possible.

That moment when a seed in wet soil cracks open and the most tender of baby sprouts pushes its way up, up, up to the light.

That moment when the root of an old tree touches the root of a young heart.

That moment when the dreams of forest and human unite and transform into something with a life of its own.

Treasure

Leo and I pull out the newspaper, making a pile beside us. It's like a birthday party, only in the middle of mirk night, just the three of us, and without ribbon or wrapping paper. But the wild anticipation—that's definitely here.

We peel back the plastic bags.

Gold flashes in the moonlight. But not jewels or coins . . .

I try to pick up the treasure to examine it from other angles, but it must weigh a ton. With both hands, I grasp it and pull it out with all my might. It's shocking that something so heavy is less than a foot tall.

It's a gold statue, solid all the way through from how it feels. I glance at Leo, who looks as bewildered as me. It's in the shape of . . . some kind of monster.

Leo tries picking it up, and when he registers how heavy it is, sets it back down again. "That thing has to weigh fifty pounds!" he says, rubbing his neck. "Is it solid gold?" he asks Gali in disbelief.

Gali gives a quick, embarrassed nod. He doesn't volunteer any further information, though.

In the moonlight, Leo and I examine the statue from all angles, mystified. There's a spray of feathers on the sides and back. Its feet have the webbed claws of . . . a dragon? And a line of spikes runs over its head, like dinosaur plates. Yet its body and legs are all right angles.

"A monster?" ventures Leo.

"Or a dragon?" I guess.

Gali presses his lips together as we toss out ideas.

"A dinosaur!"

"A robot?"

"A mechanical phoenix!"

"A chupacabra?"

"C-3PO in a turkey costume!"

"Or a turkey in a C-3PO costume?"

As Leo and I shoot off guesses, I can see Gali flush, even in the chilly half darkness. Pink spreads from his apple cheeks to the rest of his face. He looks like he wants to crawl in the bag and hide.

Once Leo and I run out of ideas, Gali cringes and whispers, "Robot rooster."

And now I see it, sort of. There's a standard rectangular robot torso and legs, but with webbed chicken claws as feet, and cartoonish wings as arms. Flamboyant tail feathers arch out from the robot's bottom. And a majestic rooster head tops it, with a huge comb like a wig, and a dangly beard-thing beneath its beak.

That's all there is to it. It's not a jointed, moveable robot like the ones Gali makes with bits of old metal junk. And as far as

I can tell, there are none of the hidden compartments of his upcycled robot art. It's just . . . a solid-gold robot rooster.

I find my voice. "But . . . *why*?"

Gali hides his face in his hands and starts shaking.

Oh no. What if this is triggering another heart attack?

"You okay, Gali?" asks Leo.

As I grow closer, I see Gali's laughing. Well, laughing and sobbing at the same time.

After a moment, he wipes his nose and eyes, but keeps wheezing out a teary chuckle here and there.

Then I see that Leo is laughing, too.

Once I get my own laughter under control, I ask, "What *is* this thing, Gali?"

"Oh, my dears. This is a ridiculous remnant of my gold mining days. When my investment started paying off, I commissioned a statue. As you know, my last name, Gallo, means rooster. And I've always liked robots."

I feel my face wrinkle up. When I look over at Leo, I see his expression is all twisted, too.

"Let me explain," Gali says, taking a deep breath. "After I came back from the jungle and donated my money to conservation groups . . . well, there was the small problem of what to do with the rooster robot. I was too embarrassed to sell it at a gold shop. I didn't know what to do with it. All I knew was that a dart of shame stabbed me whenever I saw it. So one night, under a full moon like this one, I couldn't take it anymore. I buried it. I buried it along with my shame."

I look to the back fence, at the friendly, life-sized robots he's made with metal scraps over the years. Bigger versions of the pocket-sized robots he's gifted me over my lifetime. My favorite parts are the secret chambers in their chests. "And you started making a different kind of robot," I venture.

"Indeed, Coco. That's why I make my robots from junk. That's why I hide real treasures inside—feathers, acorns, pebbles. They're the opposite of the robot rooster."

Leo pats the statue's head. "Now what?"

A look of deep relief washes over Gali. "Now we sell this monstrosity. They can melt it down. We'll give the money to Isa and her family to help save their forest." He wrinkles his brow. "But one favor."

"What?" I ask warily.

"Can you and your moms do that for me? I'm still too embarrassed to be seen with it."

Leo and I nod, amused. In a grave voice, he says, "We'll push it to the store in a wheelbarrow and keep it wrapped in grocery bags until the last minute."

Gali lets out a low laugh. "You know, by now, that eyesore is probably worth about a million."

"Dollars?" I sputter.

"Crazy, isn't it? The things our world values . . ." At that, Gali bids us good night, leaving us with the million-dollar robot rooster.

We crouch down beside it, and I run my hand over its cold tail feathers. Leo looks at me through the steam of the springs and the steam of our breaths. A hint of sunrise glints off his chocolate-brown irises. The robot rooster stands between us in all its gaudy glory.

Suddenly, we start giggling and can't stop. We're in a strange state of extreme happiness plus utter exhaustion.

The kind of state that makes you feel you're zipping down the Milky Way and landing in a pile of star flowers.

The kind of state that makes you forget to be embarrassed or afraid and instead, just throw open your arms and hug your best friend in the galaxy.

The kind of state that makes him hug you back, hard, as if you've both been away visiting other solar systems, and now you're here, together, laughing, changed by the journey, yet with hearts beating in rhythm once again.

The next morning, early spring light streams through the clouded windows of El Corazón. We all sit around the big table sipping cinnamon-chili hot chocolate—me, Leo, Gali, and the moms. The framed photo of the ceiba hangs above us like a guardian angel. Just looking at it makes me miss the jungle.

And before us, as a kind of centerpiece, stands the gold rooster robot, buffed shiny and zinging sunshine. In the daylight, I can make out more details of its features—the dozens of ostentatious feathers arching from its backside, the tiny claws and ridges on its webbed feet, and the startled expression in its beady eyes. Its rectangular torso is imprinted with gears and knobs and buttons that don't move, and screws are stamped on the unjointed knees.

"Wow," is what Mom and Nieves keep saying. "Wow."

I'm not sure if the wow is over the absurdity of it or the outrageous amount it's worth . . . but eventually, Mom says, "Well, let's start figuring out where we can sell this thing. The sooner we get the money to Isa's community, the better."

Nieves nods. "I'll look into the logistics for an international gift this large."

Gali presses his hand to his chest. At first I'm worried it's the first signs of a heart attack, but then he says, slowly, "The dart . . . it's out. The poison . . . every last drop is gone. Digging up this shame of mine . . . and transforming it into a gift . . . this was what I needed, to return the last of the gold to its true owners."

"*Gracias,*" Leo and I say at the same time, and then eye each other, silently telling the other we're owed a truffle.

"Oh," Gali says, "thank *you* for helping out an old man. For listening to your dreams. For working together."

"And we'll keep working together," Mom says, twisting her coppery locks into a messy bun and sticking a couple pencils in to hold it. Still, a few unruly curls boing out. She picks up her cup in a toast. "To friends, old and new."

We click mugs and I take a long, delicious sip of chocolate. *Old and new.* That's what I think about as spice sparks my taste buds and another wave of theobromine kicks in.

Every seven years or so our bodies are created anew. Most of our old cells die, and new ones replace them, and on and on it goes. Whether human or tree, we're not things, but processes. We're not what we used to be. We're always being reborn. I can feel this swirling inside me, these bits that live and die and live, these remnants of exploded suns and galaxies, this stuff as old as the universe.

Leo eyes me. "You're thinking about the universe and cells, right?"

"You know me well." I can't stop smiling. I can feel stardust sparkling through my atoms, my blood, the invisible roots and branches that connect me to Leo and Isa and our trees and the tiniest pinpoints of light in the farthest reaches of the galaxy.

Stardust must be shooting from my eyeballs, because Gali turns to me and says, "Oh, my dear Coco, I don't even need to ask how your heart is. I can see it everywhere."

The Way My Heart Is Now

The party is on a July afternoon, three months after our return from the jungle. It's one of those sweet summer days in the mountains, everything blooming—pink coneflower and violet columbine and yellow yarrow. Just the right amount of breeze drifts through my hair, which is long and loose and tumbled over my shoulders. A giant banner reading FAREWELL! flaps from the branches of our cottonwood.

I'm sitting in the dappled light of El Corazón's courtyard, at my favorite table closest to the steaming creek. All the other tables, inside and out, are full, but there's a RESERVED FOR RAIN FOREST CLUB sign on ours.

Of course, I'll mostly be a member-at-a-distance since the farewell sign is for me and Mom. Next week, we're moving to the Amazon.

We're moving to the Amazon.

I've loved saying those words over the past three months.

And now our friends and customers have come to wish us well.

Through a slender bamboo straw, I sip the Underground

Heart from a gourd. That's what we named this frothy chocolate shake, topped with whipped cream, sprinkled with cinnamon and rose petals, and made with cacao from the Cooperativa Felicidad.

Of the Amazonian Nacional cultivar, this is the hero of all beans. It tastes of triumph. It holds the heart-thrumming flavor of a treasure hunt, a trip into the unknown, and true friendship, new and old. Rich, earthy notes dive deep and far. Floral currents drift on a delicate breeze. The flavors are ever-changing, ever-evolving, ever-reaching out tender new branches and roots.

Around the table, my friends are sipping their own chocolate shakes from straws, loudly enough to compete with the babbling stream. Yes, friends *plural*.

Leo is sitting beside me, both of us sporting our favorite tooth necklaces. Eight other friends are squeezed in, some two to a chair. A few are kids I would've formerly labeled royalty—like Caitlyn Bland—but now, around the table, we're all part of the same club. The Heartbeat Springs Rain Forest Club, founded by Leo and me.

And El Corazón is our meeting place of choice, the new cool hangout. Donut Delite saw a drop-off in business once its regular customers noticed the donuts of flesh that had settled around their midsections.

Clank, clank, clank. I turn to see Gali coming down his

steps, without a cane. (His heart is still beating!) He waves at us, face aglow, as if we ourselves are a secret to happiness.

He's offered to chaperone the Rain Forest Club field trip to the Cooperativa Felicidad next spring break—an offer that made the moms frown at the memory of his tour-guiding skills—but made Leo and me grin. I suspect if the club doesn't raise quite enough funds, an anonymous benefactor just might hold a last-minute second-annual Home Sweet Home contest.

Gali ambles over to our table, a skip in his step.

"How's your heart?" I ask, pulling up a chair for him.

"Stronger than ever, my dears." He plops down between me and Leo.

Leo greets him with a smile, then leans back in his chair and tucks some red silk scarves up his sleeve—a new magic trick he's working on for his next show. Every weekend in the park, the crowds of tourists around him have grown bigger, stuffing his top hat with donations to our club.

Leo takes in Gali's pink cheeks and bright eyes. "Ready for surgery next week?"

"Can't wait!" Gali knocks on his chest, as if it's a secret door.

"Oh, that reminds me," I say, leaping from my chair. "Leo and I made something for you. Hold on!"

I dart inside to the kitchen and pick up the silver platter covered with a dome . . . the one that held Leo's chocolate jaguar back in March in the contest that changed everything. I speed-walk outside and carefully set the platter on the table. With dramatic flair, I lift the top.

"A chocolate robot!" Gali's eyes pop out in delight. "Oh, my dears . . . you've outdone yourselves this time!"

It looks like one of the robots he makes from metal scraps, only this one is made with cacao from the Cooperativa Felicidad. I flavored it with flowers and Leo expertly carved it. It took us three hours this morning, but it felt like three minutes. Time flies when we're together, especially since we have so much to dream up and plan out.

After everyone oohs and aahs, Leo says, "The robot's for good luck." He plucks the sugarcoated rosebud from the robot's chest and hands it to Gali.

"Dig in," I announce. "You'll get another one when you're home from the hospital."

Leo pulls out his phone. "A picture first."

We lean our faces to the cheery chocolate robot, whose expression is camera-ready, as if he's shouting an enthusiastic *Cheeeese!*

"For Isa," Leo says, and our smiles grow as big as the robot's. Isa is part of our Heartbeat Springs family, even though she's on a different continent.

"Isa!" I remember the folded paper in my pocket, the latest update from our friend. It arrived yesterday with the shipment of cacao, gourds, and bamboo straws. "We just got a letter from her."

"Sweet!" Leo says. "Read it out loud."

The others in our club echo him, their mouths already full of chocolate robot bits. "How's she doing?" Caitlin asks. "And what about cute little Lily and Marcos and Dany?"

"Magnificent." I take a bite of chocolate robot ear and wash it down with a swig of the Underground Heart. I read slowly, translating to English as I go.

Dear Coco and Leo,

The whole forest misses you!

I told our ceiba "waponi" just like you asked. She seems happy. She's still surrounded by star flowers and plants and animals. I haven't seen our jaguar again—only his tracks—but I whisper "waponi" to him, too.

My family and I fixed up Bai's old hut as a place for the scientists to stay. We're helping them identify endangered plants. And we're asking the government to make this land a protected area.

Antonio's community has been recording their sicknesses caused by oil pollution. Nieves says that with all this evidence, we can demand that the government take away the petroleros' oil-drilling permits. Then we can make them leave and clean up their mess and pay medical costs. Oh, and Antonio is working on a new comic book, a happier sequel to the last one! ☺

Tell Gali that the robot rooster money is coming in handy! We used it to set up a nonprofit to support the cacao co-op and protect our environment and health. And we bought a plane for the community! My uncle José is getting his pilot's license so he can transport our cacao and bring people to doctors' appointments.

Leo, we can't wait for you to come next year with your Rain Forest Club friends. We'll have a big gourd of chicha waiting for you. ☺

Coco, I'll see you soon, neighbor! I have so many

new dreams to tell you about and I know you do, too . . .
but for now, I'll be fermenting our next batch of cacao.

Your friend for always,

Isa

The letter warms my insides like a sunlit patch of jungle every time I read it—and I've read it thirteen times since last night.

Not surprisingly, Caitlyn gloms on to the fermentation bit in the letter. It turns out last year was her own fermentation stage. Then she went to a science camp in June, and her new-and-improved personality emerged with all kinds of surprising flavors, including a thing for biochemistry.

Wrinkling her perfectly plucked brows, she asks, "Now what microorganisms are involved in fermentation again?"

I smile—feeling actual fondness for her—and list them on my fingers. "Yeasts, lactic acid bacteria, acetic acid bacteria, endospore-forming rods, filamentous fungi."

"Very cool." Her voice is decidedly *un*-sarcastic. She's just finishing her melanger stage, and her volatile acids have dissipated.

Caitlyn Bland has transformed into someone who finds existence fascinating. And best of all, she's the super-organized secretary of our club, bringing labeled folders and three-ring binders to every meeting.

Once I tuck the letter back in my pocket, she hands out petitions we drafted that demand corporations and governments protect the environment and respect indigenous rights. Next she passes around a sign-up sheet for members to sell hot chocolate at school to raise funds for our trip. And she's even thought to bring sparkly green gel pens to give our signatures extra style.

As the papers get shuffled around the table, Nieves breezes outside, pausing to breathe in the chocolatey scene before she crosses the patio. She's carrying a tray of whipped cream–topped Underground Hearts and wearing a pristine white apron over her subdued gray pantsuit.

This is now her shop . . . hers and Leo's . . . the brand-new owners of El Corazón. She's splitting her time between working on meaningful legal cases and running the shop, with weekend help from Leo. She's grown even more impassioned about legal action against the oil company after her visit with Antonio and his family and neighbors in May. Even now, two months later, her eyes blaze whenever she tells customers about her joint mission with his community.

A few tables away, she hands the shakes to a grateful Mom and Permelia, who are chatting about chocolate-making. I catch a word here and there—*roast, winnow, grind, temper.* Permelia is taking notes intently. She'll be El Corazón's new manager— she wanted a change from the flower shop. When Nieves leans in to greet Gooey Marshmallow, he licks her nose with glee. He's been in heaven, frolicking around all day in white chocolate bliss.

Mom sips the Underground Heart, swishing it around her mouth, letting every one of her taste buds savor the flavors and textures. Once she swallows, she gives Nieves a thumbs-up. Mom's back to wearing her flouncy, old-fashioned clothes . . . today it's a silk turquoise tea dress that makes her red hair twist look extra fiery. Her laughter rises bright and free above the chatter.

With so much happiness and hope and theobromine filling the courtyard, I'm caught off guard by a quiver in my lip and something welling in my throat. Quietly, I walk over to the tree and settle in my nook, wondering why I'm on the brink of tears.

Leo's head pokes into the cottonwood nook. Sunlight dapples his face, and one honeyed beam lights up his irises. "You okay, Coco?"

I sniffle and blink and smile. He must've noticed that tremble of my chin. "A little sad," I admit, "but mostly happy . . . and a tiny bit scared . . . and a lot excited. All mixed together."

He settles beside me in his spot. "Me too."

The FAREWELL banner flips and flaps above us in the branches, and the creek bubbles and gurgles, and people munch and chitchat on the patio. In our hidden place, I lean back against the trunk. Leo does the same. And then, little by little, our heads tilt toward each other, as if they're planets or moons, drawn together by gravitational force. I can almost feel our neurons sparking each other's like one starburst after another.

One thing is certain: No matter what, we'll be friends for a long time to come.

My eyes drift closed. I hear the *thump thump thump* of the hidden springs and the soft music of tree messages and secrets to happiness whispering around me. I feel my heart wending with the roots of the cottonwood and ceiba, with the threads of Leo's heart, with all my friends' and family's. I think of the universe and every atom in it and I know that whatever happens, my heart can grow to embrace it all.

The Ceiba Tree

AMAZON RAIN FOREST

Waponi.

Author's Note

Ever since college, when I did my capstone anthropology project on cultural and environmental issues in the Amazon, I dreamt of going there. And finally, two years ago, my dream came true. I took a life-changing trip to a remote part of the Yasuní National Park in Ecuador, staying in a cooperative ecolodge run by a Huaorani (aka Waorani) community.

Since I'm fluent in Spanish, I was fortunate to have fascinating conversations with my Huaorani hosts, learning about their hopes, goals, and feelings about the cultural and environmental changes happening in their lives. I'd planned to return soon to visit my new friends to help them with their own creative projects, but sadly, the ecolodge closed for safety reasons. An oil company began doing seismic oil exploration in their territory. This involves setting off explosives throughout the forest to decide where to drill. Their forest had become a danger zone.

When I heard this news, my heart broke.

Yet it made me even more determined to bring this story into the world.

As you can guess, the environmental and cultural issues in

this book reflect reality. The Huaorani and their indigenous neighbors in the Amazon have been facing the expanding threat of oil drilling, mineral extraction, and logging for decades now. Some people have been sickened by pollution and displaced. Some have been forced to engage in destructive jobs to survive. And some have found sustainable ways to protect their homes through ecotourism or cultivating crops like shade-grown cacao.

There are many examples of brave indigenous people standing up to destructive environmental practices. But tragically, many of these activists have been threatened or killed as a result. Although this book is a work of fiction, I've woven in the kinds of real-life situations that are occurring throughout indigenous territories in the Amazon.

The elements of this book that some readers might consider "magical" relate to the spiritual worldview of the Huaorani people. My new Huaorani friends told me they recount their dreams to each other because dreams have meanings that should be shared and acted upon. They told me that the spirits of deceased loved ones can take the form of powerful jaguars. They brought me to a waterfall for a spiritual cleaning, and afterward, my soul felt as sparkling as the morpho butterfly flitting past us.

The anthropologist in me made a great effort to weave accurate cultural details throughout the story. The sources of my research were a mix of books, documentary films, interviews, and participant observation. My Huaorani friends generously shared with me their cultural practices: painting our faces with achiote, shooting blowguns, climbing tree trunks, fishing for piranha. They shared their intimate knowledge of the forest, showing me which vine to use for the poison in blowdart guns, and which plants to use for shampoo or toothpaste. They shared folklore, mythology, and beliefs, which often feature the sacred ceiba tree.

A few elements of this book walk the line between fiction and reality. Although the star flower came from my imagination, there are many plants in the Amazon that indigenous people have long valued for their healing properties. Sadly, some of these plants are threatened with extinction because of the environmental damage of recent decades. Scientists estimate that due to human activity, species are becoming extinct at a rate of between one thousand and ten thousand times the natural rate of extinction. The organisms within an ecosystem are often so interdependent that if one piece is taken away, the entire system could collapse. This is what I envisioned could happen with the star flower and the ceiba.

The Amazon is staggeringly rich in biodiversity. Even though the Amazon only covers 1 percent of the earth's surface, it is home to one-third of our planet's remaining tropical forests. The Amazon is also home to 10 percent of the earth's known species of plants and animals. Incredibly, every two days, a new plant or animal species is discovered by scientists in the Amazon. Although the precious flower species of my story is invented, discoveries like this are common and help identify critical habitats that need special protection.

Interestingly, the poetic idea of the "Mother Tree" has some scientific truth. Ecologists have found that the oldest trees in a forest community oversee how their resources are distributed.

If the Mother Tree is chopped down, the trees around her could suffer. Experiments have shown that there is an underground network of chemical messages relayed by fungal threads called mycelia. These threads have a symbiotic relationship with tree roots, meaning that both the fungus and trees benefit. Forest ecologists have compared this network to an underground brain.

These scientific ideas reflect the cultural ideas of the Huaorani in some ways. Like many other indigenous groups, the Huaorani believe that plants have their own consciousness and the forest has its own wisdom. These scientific and cultural ideas inspired me to create the fictional character of the ceiba tree, who communicates her plea across continents.

I see the bones of this story as real . . . just fleshed out with magic and imagination. I think we need both the scientific and the spiritual to feel the *thump thump thump* of the underground heart . . . and then we need to take action to protect our world. For ideas on how you can help conserve the wildlife of the Amazon and support its indigenous cultures, please visit my website at lauraresau.com. *Waponi*.

~Laura Resau, Fall 2017

Indigenous Language Spelling Note

The traditional, Spanish-based spelling that my friends use for their ethnic group is *Huaorani*, although recently *Waorani* has become a more popular spelling. Similarly, the traditional spelling is *Quichua*, while the more recent spelling is *Kichwa*. I've chosen to use the traditional spellings because that's how my friends refer to themselves.

Acknowledgments

Thank you to everyone who helped with this book over the years. You each have a special chamber in my heart.

I couldn't have written this without the generosity of my Huaorani hosts, guides, and friends in the Ecuadorian Amazon. Pegonka Rolando, thank you for sharing unforgettable stories and knowledge with me—like how to shoot a blowgun, climb a branchless tree trunk, start a fire from scratch, clean my spirit in a waterfall, imitate macaw calls, and throw a spear . . . to name a few.

Obe Beatriz Nenguimo Nihua, thank you for meaningful conversations about indigenous healing, our children, our ideas, and our dreams. Luís Onke Enquere, thank you for fascinating chats about your family history and illustrated book projects, and for your amazing piranha-catching skills. And thank you to everyone else for opening your homes and hearts, sharing laughter and dancing, and making me feel so welcome: Fausto, Gabriel, Pedro, Elizabeth, Remigio, Veronica, Laura, Carmen, Fredy, Bai, Beba, Josefa, Bertha, Rosario, Fernanda, Inés, Vicky, Bromelia, and anyone else I've missed. *Waponi* to you all!

Writing a book is truly a group project, and I couldn't have done it without the thoughtful comments of early readers. *Muchísimas gracias* to my patient Ecuadorian guide and friend, Javier Huera Santa Fe, for leading me into the remote Amazon, enlightening me in so many ways, and commenting on this manuscript.

Endless gratitude to my big-hearted writer friends for offering encouragement and suggestions on early drafts—Karye Cattrell, Laura Pritchett, and Todd Mitchell. *Gracias* to my *amiga del corazón*, Gloria García Díaz, for giving feedback on the Mexican culture and Spanish language aspects of this manuscript and adding lots of *felicidad* to my life. Thank you, Mika Mason, my bilingual tween reader and creative writer friend—your enthusiasm fueled me onward. And thanks to my supportive writing community here in Colorado and my EMLA community that stretches from coast to coast. Best colleagues ever!

A heartfelt thank you to Alix and Toby Gadd, owners of the extraordinary Nuance Chocolate, for giving me a delicious tour of your chocolate factory and shop, sharing your expertise on craft chocolate-making, inspiring me with your poetic chocolate descriptions, and commenting on all things chocolate in my manuscript. I feel so lucky to live just five blocks away from the best bean-to-bar shop in the world! I truly couldn't have written this book without you (and a steady stream of your chocolate).

A huge thanks to Ryan Finchum for commenting on this manuscript in your limited spare time between running Colorado State University's Protected Area Management and Training program and working on meaningful conservation projects with indigenous communities in the Amazon. (You amaze me!)

Thanks to Les Sunde for inspiring me with rusted robots and other charming creations made from abandoned junk . . . and to Maria Singleton for building such a warm community around them. Wonder and wisdom abound when I'm with you two happiness-makers.

It's been a joy-filled dream working with my agent, Erin Murphy, and my editor, Andrea Davis Pinkney. Erin and Andrea: You are two of the smartest, kindest, and most creative humans I've ever met. A thousand thanks to you both, as well as insightful associate editor Natalia Remis and the rest of the incredible team at Scholastic.

I'm eternally grateful to my story-loving, nature-loving, chocolate-loving family. Chocolate kisses to my husband, Ian, my own secret to happiness . . . I appreciate that you didn't even blink when I told you I was going on a solo research trip to the remote Amazon. And thank you to my favorite chocolate snob of all—my son, Bran. You've always inspired me with your pride in your chocolate-concocting Mayan ancestors, who—as you say—ROCKED!

Thanks to my mom, Chris Resau, for generously commenting on this manuscript . . . and more important, teaching me from a young age that chocolate is an essential food group. Thanks to my sky-gazing scientist dad, James Resau, for showing me the wonders of existence, from microscopic cells to far-off stars. Thanks to my late grandfather, Howard Resau, for being with me in spirit as I wrote. You loved trees so much that your last words to me were about the two beloved giant spruces outside my writing room window.

Hugs to all the trees who have whispered secrets to me over the years, from the magnificent ceiba I met by the Shiripuno River in the Amazon to the magnolia whose top branches cradled me when I read books during my Baltimore childhood, to the willow who faithfully served as Bran's imaginary pirate ship here in Fort Collins.

And most of all, thank *you*, dearest readers. Can you feel our heart-roots intertwined?

I can.